BENEATH

MAUREEN A. MILLER

BENEATH
SERIES

BENEATH
HORIZON DIVIDED

TABLE OF CONTENTS

PROLOGUE

She was going to vomit.

Stella Gullaksen looped her arm through the tuna tower ladder. The LED spotlights cut through the storm, revealing a pool of seawater on the cockpit floor of the sport fishing boat. The brine was creeping up to her calves now. Across from her, Col, her best friend's brother, wrapped a rope around his arm like a boa constrictor. Dark hair was pasted to his forehead, and his eyes were lost in the night, but the bright red coil in his free hand was visible enough. He nodded at her and tossed it.

Stella clawed at the darkness, squinting against the blinding fusion of rain and saltwater. The rope unraveled, winding through the water, eluding her grappling hand. Finally, she latched onto it and read his encouraging nod to secure it around herself. Trembling fingers attempted the task, but another black wave smashed into the hull, cascading against her hip and nearly tossing her over. She clung to the aluminum rigging.

This was to have been a weekend fishing

excursion, a last respite before her freshman year in college. Stella's best friend, Jill Wexler, was also a freshman at the same college. They met each other as freshmen in high school when Stella moved to Monmouth County from Pennsylvania. They were polar opposites in personality, but somehow, it worked, and they had been attached at the hip since.

Jill's parents owned the STARKISSED, a 32' Topaz Express saltwater fishing boat. It was a tight squeeze to fit Donald and Anne Wexler, their eighteen-year-old daughter, Jill, and their twenty-year-old son, Colin, along with Stella. It was only for a night, though. It took too long to reach the New Jersey underwater canyons, where yellowfin tuna fishing was at its best. They had to spend the night at sea and were due back into port late tomorrow evening.

Inside the cockpit, she saw Don Wexler hunched over the steering wheel, smacking the radar display. His curses were loud enough to carry over the maelstrom.

"I checked with the Coast Guard. I checked the satellite. The weather was clear!"

The defense seemed lame, given their current predicament. Did it matter what the weather report claimed? They were over a hundred miles off the coast of New Jersey in the center of a mean tropical storm. The fact that it was the middle of the night was just a cruel bonus.

Stella looked frantically at the cabin hatch, now submerged under several inches of water. Jill was down there, along with her mother. Only a few moments ago, Stella had been with them. When the storm struck, her stomach was the first to protest. She rushed up to the cockpit in search of air and, instead, emerged into chaos.

The hatch burst open, and the blonde head of Anne Wexler cracked through. She held her hand over her eyes to shield them from nature's assault. Water poured into the cabin. The blonde head disappeared, replaced by Jill's tawny ponytail. She tripped up the small staircase and crawled through the pooling water until her brother's arm latched onto her. Anne's head reappeared as she climbed out of the cabin, hauling an armful of life vests. To Stella's horror, Don hollered something to the effect of; *it's too late*.

Another wave came. This one taller than the fourteen-foot tuna tower. It struck with the force of a speeding tractor-trailer.

Stella no longer dwelled on her nausea. She was the first to enter the sea as the STARKISSED slapped onto its side, surrendering to the force of the breaker.

Stella surfaced, reaching for the slick hull. It was nearly inverted now, and she kicked back away, afraid it might drag her down.

An eerie glow from the submerged lights wrapped around her legs. She watched in horrified fascination as they twitched frantically.

"Help!" she choked.

Saltwater slapped her in the face. There was no sound other than the angry stream of the ocean.

"Jill? Mr. Wexler?"

She coughed and tried to blink the sting of salt from her eyes. The storm had come on so suddenly that no one had time to put on their life vests. As the lights from the boat faded into the depths, Stella took stock of her grim predicament. She was in the middle of the Atlantic Ocean, being pummeled by a rogue gale with only the waning strength in her muscles to keep her afloat.

Before the notion of her demise even formed, another shadowy wave towered above. It seemed to labor, toying with its prey before it drilled down upon her.

Under its force, Stella plunged down—down—down—into the obscurity beneath.

CHAPTER 1

Tumbling.

It felt like a free fall from a passing jet, yet that was impossible. Water was resistant. Still, down she went, a strong suction overruling all her attempts to claw to the surface.

The surface.

There was no delineation of sea and sky. Everything was black. The lights from the STARKISSED were long gone. All that remained was the disorienting gorge of oblivion that now tugged Stella deeper until her chest began to ache and her limbs grew numb.

It felt as if a beast had crawled into her ear and was swelling inside her head. She was conscious enough to pinch her nose and blow out, which offered minimal relief.

How long had she held her breath?

Any moment now, her lungs would overrule her brain and demand nourishment. Any moment now, the reflex to breathe would yield water rather than oxygen. The end would soon follow.

Down.

Down.

She had hopped an express elevator to the bottom of the sea.

Jill.

Her best friend was likely dead already. Was there an afterlife? Would they meet again? Would it be soon because they had perished in such close proximity?

Death had not claimed Stella yet, however. The pressure remained in her lungs and ears, but the feeling of free-falling persisted. How long had she been underwater? Ten minutes? Ten seconds?

Down.

Down.

She felt a tug.

Not the persistent force that dragged her down. This tow hauled her sideways. It was vigorous enough that her arms and legs dangled helplessly before her as if a hook had latched around her waist.

Breathe.

There it was. The first all-out demand to draw air into her lungs. Why did she fight it? Simply to last a few more seconds? There was no hope. The deep-sea currents were having their way with her.

Breathe.

Stella felt the drag of the undercurrent, but she couldn't see anything. She tried to pry her eyes open. The water was so cold that she thought she might freeze to death before her lungs gave out. Hypothermia. That's right. Her heart was just going to stop. Wasn't that an easier way to go?

Oxygen deprivation was taking its toll. She swore she saw light. Was it the end? *The* tunnel? The path to the afterlife?

It sure wasn't what she had imagined. They spoke of a bright light—so beautiful—so beguiling—something you were drawn towards—an undeniable euphoria.

This was not so magnetic. It was subtle. A soft glow that she couldn't really focus on as she was yanked like a dog toy, powerless to swim against the pull.

Vaguely aware of passing through a narrow channel, Stella felt the pressure begin to ease. The force dragging her began to taper. For the first time, she regained use of her arms and legs, flailing them in a desperate attempt to rise.

Breathe, her lungs and brain commanded.

Wrinkling her nose, she struggled not to inhale.

Something slithered by her. A fish? An eel? Disoriented, she tried to find it again in the murky water.

There!

Stella's body jerked in surprise. She swore she saw the red rope that Colin had been holding. Confident that she had now suffered brain damage, she reached out, expecting to connect with the tentacle of a squid. Her fingers wrapped around the coarse material, and she instinctively tugged. It might have tugged back, but she lost consciousness, finally surrendering to the sea.

Stella jerked awake.

The racking cough that threatened to split her chest open had roused her. A firm hand clutched her shoulder, easing her onto her side. The position offered relief, and the cough soon tempered into a soft wheeze.

Shaking feverishly, she cracked open her eyelids, but the view didn't stem her confusion. Everything was dark. Not black, but heavily laced with shadows. The walls looked dank, cave-like, lined with salivating teeth. Stella blinked. No, not teeth. Icicles. Rock icicles. Think. Think. There was a word for it, but her brain was so fuzzy.

Stalactites.

Stalactites?

Stella pried her face off the gritty floor. Pebbles stuck to her cheek. She swatted at them, puzzled by the granular surface. Planting her palm on the sandy bedrock, she searched the low, barbed ceiling. The cave was long with a narrow ledge that she now rested on. A few feet away, gray water lapped with deceptive innocence. Stella yanked her feet away from it.

She was about to climb onto her knees when she remembered there had been a touch on her shoulder. Flipping back onto her butt, she gaped up at the drenched figure kneeling behind her.

"Colin!" she croaked.

Colin Wexler looked daunting in the shadows. Dark hair clung to his temples, and the muscles along his jaw clenched in resolve. The wet t-shirt clung to his chest, which hefted under each labored breath. His anxious gaze roved over her.

"I didn't think you were going to make it," he rasped. "You weren't breathing. You weren't responding to CPR."

"You—you had to do CPR on me?"

The situation was too dire, and she was too shaken to imagine Colin's hands on her chest. Instead, she focused on his words. "I wasn't breathing?"

"No." He shook his head, his gaze shifting towards the water.

Stella followed his eyes. Together, they watched the ripples, hearing the soft splashes reverberate under the low ceiling. The pounding inside her ears overpowered the sound as she struggled to regulate her breathing. Another cough bubbled up in her throat.

"Where are we?" she whispered hoarsely.

Colin climbed to his feet. He had to be just over six feet tall, and his head nearly collided with the limestone daggers that clung to the cave roof.

"As best I can guess," he dipped at the waist to peer down the tunnel, "we might have been caught in a downwelling current." He read her confused expression and added, "A descending current. Or, at least I've heard of such a thing. It could have happened down in the canyon. We must have—" he glanced around incredulously, "—we must have been sucked into a cave."

"A sea cave?" she tested the theory out. "Do you realize how deep it would have to be if we're in a canyon? Wasn't the depth finder reading something like 500 feet when we were fishing?"

"Yeah," he stared at the water, "the canyon would be much deeper. At least a thousand feet deeper."

Stella usually studied the depth finder out of boredom when she went on fishing trips with the Wexlers. It was like following the signs as you drove up a mountain—*2000 feet above sea level. 3000 feet above sea level*—except in reverse.

She knew about submarine canyons because she had researched them the first time Jill's father mentioned taking them out fishing there. As you start to leave the coast behind, the ocean floor descends into what they call the continental slope. Submarine canyons are like deep valleys cut into that slope. They cut deep. Real deep. They're also the *home of some mighty fine tuna fishing*, as Don Wexler would say.

"So then—"

"How are we alive, and how is there oxygen 2000 feet below the ocean surface?" Colin voiced her unspoken questions. "I don't know yet."

Stella swallowed down the next obvious query. *How is there light in this cave?* He was already agitated, and heck, he had just saved her life. Why rile him?

"I'd like to figure out where the hell we are," he continued, "but we can't go investigating yet. If two people from the same boat were caught in the same current, then—"

"Then *Jill*—" she cried. "Your parents. They could end up here!"

Scrambling to the edge of the rock shelf,

Stella tried to detect anything in the murky pool. Colin knelt beside her. They stared in silence, willing the water to offer up another victim. All that could be heard were their labored breaths and the steady drops of water that fell from the jagged ceiling.

Could it be true?

Could they be down in one of the deep-sea Atlantic canyons?

It had to be. They were a hundred miles off the coast. No land was in sight, and the ocean floor had been 500 feet beneath them. The ocean floor would not have an oxygen-sustaining cave. So where else could they be?

Stella eyed the swollen drops of water at the tip of many of the bulbous mineral daggers. On cue, one fell and splattered against her soggy sandals.

One drop.

How many more would there be when the entire Atlantic Ocean was above you?

CHAPTER 2

"How far back does this cave go?" Stella asked.

They sat side by side, staring at the water, willing it to produce Colin's family.

"Maybe they're inside already," she suggested in a soft voice.

Colin's shoulder flinched. She wanted to reach out and touch it—to offer comfort. He was mourning the loss of his family, and he was doing it stoically. Little emotion was revealed in his profile—just the sharp line of his chin as if he was grinding his teeth. All the muscles in his body were taut, prepping to dive into the subterranean lagoon.

"I wanted to say—" she hesitated, "—I wanted to say, *thank you*. Thank you for saving me."

Colin looked at her, and his full lips twisted. "You shouldn't thank me. I just prolonged your agony." He jerked his chin towards the black pool. "*They* were the lucky ones. They aren't going to suffocate in a cave deep beneath the ocean."

Stella gasped. Anxious, she eyed the low ceiling. It closed in on her with grisly fangs ready to gnash.

"Look, I'm sorry," Colin whispered. "We'll—we'll figure something out."

Empty words, but she appreciated the sentiment.

After a shared silence, she cleared her throat and offered, "Why don't you stay here in case someone else—" she paused, "—appears. I'll go investigate a little deeper. I mean, there seems to be light coming from somewhere—"

Colin rose and crossed over to a pockmarked boulder the size of a couch. He stooped behind it and retrieved an aluminum cylinder, the illuminated end casting a tempered glow.

"I had this strapped to my wrist when I fell overboard. It cut out at some point. It's supposed to work up to 300 meters. I was surprised to see it turn back on inside this cave."

Stella jumped on any nibble. "Then maybe we're not that far from the surface."

Colin shook his head. "There's no pressure in this cave—that's why it's working. But the batteries are dying out."

"The light coming from it is so weak, and yet this cave seems to glow—"

A nearby splash made them both jolt. Colin rushed towards the rock ledge, getting down on his knees and peering over the edge into the dark water. A hand shot up from the pool, groping the slick shelf and slipping back into the depths.

"Colin!" Stella screamed.

Colin launched into the water and disappeared beneath the surface. Stella sank to her knees, searching for any sign of him, but it was like looking into a tar pit. The surface rippled in agitation, and Colin's dark hair cracked through. He reached for the ledge, and Stella grabbed onto his arm. At that moment, another figure surfaced, coughing and moaning. It was Don Wexler, Colin's father. Colin grasped him around the chest and hauled him tight against the rock shelf.

"Get him," Colin sputtered.

Stella scrambled closer, clasping her hands around Don's upper arm.

"Okay," she said. "I have a hold of him."

Colin clambered up onto the ledge and grabbed the other arm as they hoisted the man out of the water and sprawled him chest-down on the rigid surface. Don's cheek rested on the rock floor, water dribbling from his pale lips.

One trait Stella had always associated with Jill and Colin's father was his perpetual tan. The man was tan year-round. If he wasn't out on the STARKISSED, he was standing on a pier with a fishing pole in his hand. In the other hand was his cell phone, where he'd stay on top of his financial advisor duties.

"Dad!"

Colin flipped Don Wexler over. His ashen face was swollen, his eyelids puffy. Stella feared the worst as Colin hunched over him, adroitly applying CPR. She crawled to join him.

"How can I help?"

"Put your fingers under his neck and tilt his head back."

With shaking hands, she complied, wondering if her flesh felt as cold and clammy as the skin she touched.

Out of the corner of her eye, she caught motion. A slim white arm shot out of the water. It reached up into the air, fingers clawing futilely at the void.

"Get her!" Colin commanded as he stooped to blow air into his father's lungs.

Stella scrambled on her knees, feeling the crusty surface dig into her flesh. She leaned over the ledge, but the dark water had reclaimed any sign of life.

"I don't see her," she whispered, knowing what she had to do and trembling at the thought.

She had recognized Jill's braided leather bracelet, a gift Stella had given her on her birthday. Anger suddenly infused her. She was not going to let this ocean claim her best friend.

Stella dove into the pool and surfaced quickly to get her bearings. The waning glow of the flashlight cast Colin as an eerie, hunched eclipse, like a gargoyle perched on a rooftop. She tucked her head back under the water, but a few inches down, all traces of light vanished, leaving only harrowing blackness. She splayed her arms out and kicked her legs widely, hoping to connect with something. Eventually, the plan worked. Her foot brushed against an object. Not rock. Something malleable.

Stella spun in that direction and nearly sucked in the entire ocean when a manacle snatched her calf. Instinct was to jerk away, but she groped down her leg until she felt Jill's hand and latched onto it, pulling for all she was worth. As they rose, she felt the lithe form pull up alongside her, and together, they reached for the ledge, erupting with a severe cough.

Scrambling up onto the rock shelf, Stella immediately spun around, grabbing Jill under her armpits, trying to hoist the young woman from the sea. Frustrated by her waning strength, Stella growled. Aid came quickly in the form of two powerful arms that paralleled hers. Colin reached in, and together, they hauled Jill from the depths.

Jill's stark coughs echoed under the low ceiling. Her wet ponytail clung to her neck as she struggled onto her hands and knees. Dark blue eyes ringed with red spokes climbed up to meet their gaze.

"You—you're alive," she choked out. "Mom? Dad?"

Colin reached to help her to her feet. "Dad is here. He's breathing now."

Jill searched behind her brother. Some of the tension left her face when she spotted her father reclined against a boulder, methodically rubbing his chest. She went to him, collapsing onto her knees at his side.

"Dad, are you all right?"

Don patted her arm and nodded, though he still looked pale and puffy.

"Mom?" she asked in desperation, her head swinging in search.

Stella saw the same disbelief register on Jill's face that she had experienced on the first view of their surroundings.

"Colin," Don's voice cracked. "Have you seen her?

Colin was standing beside Stella. She could feel his tension—his desolation. He had already saved two people, yet he must have felt it was not enough.

"No," his tone was husky. "But, it took a while for Jill to surface, and she is safe—"

Jill huddled with her father, reverting from an eighteen-year-old young woman to a child seeking the protection of her parents.

Stella took a retreating step. She was uncomfortable under this raw display of family anguish. Even now, she felt as if Colin was staring at her. What was he thinking?

It should have been you instead of our mother.

Stumbling back another step, she found a spot to sit, removed from the grieving family.

What was her own mother thinking? Caroline Gullaksen didn't even know that her daughter was missing yet. These fishing trips with the Wexlers had become so commonplace over the years that Stella merely texted her mom when she left the pier and texted when she returned the next day. There was no cell coverage out at sea, and her mother was working anyway.

There were so few similarities between the Wexlers and the Gullaksens. The Wexlers were a semi-affluent, *whole* family. Stella was an only child. Her parents divorced when she was thirteen. Initially, she spent her summers with her father as part of the custody settlement, but then he had remarried, and his priorities…shifted.

Stella's mom worked for a pharmaceutical

company. Her evenings were spent running an online ceramic shop—pieces she crafted in their garage, sometimes in the middle of the night. Caroline Gullaksen was a busy woman—there was no doubt about that. Her ferocious attack on life was intended to keep them settled in the house that Stella's father purchased and could not afford. His income as a real estate agent was minimal, a loophole that significantly reduced his responsibilities toward Stella's welfare.

Stella's academic scholarship eased some of the financial burden on her mother, but still, the woman was possessed with never making them feel like they were treading water.

Stella snorted at the pun.

"It must have been a rogue current," Don pondered from his reclined position against a boulder, "but one with such force and speed to take us down to such a depth that we're— we're," he looked around, confused, "*below* the ocean floor? We were over a canyon." He tipped his head back, inspecting their seeping den. "But, if we went into that—"

"Yeah," Colin interrupted. "I've tried to work out the math. The minimum I could calculate would be well over a thousand feet. More like two."

His father mulled that over. "If it was a thousand—well, there have been fantasy stories about men free-diving that far. *Fantasies*, though. Most professional divers can't go further than 400 feet. How we didn't crush our lungs—"

His eyes teared up, and his throat locked. Jill linked her arms around her father's neck and wept into his shoulder.

"There's still a chance," Colin whispered, futilely staring at the black pool. His eyes swerved, spanning the low ceiling. "Maybe there is another entrance. Maybe Mom got pulled in through another vent."

Don shook his head.

"The more entrances there are, the less likely this air pocket could have formed."

Colin considered that, but his dark eyebrows dipped. "It's still worth exploring."

"I'll go!" Stella sprang to her feet, eager to do something—*anything*—but wait.

"Not alone," Colin commanded.

As much as she wanted to give this family their privacy, she was still human. Fear of the unknown nipped at her stomach. Having Colin at her side would ease some of those nerves.

"I'll be fine." There was an emptiness to her declaration.

Colin reached down and touched his sister's shoulder. "Stay here with Dad until we return."

Troubled eyes looked up at him. "And if you don't?"

"I don't think they can go far," Don assured, patting his daughter's arm. He nodded at Colin. "Seriously, son. Don't go beyond yelling distance. Wait until I can join you."

"We won't go far because we're leaving the flashlight with you." He paused. "Just in case."

Stella wrapped her arms around herself. What would happen when that light failed? They would be trapped in an obscure coffin two thousand feet under the ocean surface. Could there be a more horrific plight? The most dreadful nightmare could not do this crisis justice.

Colin stirred, shaking her from her panic.

"Come on. Stay close," he instructed.

Close.

There was no problem with that command. No way was she going to be left behind in this subterranean abyss.

As they started forward, her toe clipped Colin's heel, causing her to stumble and plant a palm on his back for support.

"A little too close," Colin muttered over his shoulder.

Stella's hand snapped back. It wasn't the first time she had inadvertently touched her best friend's older brother.

In high school, she had taken many fishing trips with the Wexlers. It was common for them to spend the night at sea so that Jill's dad could reach the best fishing spot. The cabin was tight on the STARKISSED, and Colin usually slept on the bench seat beside the kitchen table while the three females monopolized the V-shaped bed.

On one occasion, she, Jill, and Anne Wexler retired into the cabin for the night while Colin and his father remained up on deck. Stella and Jill took the bunk on one side of the V, and Anne slept on the other. At some point, the boat pitched slightly on a wave, and Stella rolled off her tight perch into the gap between the mattresses. Expecting to hit the floor, she instead landed on something pliant—something strong—something that smelled like the sea and Irish Spring.

Stella was a junior at the time. She had already been kissed and maybe pawed a little, but she still had very little knowledge of what a man felt like. Now she was pinned to a broad chest with her legs twined between his. Planting her palms on the carpet, she clambered for balance. Heat rushed to her cheeks, and every move she made to dislodge herself only made matters worse.

Colin didn't say a word. Powerful arms hefted her back onto the mattress, and just like that, his silhouette climbed through the hatch and back onto the deck.

Ever since that incident, she had a tough time looking him in the eye. It wasn't just because of the awkwardness of the situation. The truth she concealed was that she had a big-time crush on her best friend's brother.

The first time she met Colin Wexler, she was just a freshman in high school. He was a junior. The age difference seemed astronomical at the time. It wasn't until Colin started college that she came to grips with the fact that he was way out of her league. He was an adult now. He was working towards a career. He brought a girlfriend home over spring break. *A mad, hot one.*

Yeah, Colin Wexler was beyond her reach. But, heck, it had been fun fantasizing, especially after that incident in the middle of the night.

Once Colin started his junior year in college, he rarely had the time for the bi-monthly trips in the summer. He was taking summer classes in order to graduate with two degrees. There was little opportunity for her to see him anymore, let alone avoid eye contact.

And now, here she was, standing close enough to feel the heat of his body. It was all so surreal. Colin had been right, however. They had received a temporary stay of execution. Instead of dying quickly in the ocean, their death would be slow and agonizing. This futile attempt to search the cave—it was a distraction—*hope* to counter the despair in Don and Jill's eyes.

As they moved deeper into the cave, Stella explored the undulating ceiling. In some parts, the roof arced high and was lost in shadow. In others, it dipped low enough that they had to hunch over.

"Careful," Colin warned. "There's a row of rocks up ahead that we'll have to climb over. I think there is a chamber beyond them."

The flashlight's glow was waning behind them. Stella glanced down at the rocks only to find that her feet had surrendered to the shadows already. How could they climb something they couldn't even see?

Colin turned around. She could feel the warmth of his breath against her forehead. She nearly leaned into it.

"Put your hand on my shoulder and climb on top of this boulder. It's pretty level and wide enough for us both to fit. Don't jump off of it. Wait for me."

Stella nodded numbly. She curled her fingers around his shoulder and used the leverage to heft onto the three-foot-high boulder. Instinctively, she crouched, expecting to collide with the ceiling, but the shadows had claimed it as well. It could be an inch above her head or several yards for all she knew.

Colin scrambled up next to her, and they paused to listen momentarily. Stella heard his ragged breath. She heard a slight wheeze in her lungs. She listened to her friend's whimpers and her father's low, assuring murmur. She heard the blood thumping in her ears and the monotonous *drip, drip, drip*—a cadence of death.

"Col," Jill called from behind them. "The flashlight—it's going out."

Sure enough, Stella noticed it with dread. The beam offered a rusty yellow glow, its circumference half the size of what it was a few moments ago. She looked ahead, thinking that any chance of searching the far end of the cave was futile. Even now, she could feel Colin shift, ready to leap back down.

"Colin, wait." She touched his arm. "Do you see something ahead?"

She squinted, wondering if her mind was playing tricks on her. Maybe she was having a stroke. Narcosis.

The tall body beside her moved. He didn't say anything, but she could sense his focus.

"Light?" he asked quietly.

"Yeah. I keep thinking I'm imagining it, or it's some reflection from our beam. I mean, the walls are moist, right?"

Colin's silence troubled her. Finally, he said, "You're probably right."

"What are you guys whispering about?" Jill asked over a cough.

"Nothing. Just stay right there. If the light goes out, we need to know you're in the same spot. We'll find you." Colin looked back into the void. "Just give us a couple more minutes—"

Crouching and blindly dropping down to the cave floor, Colin reached up to give Stella a hand.

"The way the light is intersected, it appears to be around a bend," he suggested.

With the glimmer still in the distance and the boulders blocking out what little glow remained from the flashlight behind them, they progressed blindly. Stella nudged her toes out before her, testing the terrain for obstacles, but found this portion of the floor to be smooth and slippery.

"Maybe it's some sort of phosphorescence," she offered, careful to duck as the ceiling dipped.

"A pool of bioluminescent plankton," Colin considered. "Maybe. I can see where the passage turns now. It looks very narrow."

Narrow didn't concern her. What was there to be afraid of, claustrophobia? If she suffered from claustrophobia, she would have been a catatonic pretzel by now.

"What if we get disoriented and can't find our way back?"

They had progressed enough that Jill and her father were no longer in view. Along with the flashlight, they had been an anchor of sorts.

Now, Stella wanted nothing more than to link her arm through Colin's—not because of a childhood attraction but for the connection with another human being. If she lost him, she didn't want to die down here alone.

"We'll find our way back," he assured. "Just stay close behind me."

Oh, I can do close. No problem.

They moved in tandem, their fingers dragging along the moist wall for leverage. As they curled around the bend, Stella noticed a crack in the wall across from them. Not a crack so much as a fissure, possibly even another chute, another avenue to pursue. The ambient glow barely reached into its obscurity. She was about to return her gaze to the path ahead when a shadow passed through that chasm. A phantom cloud. There, and then gone.

Straining to distinguish anything in the blackened chute, she lifted her hand to tap Colin on the shoulder. Stopping just short of touching him, she shook her head and dismissed the vision as a byproduct of the creepy environment.

Cautiously negotiating the path, carefully emulating Col's steps, she cast one last glimpse back at the fissure.

Luminous eyes stared at her from its depths. Stella screamed.

CHAPTER 3

"What the hell?" Colin swung around.

Stella barely heard him over her thumping heart.

"Stel?"

Wraithlike spirals of condensation twisted through the cave, like the diaphanous gown of a banshee.

"Stella, dammit, what is it?"

"I—I—" Her hands were shaking. She clenched them into fists. "I saw a face."

"A face?"

He followed her gaze to the crack on the other side of the cave. Awareness snapped his body as large hands clasped her shoulders and swung her towards him.

"*Mom?*"

The desperation in that plea tugged at her heart. But no, what she saw looked nothing like the vivacious Anne Wexler. In that split second that she even now suspected was a delusion, she had witnessed a gaunt face, ashen with deep black shadows carved around shimmering eyes.

"No," she choked.

The mist continued its nebulous trek through the cave. It must have been an effect of this natural phenomenon that had deceived her.

Colin stared at her, his eyes barely visible in the waning light. How could she have witnessed that face in the wall so clearly if she could hardly see *his* face?

Simple. She imagined it.

"I'm just edgy," she explained. "I'm sorry."

The fingers on her shoulders relaxed slightly, but he still held onto her.

"This place—" his chin lifted as he searched the ceiling, "—will destroy our minds if we let it."

Stella almost sagged with relief. He understood. He understood that the fear of dying in this deep tomb far outweighed the actual fear of death.

"We should get back to Dad and Jill."

Yes. Strength in numbers.

"But," her cursed curiosity decided to intercede, "there is still light up ahead."

Even now, she could see the glow beyond Colin's shoulder. It enabled her to observe the clouds of condensation undulating in the humid tomb. Gleaming eyes had reflected off of it.

"Maybe I saw some sort of deep-sea creature," she whispered, still searching for an explanation.

"Maybe," he agreed without conviction.

Nonetheless, Colin had turned back towards the light, his broad shoulders nearly obscuring it.

"But, you're right," he agreed. "The only way we're going to get out of this place is to keep searching. There has to be—"

He didn't finish the sentence. There was no need. What else could there be? An elevator? They were over a thousand feet under the ocean surface, at least. It was physically impossible to swim. Their fate was sealed. Curling up into a four-person ball didn't seem like a viable alternative yet. As long as there was still air in her lungs and power in her legs, she was going to explore this cave of damnation.

"Let's just make it around this bend," she suggested.

The truth was that she was actually looking forward to college. This year, she started on her path toward a BA in Journalism with classes like Media Law and Ethics and the Culture of Journalism. Being a journalist was a childhood dream of hers. She was the editor of her first newspaper at the ripe age of 9. It was a hand-typed periodical chronicling her friends' activities, which she printed out three copies of, stapled them together, and handed them to the three subscribers: her mother, her father, and the next-door neighbor.

In high school, she started her blog, *Stella Says*. Despite the effusive title, no one really cared what she had to say. She didn't use it as a soapbox. There was no political rhetoric. It was simply a showcase of her random thoughts for the day. People always accused Stella of having her head in the clouds. If that was the case, it was only because she wanted a bird's-eye view. She needed to see the whole picture. She hated gaps. She hated missing information.

If there was some way to return from this

catastrophe at sea, just think of the documentary she could compose.

"Do you notice that?" Colin interrupted her thoughts.

"What?"

Unconsciously, she turned back towards that cleft in the cave wall, but no one was staring back at her.

"The echoes of our voices…they're growing fuller. Acoustics can be erratic in caves, but I get the impression that the chamber ahead is much larger."

Stella sensed a breeze across her cheek. It felt foreboding—a harbinger of danger. But successful journalists had to possess nerves of steel. They had to be able to walk into unsavory situations and emerge with answers.

She squared her shoulders and declared, "Let's go find out."

"Colin!" Don's voice sounded muffled, and yet it amplified off the walls. "Col, come back here."

Colin's body braced. "Are you okay?" he yelled back.

There was no answer.

Colin cast one last skeptical glance into the abyss and murmured, "We'll finish this after we check on them."

"Colin, you can't leave us like that," his father reprimanded. "Not now."

"We agreed that Stella and I should try to see if there was another access pool."

Despite the severity of their situation, Stella could tell that Colin was slightly annoyed by the censure. After all, he was right. They had agreed it was best to investigate. What if Mrs. Wexler was here already...maybe only yards away?

"Yes." Don sounded tired. "But not for so long. The flashlight is failing. If it goes, we better stick together."

Stella crouched down next to Jill. Her friend was sullen, not even acknowledging Stella's touch when she wrapped her arm around her for support. It was such a clash with Jill's typically vivid personality. Stella was the inquisitive one. Always studying, constantly searching the internet to answer whatever bizarre question popped into her mind. *Whatever happened to Einstein's brain after the autopsy? Why don't satellites show better images of the Apollo missions to the moon? What if we built an underground tunnel from San Francisco to Los Angeles, and an earthquake struck?*

In contrast to Stella's relentless inquiries, Jill Wexler was embarking on a language arts degree in hopes of becoming a teacher. She loved kids, and most of their weekend plans in high school were thwarted by Jill's babysitting duties. Jill was the Pied Piper, and the whole neighborhood flocked to her.

Jill used to tease Stella about overanalyzing. Jill would sit down on a lawn chair and hunch over with her elbow on her knee and her fist to her chin, mimicking the bronze sculpture of *The Thinker*.

"This is Stel," she would say. "Always

thinking."

But now, Jill, the bubbly eighteen-year-old with deep golden hair and sky-blue eyes, was withdrawn. She had even started humming—a distraction technique. Stella tried to identify the tune. It wasn't even from Jill's repertoire of favorites.

Stella clutched her friend tighter and murmured a boost of confidence, but it seemed to fall on deaf ears. Jill stared blindly at the gritty floor.

Glancing up, Stella found Jill's father in the same state. Occasionally, his head would roll back as he searched the black pool, but forlorn, he would drop back into his catatonic state.

Standing beside them, Colin looked morose, his palm flat against the wall. It supported more than his weight. It was a crutch to allow him to think. She could see the wheels turning—analyzing—calculating. Remaining steadfast by his family's side, he towered over them with a dark intensity that dared anyone to attempt them harm.

With nothing else worth focusing on, Stella continued to study his features. His deep chestnut hair was beginning to dry. It was cut short with a few natural spikes poking up above his forehead. His jawline was blunt, locked in contemplation. The red Rutgers t-shirt was still damp, clinging to a muscular, broad chest. His gray cargo shorts revealed long, tanned legs. She waited for him to break from his spell and suggest a plan, but he was caught up in his family's melancholy.

So that's it. That's what they wanted. They

37

wanted the four-person huddle of death. She couldn't do it. Maybe she had imagined things in the adjacent chamber, but it was better than staring at a black pool—a one-way ticket to the insane asylum. Stella understood that they were waiting for that tepid portal to emit their mother—their wife. But no one was going to come through that gateway for her. She had to be independent. She had to find her own solace.

Stella slipped from Jill's side without a reaction from her despondent friend. She stroked Jill's moist hair and whispered, "I'll be right back. Stay strong."

A slight flinch of Jill's shoulder served as the only acknowledgment. Stella tried to make eye contact with Jill's father. His shoulders were hunched, and his arms wrapped around his knees. He leaned slightly under the weight of his daughter resting against him. Colin crouched to join them, grabbing a rock and tossing it into the water. The ripple effect made their heads rise in unison, and in harmony, they all sank again.

Stella crept away.

Sure, she was scared. Out of her mind, scared. But she had to move. She had to keep moving. If the glow proved to be just a figment of her imagination, she would be back soon.

Climbing the row of boulders that dissected this grotto from the chamber next to it, Stella's sandal skidded on the moist surface, and she scraped her thigh as she slipped down the other side. Ignoring the mishap, she blinked, acclimating to the loss of light. Nervous fingertips touched the wall for guidance as memory directed her. Eventually, a diffused glow made objects discernable again. Soon she found herself across from the sharp slash in the opposite wall.

Stella squinted into that crevice, prepared to meet the simmering eyes of a subterranean phantom. It was empty, though.

Forcing herself past that sinister lair, she hiked forward, feeling a tickle of wind flutter her bangs. The walls brightened as she progressed. There was an erratic bob to the glow as if the source was in motion.

Casting a glance behind her, the path to the Wexlers was no longer visible. A yawning blackness had claimed it, seeking to obliterate her route. Stella took a deep breath. The pungent smell of brine filled her nostrils. Focusing on the pulsing glow, she followed the natural bend of the cavern until she heard something.

She froze.

Curse her chest. It wheezed. That thin whistle was all she was able to hear. Another step. Another few inches closer to the light. Suddenly, a shadow formed on the wall. A nebulous hulk that loomed across the craggy surface and then vanished. Stella refused to give in to fear. She crept forward and heard a slothful tread. It was so close.

Another curve, and she emerged into a vaulted cavern. The hint of wind continued across her face, but the breeze was warm—the cavern sultry. It was a shock. She had expected a biting chill in this underwater wasteland.

The light that she had chased was stationary now. Tucked behind a boulder, its gleam cast a halo around the rock's perimeter. Stella took another step and then shrieked. A figure stepped into the light. A man. A man with a gaunt face and simmering eyes.

A hand clamped down on her shoulder.

Stella's heart convulsed.

"What the hell?" Colin hissed behind her.

The figure retreated so that half of his body was consumed by the shadows. What remained visible was a medium-sized man in a knitted sweater, the cuffs unraveled, casting spaghetti noodles of wool around his wrists. Black pants hung loose, the knees patched with another swathe of fabric. A black knit cap revealed a fringe of graying hair over a thin, angular face. The eyes she had thought were simmering were merely reflecting off whatever the source of light was. The man bent into that glow, and when he rose, a yellow radius ensnared him. In his scarred hand was a lantern.

Stella's heart thudded.

"Who are you?" Colin asked as he stepped out from behind Stella, strategically guiding her behind him.

She wasn't about to protest having Colin's wide shoulders as a barrier between her and this creepy specter. She hiked onto her toes to try and gauge the man's reaction. Was he even real? Were she and Colin jointly deranged?

One graying eyebrow cocked inquisitively as the man studied Colin. He scratched under his hat and cleared his throat.

"Sorry," he muttered.

Sorry?

Stella clamped down on her fear. She cracked her head around Colin's arm and demanded, "*Sorry?* For what? Who are you?"

Colin turned and narrowed his eyes at her.

"I'm sorry you found your way down here," the man uttered in a hoarse voice. "You must have been traveling with the woman?"

Colin tensed. "*What* woman?"

"A woman surfaced in the grotto not too long ago. She is not well, but we're trying."

We're?

"Blonde?" Colin barked.

"Yes, yes," the man kept his face averted. He was looking deeper into the chamber.

"Are there more of you?" the man asked.

"More of *us*?" Stella quipped. "How many more of *you* are there?"

"*Stella*," Colin lectured.

Pressing her lips tight, she contained herself, but the questions were brewing, boiling up in her throat.

"Yes," Colin responded. "My father and my sister are behind us."

The man peered over Colin's shoulder. "Do they need medical attention?"

"Why, is there a hospital down here?" Stella retorted.

I mean, come on, seriously.

Colin gave her another quelling look. She glared back.

"My father is having trouble breathing, but he's recovering."

The man nodded. "Why don't you go back to him? We'll come for you."

"*We'll?* How did you get down here?" Colin asked. "How do we get back to the surface?"

Thank you, Col!

At least he was coming around and finally asking the critical questions.

The man lifted his lantern, bringing the light closer to his face. A chill jolted through her. This wasn't the gaunt visage she had witnessed in the crack in the cave wall, but this man looked equally disturbing. He was pale to the point that his skin appeared translucent, with black lines scoring across his cheeks. Veins, no doubt, but their contrast was so pronounced under the thin skin. Shadows clung under gray eyes like the black grease football players use to reduce glare. His eyes seemed lifeless—little granite pebbles inserted in his lean face.

"It's easy to get *down* here," he uttered in a thick voice. The granite eyes shifted between her and Colin as he added, "It's impossible to get back up."

CHAPTER 4

Don Wexler studied his son in the waning light. The beam offered a tarnished blush that was amplified only by the border of absolute darkness.

"It's okay, son." He nodded, resigned. "It's time for you to sit down with us. You tried."

Even without the light, Stella could sense Colin's frustration. It crackled through the air. He loomed tall under the stalactites waiting to feast on his head.

"I'm not imagining things, Dad. Stella saw him, too. We're both completely lucid. He said—"

Stella understood Colin's reluctance to divulge the news about his mother. Don already thought his son was delusional. He would find it cruel that Colin would bait him in their final hours.

"He said what?" Don prompted in a husky voice.

"Never mind." Colin turned his back to the group huddled on the ground.

Stella wanted to go to him and offer some notion of comfort. Perhaps she should speak up and validate what they had seen.

Watching Don and Jill absorbed in their grief, Stella searched the channel from which she and Col had just emerged. There was no glow. No hint of life. The void encroached now with bleeding fingers of obscurity slowly fisting around the grotto.

Maybe Don was right. Maybe she and Colin *were* delusional. How could they have seen a human down here—over a thousand feet from the surface?

Stella folded onto her knees, tucking her head and focusing inward, conjuring up an image of her mother making meatballs in the kitchen. Caroline Gullaksen used the back of her hand to scratch her nose, her palms speckled with parmesan and eggs.

"Stell, can you get me a paper towel?"

Stella yanked a paper towel off the rack and taunted her mother with it. "Do I get to pick the movie tonight?"

"Heck, no. You'll pick some science fiction crap about sharks in outer space."

"Then, *no* paper towel for you."

Caroline wrinkled her nose to avert a sneeze. "Fine," she relented. "Sharks in space it is. Now hurry!"

Stella wiped her mother's nose. "A double feature?"

Cool fingers touched hers, yanking Stella from the memory. She opened her eyes, but there was barely any light to register the source. She recognized it, though. Jill had reached for her hand and tucked it against her hip. The muffled drum of a pulse beat there. It was reassuring. When the light finally failed, at least that stabilizing throb of life would still persist…for a little while.

It felt good to have the touch of her best friend at her side, but she wished…she wished Colin would hold her. If she was going to die, couldn't her last wish be to die in his arms?

Okay, pathetic as hell, Gullaksen.

Colin had never even glanced at her that way…, but still, it was her death…and that was her wretched wish.

In the blackness, Stella heard the shift of Colin's shoe. He was still standing. He knew nothing of her desire. He would forever be the elusive older brother of her best friend, a man put on this earth for Stella to fantasize about.

She drew in a shaky breath laden with the dank scent of stagnant seawater. Their power huddle could not stave off the darkness. It grew into a yawning despondency aimed at burying them alive.

When the last spark of the flashlight faded, Stella heard Colin curse. Her heart kicked up its pace, and she started to hyperventilate. Jill's whimpers dissolved into a keening moan. Don chanted hopeless words of assurance. The tomb closed in on them.

Light.

A pulsing light to match her heartbeat.

A shadow…two shadows…scaling the cave wall until they grew into macabre giants.

Stella planted her palms on the moist ground to hoist into a half-crouch. The light resumed at a less frenetic pace as the shadows shortened, eaten by the blunt stalagmites that formed a stockade around the pool.

Her eyes hungrily latched onto the bobbing lantern as it rounded the corner. She feasted on *it* rather than the pale, gnarled fingers that clutched the handle.

Only after the gasps sounded beside her did the source of this miracle register. She rose when she saw Colin step towards the approaching couple.

Two people down here!

An equally haggard woman joined the man she and Colin had seen. She wore a calf-length dress that might have once been white but was now deeply marbled with diverse stains. Dark hair peppered with gray was curled up into a loose bun that eclipsed the woman's head. Wide eyes flickered for a second as the man raised the lantern.

Was this the face Stella had seen in the shadows?

"What the—?" Don muttered as he struggled to his feet.

Jill inserted herself under her father's arm for support, looking like she couldn't handle much more trauma.

"I imagine our presence here comes as quite a shock to you," the stranger stated in a hoarse voice.

"Shock?" Don laughed hollowly. "You think this shocks us?"

The high pitch alarmed Stella. It caught Colin's attention as well. He stepped in between the couple and his father.

"My mother. You said—"

"We will take you to her," the man stated

with a nod.

"Anne!" Don stumbled away from Jill's clutch.

Colin's solid arm proved a barrier, thwarting his father's attempt to charge forward.

"Who are you people?" Don cried out. "Did your ship go down in the storm, too? Where are we? Where is my wife?"

"Dad," Colin clasped his father's shoulders. "Easy. The answers will come. Let's find Mom."

Don composed himself somewhat, but Stella worried about his stability—physically and mentally. Glancing at this bizarre couple in their curious, frayed attire, she was concerned about her own mental state. Had she already died and been stuck in some deviant universe? A quick fact-check of her life convinced her that she would head north after death, but apparently, this tribunal had other plans.

"Come with us," the man uttered. "We know you will have many questions. Let Sarah check you out, and then we can talk."

Well, whatever direction death was taking her, Stella wanted to hear these answers.

Unconsciously, she patted the back pocket of her shorts, but her cell phone was not there. It was back in the cabin of the STARKISSED where she left it on the counter. The recorder would have come in handy because this was about to be the interview of a lifetime.

"Who is Sarah?" Stella asked as she fell in

directly behind the couple.

The man glanced over his shoulder, his step wavering to accommodate Don Wexler's slow pace. Don's gait improved after the first step or two, and now his expression looked resolved.

"Sarah," the man nodded at the huge bun at his side. "My wife. She is a nurse."

Stella studied the back of the soiled dress with new interest. The style seemed outdated, but somewhere beneath the grime, she noticed the haunting semblance of a nurse's uniform.

"I am Etienne," the man continued, although now he faced forward, and his words were distorted by the volleying acoustics. "Etienne Fournier."

"How long have you been down here?" Stella probed. "Did the storm capsize your boat, too?"

Cool gray eyes turned back to stare at her. He reminded her of a raccoon with heavy black shadows etched around those dissecting orbs.

"The storm?" he echoed wryly.

The woman, Sarah, turned her head to look at him. Under the glow of the lantern, it was a meaningful exchange.

"Yes, the storm sent us down here," he affirmed in a hollow tone.

Stella stared at the back of Sarah's head. The bun dipped low but not low enough to conceal the painfully thin neck. The stitching where her shoulders should be hung low on her arms. The woman had lost significant weight, and the belt around the waist was cinched with a knot rather than the holes it originally came with.

Etienne also bore signs of malnourishment, but his frame was large enough to distract from it. He was nowhere near as tall as Colin, who now ducked his head as they traveled through the narrow tunnel. She tried to make eye contact with him—to give him a, *What the hell is going on?* look. He averted his gaze before she could connect.

They followed like bugs attracted to a light bulb. The lantern was a temptress. Stella peered through the tarnished glass, noticing that it was fueled by oil.

The tunnel emerged into a vaulted chamber, the vast space apparent by the shift in resonation. She could no longer hear the echo of her own breath. Still, the scope of the lantern cloistered them in a tight, glowing sphere, keeping the unknown at bay.

Stella felt perspiration bead up on her forehead. The cave walls were recessed enough that all six of them could walk abreast if they wanted, but they stuck to their tandem. Etienne and Sarah in the lead, followed by Colin, with Stella a step behind. Don and Jill stumbled in the rear as their chins tipped up in inspection.

"It's so warm in here," Stella observed.

She wore only the navy drawstring shorts and red tank top she had fallen asleep in. The outfit had primarily dried, but she expected to be freezing. There was no sunlight. No source of heat. The ocean had steadily grown glacial as she descended. So why was she sweating? Was she ill?

Etienne's arm stretched out, the tattered wool hanging loosely from it. A contorted finger pointed to the right.

"There is a chute over there that leads into an antechamber. At the far end of that antechamber is another cavern. Stay clear of that area. It is dotted with hydrothermal vents. Temperatures can reach 200 degrees," he paused and clarified, "Celsius."

"Hydrothermal vents?" Don echoed from behind.

Stella wasn't sure if he sounded shocked or just had no clue what Etienne was talking about.

Doing a quick calculation in her head of 1 degree Celsius to 32 degrees Fahrenheit, she thought it was no wonder she was in such a sweat.

"Yes, the thermal vents are what sustain us down here," Etienne continued with a slight accent Stella couldn't place. The name was French, but the inflection didn't quite match it.

"There is an intricate tunnel system that allows us to exist at a safe distance from the heat. These natural chimneys are providing us with oxygen."

"How?" Colin beat her to the question.

The silhouette of a grin appeared over Etienne's shoulder. With the lantern behind his face, it looked more like a jaw x-ray.

"There will be time to answer your questions. Let's get you settled and reunite you with your mother."

Stella felt a rush at her side. Jill stormed by, sidling up alongside the man.

"Where is she?" she demanded.

"Not far." He was tolerant. Patient. "There is another grotto near here. That is where your mother surfaced. Most come up in the pool you did, but it depends on the tug of the current and whether a nearby vent is spouting."

Most?

"How is she?" Jill nearly latched onto his arm. It looked as if she wanted to yank the wiry limb until she got the answers she desired.

Etienne turned to look at Sarah. Did the woman speak? Only a tight nod of her angular chin served as communication.

He returned his attention to Jill.

"She is not conscious yet."

"What?"

This time, Don jerked forward, only to be stopped by Colin's grasp.

"Dad, wait until you see her."

Anger, confrontation, demands—they would yield nothing down here.

"Dammit, if I had just grabbed onto the first aid kit—" Don's voice faded.

"We have medical supplies here," Etienne assured.

Right, Stella mused. *Maybe they had internet too.*

The likelihood that these two bedraggled individuals possessed anything of value, including their cognizance, was rapidly decreasing. Any further questions would likely be deflected, so they trudged in silent pairs, still lured by the light.

Above all else, keep to the light.

A breeze brushed Stella's hair from her face. In front of them, a natural archway came into view.

Etienne hesitated. He turned away from this

portal and scanned their faces.

"You'll be safe here."

With no need for the lantern anymore, he dropped his arm and stepped out of their way.

As Stella moved past him, she clutched her heart.

"No freaking way."

CHAPTER 5

Jill gasped. Don let loose an expletive. Colin remained impassive, but Stella thought she caught a tremor in his hand.

The enormity of the chamber stole her breath. Stella felt like a tiny spec in a grand theatre. Torches and lanterns dotted the walls, some so distant they seemed like a chain of fluttering fireflies. Even the fireflies could not reach the great heights of the vaulted ceiling. The soaring natural dome crested over multiple summits. It was the closest peak of bedrock that arrested her attention—or rather, what lay at the foot of it.

Buildings. Crudely formed from wreckage. Some dwellings were crafted from wooden ship carcasses, while others were more abstract configurations. The door from a yacht nestled into the fuselage of a warplane. A cargo container was capped with the skeletal remains of a ship's bridge, forming a multi-story edifice.

These diverse habitats wrapped around the base of the lofty rock pinnacle and continued down a man-made avenue carved through the gritty cave floor. Aluminum railings scaled the rock peaks, leading to even more dwellings. Stella noticed a wooden crow's nest jutting out of the crag, a vantage point to survey this freakish city.

Dizzy, she grabbed onto the hemp rope railing that flanked the path and then yanked her hand away, finding the accent just another bizarre touch to this subterranean realm.

"We call it the Underworld," Etienne murmured with reverence. "I'm a bit of a Greek mythology buff. In fact, the stream you see over there, we've named it the Styx."

Don stepped forward. A furrow etched across a forehead that was usually concealed beneath a baseball cap. For the first time, Stella noticed how much gray had overtaken his dark hair.

"How quaint," he spat. "Now let me see my wife. Then—" he hesitated, "—then maybe I can start to absorb all of this."

Sarah turned around. In this enhanced lighting, Stella could finally see her face. It was thin and triangular, with the wide-eyed appearance of someone with a thyroid problem.

"I'll show you to the infirmary," she spoke softly, her head bowing under the heightened agitation.

"The infirmary," Don jibed. "Of course."

Stella couldn't blame his sarcasm. What was next, a movie theater? She stared around the ramshackle maritime village and wondered who the makeshift houses were for. She didn't see anybody, but something Etienne had said made it sound as if there were others.

Recalling one of the Greek mythology books she had read, she tried to remember what it said about the Underworld. Wasn't it the kingdom of the dead?

"This way," Sarah beckoned with a thin finger.

She led them to an airplane torso. The wings were sheared from the aluminum body, and wood paneling closed off both open ends. A tarnished red cross plaque hung inside one of the square windows. Etienne tugged on the handle of a doorway marked *Emergency Exit* in red letters. The hatch swung open, and he managed a brisk step up into the fuselage, beckoning them to follow.

Sarah stood below the hatch like some ghoulish stewardess in her soiled uniform, smiling and offering Don a hand. He looked at it and then up into her eyes and shook his head.

"*Thanks, I'm good,*" Stella heard him say.

Stella felt someone watching her. She turned to see Jill hesitating on her approach to the gutted plane. For the first time down here, she witnessed a flash of clarity in her best friend's gaze. Golden eyebrows lifted in silent inquiry. *Is this really happening?*

Shrugging, Stella reached for her friend's arm.

"Let's go in together," she offered.

Jill's lips curled up gratefully. Using Stella's shoulder for support, she climbed the steep step, and Stella quickly followed. The whole chassis shifted slightly when Colin clambered up behind them. Once he was inside, the floor stabilized. A quick survey of the surprisingly wide belly of the old aircraft determined that the ceiling was high enough for Colin to stand upright and wide enough to house side-by-side cots. Two sets of them. One of these cots held a figure wrapped in a blanket. Stella noticed blonde hair spilling off the back end of the short cot.

"Mom!" Jill bolted and dropped to her knees before the inert woman on the gurney.

Don crouched down beside her, his palm cupping Anne Wexler's forehead. "Annie, can you hear me?"

There was no response. Stella peeked over Jill's shoulder to check the rise and fall of the blanket. Anne was still alive.

Desolation dimmed Don Wexler's hazel eyes.

Sarah, the nurse, spared his unvoiced question.

"Only time will tell," she offered gently.

Don's glance flicked around the gutted plane in disgust.

"This isn't an infirmary," he fumed. "This is a rusted plane carcass with—with—" he searched the contents of a three-legged metal table supported by a wooden wheelchair, "— with a few glass bottles of God knows what and a bunch of other rubbish."

His eyes volleyed frenetically between Etienne and Sarah. "You can't take care of my wife. Are you playing some kind of game down here? Have you all lost your minds? This is some sort of mass hallucination."

Sarah cringed and rushed over to the metal table, snatching up one of the tarnished bottles.

"These are antiseptics. They are unopened, and one even has an expiration date of 1996."

Stella flinched. She sensed the roar of the lion before it even sounded.

"Well, isn't that just swell!" Don barked. "Maybe you have some Frankincense and Myrrh down here too."

"Dad." Colin placed a hand on his father's shoulder. "We should all be dead already. There's no sense in getting angry."

Don shot him a contemptuous look. "Aren't you just the festive one."

His profile bore similarities to Colin's. Both possessed dark features, but Colin's eyes were a deep evergreen, like the depths of a forest, unlike his father's tepid shade.

Stella sensed an animosity between the two men that must have been established long before they went out to sea. Their silent face-off made for an awkward stillness. It was disturbed by a faint rattle from Anne's chest. Don quickly stooped over her.

"Is there anything in this *infirmary* that can help her?"

Sarah looked sympathetic, but with that gaunt visage, she seemed like she belonged on the gurney as well.

"We've got her breathing, and her blood pressure has stabilized. Her body temperature is too low at the moment. It's warm in here, and I have her wrapped in several blankets, but if you really want to help her," she paused, "I suggest you hold your wife."

The brevity left Don's face. He slipped his arm beneath Anne's shoulders and dipped his forehead against her throat as her head lolled to the side.

"Momma," Jill whimpered.

Colin clutched his sister's shoulder. "Stay with her," he whispered. "Let me see if I can find out anything more."

Jill met his eyes. "Okay. But don't go far."

Her warning was sobering. Colin's jaw muscle clenched as he nodded and squeezed her shoulder. He looked down at his mother and Stella could see the pain on his face. He cast a quick glimpse at his father, but the man was oblivious.

Colin turned to confront Etienne.

"Can we talk?" he demanded in a husky voice.

Etienne dipped his head in assent and pivoted to step down through the hatch. Colin started to follow and then paused to glance at Stella. She held her breath.

"Do you want to stay here?"

"No," she muttered.

If Colin was going to grill this disheveled mariner, she wanted to be there.

He climbed down out of the plane—oh, excuse me, *infirmary*—and turned to offer her a hand. She took it, grounded by the strength in that grip.

Casting a quick glimpse back, she saw that Sarah remained behind with the patient. It was minimal comfort, yet consolation nonetheless.

Outside, the view still stunned her. Torches handcrafted with cloth tips lined a crudely carved path in the cave floor. The path was flanked with jagged bedrock, and on these pitted slopes, heaps of wreckage were fashioned into small houses and lean-tos. Stella saw a pair of deck chairs seated before a cabin door latched onto an inverted hull, its white façade stripped down to raw wood.

"This cabin is free," Etienne remarked as they passed the upside-down boat. "As is the one next door. They're yours now."

Stella glanced at the *cabin* next door. It looked like an orange cargo container had been sliced in half and the circular turret of a fishing vessel attached to the open gap. Ragged shards of tarp acted as curtains hanging from glassless window frames.

"Oh, I'll take the one with the sunroom," she muttered.

Colin heard her but did not react.

"You, Jill—" he hesitated, "—and mom can have that one. Dad and I will take this one. We'll need some rest."

Stella studied his face and saw that he, too, found this all absurd. That gave her some comfort. But their host seemed keen on their approval, so they offered him weary smiles.

"Good," Etienne beamed.

"Thank you for your hospitality," Colin offered cautiously. "But you can understand that we're eager to learn more about this place. It's pretty unbelievable that you've been able to survive down here—that *we've* survived."

Good ole' Col. So pragmatic when all she wanted to do was grab this eccentric man by the collar and rattle him until answers tumbled out of his yellowed teeth.

What's the matter, no dentists down here?

Even as she thought it, she took a quick glimpse, half expecting to see a DENTIST sign on an upturned airplane wing.

"Of course." Etienne's good spirits dimmed slightly. "We're going up there."

He pointed up a hill of packed rock that formed a plateau, the spot where she had seen the crow's nest.

Following him, they passed by a basketball pole and backboard, the ring void of any net. It stood askew, another tarnished slant on reality. Stella jolted when she saw a figure huddled in the deep shadows beneath it. She barely distinguished the form, but the dark eyes tracked her, shifting with her motion. Pinpricks of panic erupted on her arms.

"Col," she whispered.

"I see," he replied softly.

"You offered us this—" Colin searched for a word, "—lodging. How many others are here?"

As they climbed up the slope, Stella held the rope fence for support when the granular surface became slippery.

"A few," Etienne hedged.

"Where are they?"

"Please," Etienne held his hand out. "You will meet them in due time, but right now, there is someone I'd like to introduce you to. Together, we'll be able to answer most of your questions."

Finally. Stella's steps accelerated.

At the top of the plateau, the wooden crow's nest perched above the ghostly village, its decaying pole penetrating deep into the red, gritty surface. Drawn towards it, Stella cautiously touched the wooden basket, afraid of coming away with a splinter. From here, she could see the top of the old airplane that now held most of the Wexler family. A light glowed from within, but there was no motion.

Who had been lurking in the shadows?

"Stel," Colin called. "This way."

Pivoting to follow, she noticed a slight waterfall trickling through the ceiling of the cave. It spilled into a black stream that fissured through to another chamber. The sight of water leaking from above didn't inspire confidence.

She was going to point it out to Colin, but she caught him eyeing the cascade. The telltale nudge of his chin upwards meant he harbored the same fears. There was an entire ocean above them. How long until this narrow torrent exploded and consumed them?

"Here we are," Etienne interrupted their thoughts.

At first, Stella couldn't even recognize what was before her. A barnacle-encrusted wall nearly blended with the copper bedrock behind it. A window poked out of the barrier of shellfish, and it was the faint glow from inside that drew her attention. The light flickered as a shadow passed before it.

Etienne disappeared behind the wall and then poked his head out to summon them.

It was hard to read Colin's eyes in the limited light, but she could tell by his stiff posture that he was on high alert.

Around the corner of the barnacled wall was an open doorway, or the facsimile of one. A rotted wooden panel rested against corroded metal. Etienne pushed it aside, and light spilled onto the granular floor. Stella looked up, but Etienne's silhouette now filled the gap as he dipped his head and stepped inside. She followed, able to stand upright within the improvised hut. It looked like a section from a cabin. Not a cruise ship cabin, but something more utilitarian, like a naval vessel. It was as if the berth had been severed, losing one wall to some unknown fate. The remainder was lodged tight against the rock face of the peak, and along that earthen wall, a desk sat with an oil lamp that warmly lit the quarters. A metal bunk jutted from the façade.

On the inside, all barnacles had been shaved off meticulously by hand. A burlap bag covered the metal bunk, serving as a mattress or blanket. A few crates were stacked in the corners, and atop these were some maritime gadgets she couldn't identify.

A warped painting of an old clipper ship hung from a spike hammered into the bedrock wall. As bizarre as that touch was, everything paled compared to the daunting figure now rising from the desk.

"Welcome," the man extended his hand.

He was tall—not as tall as Colin, but he towered over Etienne. Thinning pale blonde hair mixed with silvery strands ran slightly long. It flared around the collar of his tattered jacket. He wore a uniform of sorts, navy pants, and jacket where a gap in the wool revealed a stained white t-shirt. On the open lapel of the jacket, Stella could make out some of the stitching. N-I-C-H-

O

"My name is Frederic. Frederic Nichols," he offered, his sinewy hand still hovering in empty space.

To spare the discomfort, Colin finally reached forward to shake it. Stella noticed the muscle in his forearm spasm on contact.

"Colin Wexler," he stated flatly.

"Nice to meet you, Colin." Frederic cocked his head to the side, and Stella felt herself under a penetrating gaze.

Frederic appeared slightly younger than Etienne, but both had such a gaunt countenance that it was hard to gauge age. Cerulean eyes stared at her from under hooded lids. Blue veins scored paths down each temple and disappeared back into the hairline. There was a sharp angle to his cheekbones, and his chin was very pointed. Still, there was something vaguely appealing about him, as if, at some point in his life, he had been very handsome. Before her now was a ghostly version of that long-forgotten youth.

"I'm Stella," she declared and then cleared the frog in her throat. "Stella Gullaksen."

"Swedish?" His blonde eyebrows raised.

"My father was Swedish," she mumbled.

Naturally, her father was alive and kicking, but she had begun referring to him in the past tense somewhere along the line. "Two generations ago," she added.

"Of course." He nodded with a fascinated smile.

Seeking a break from Frederic's sharp eyes, her glance probed the lodging. A wooden collapsible chaise lounge was folded up in the corner. Next to it was a bucket of water with a clean cloth hanging from a wall spike.

"You are the children of the woman we found earlier?" Frederic asked.

His tone was deep, with a strange inflection. Subtle but distinctive.

"I am her son," Colin affirmed.

"I'm just a friend," she muttered.

"Do you have any medical experience?" Colin asked. "Can you help her?"

Frederic's lips thinned, but there was compassion in his steady gaze.

"Sarah is best equipped to care for your mother. She is a medic," he assured. "It appears your mother went a long time without oxygen—"

"We *all* went a long time without oxygen," Colin interrupted.

"She did not emerge from the water as quickly as you all did. And we did not notice her immediately. She surfaced in one of the back caverns."

"You noticed us?" Stella asked, thinking of Colin's mouth pressing life into her, and yet no one came to assist.

"We heard both of you," Frederic's eyes shifted between them.

"And you didn't come to help when my father surfaced?" Colin accused.

Stella touched his arm. His gaze dropped down to that connection, and he collected himself.

"You were all in a mild state of shock from the trauma of waking up in here," Etienne spoke up. "If we were to suddenly appear, it would have been too much for you to assimilate."

"I can assimilate a lot." Colin's voice deepened. "I can assimilate that you have yet to tell us where we are, how we survived, and how we're going to get back to the surface."

Stella executed a mental fist pump.

Etienne and Frederic exchanged a lengthy glance, and then the shorter man sighed.

"Let's step outside," Etienne suggested.

The quarters were a little cramped for the four of them.

As they filed out onto the earthen path, he explained, "We were once as bewildered as you. Frederic, Sarah, and I were aboard the DONOVAN, a trawler owned by the Fisheries and Research Board of Canada."

Following out of the cabin, Colin hesitated and held out his hand, prompting Stella in front of him. They approached the rope railing at the edge of the plateau and looked down at the cavern floor.

A thin stream of black water curled past the crude abodes and around the base of the very peak they stood on. Mist hung in the air, trapping the smoke from the torches to create a low, hazy ceiling.

"What happened?" Stella asked, dragging her eyes from the gutted military plane below.

"We were at sea pretty late in the fall— probably too late. We were trying to get in some last-minute lab work," Frederic explained. "I was the hydrographic equipment handler."

Stella searched Colin's face for a translation. She knew he was more familiar with the sea and its sciences than she would ever be.

"Hydrography—" he read her questioning gaze. "They basically map out the sea floor."

He turned to Frederic for verification.

Frederic nodded, pleased. "Yes. We measure depths, search for obstacles."

"Then you would have known the depth you were at when—"

"Just before we sank," Frederic filled in. "Yes, I was in the lab. The continental shelf was at about 150 meters there," he paused and explained, "about 500 feet."

"500 feet!" Stella exclaimed. "If we had oxygen, we could possibly survive an ascent."

The grim faces around her stole some of her enthusiasm.

"True," Frederic agreed, "but that is not where we are. When the abandon-ship alarm sounded on the DONOVAN, I was literally charting the floor beneath us for a map I had to submit. We were crossing over a canyon at the time. I recall it vividly because I was working with the Hydroplot system, and it was passing back data that confirmed the canyon's existence. I had been trying to plot the canyon depth, which was growing deeper by the minute. At the time of the abandon-ship, we were at 1840 meters or about 6000 feet."

"Well over a mile," Colin calculated.

"Whoa." Stella's hand snapped out. "You think we're over a mile under the ocean surface?"

Frederic shrugged. "Close to it. The storm was fierce. The DONOVAN was tossed around by the waves. Some life rafts made it into the water. The labs were on the second to the last deck. Etienne was across the hall from me, and Sarah was on the same level in the First Aid Center. We tried to reach the main deck, but by then, the DONOVAN had started listing too far for us to climb."

Despite the heat and humidity, Stella clasped her arms about herself as she listened intently.

"What happened?" she asked.

"We made it astern," Etienne filled in with his hoarse voice, "but a wave came—it knocked us over the railing."

That sensation was all too real for her. She recalled the surf crashing down and tossing her into the ocean like she was chum for the tuna.

"I tried to hold onto Sarah, but the churn of the wave yanked us apart. And then I was caught in a current that hauled me down no matter how hard I kicked against it." Gray eyes looked haunted. "I knew I was going to die. I knew I'd never see my wife again."

"But you didn't die," Stella offered feebly.

Etienne's pale lips twitched. "True. I was caught—" he looked towards Frederic, "we were *all* caught in this strong down-current. We descended so fast."

Frederic interrupted. "Even in the confusion of darkness, I knew we had traveled well greater than 150 meters. There was nowhere else for us to go. We had to have been dragged down into the canyon. No one had done any studies on the currents there yet. Whatever we were experiencing was something undocumented."

"No shit," Colin mumbled.

Stella shot him a glare, but he remained resigned.

"And you all surfaced in the same cave we did?" he asked.

"I did," Frederic stated. "Sarah and Etienne surfaced in the cavern where your mother emerged. You can imagine our surprise when we found each other."

"Yes, I *can* imagine your surprise," Colin replied with a hint of cynicism. "Can you imagine *our* shock at seeing this?" His arm swept at the peculiar village below.

Stella was studying Frederic and Etienne's faces. Etienne followed the sweep of Colin's arm, and an expression of subdued satisfaction passed over his gaunt features.

"This is the product of years of salvage. That siphon had dragged more than us down here. Wreckage from a host of ocean disasters has turned up in our pools."

Our pools.

Still scrutinizing his expression, Stella thought Etienne seemed awfully possessive. And honestly, downright creepy. He kind of looked like a rodent. Small face. Upturned nose. Sunken eyes. Fuzzy hair. Gray.

Frederic, by comparison, seemed slightly more refined but no less disturbing.

"Some of this seems really old," Colin observed. "Like the airplane chassis that is serving as your infirmary. That looks like it's from World War II. Was some of this here before you arrived?"

Frederic nodded. "Indeed. We spent a long time just scavenging what was already here, but flotsam kept streaming in. This place is like a vacuum. It sucks in everything that passes by above."

"And how long have you been down here?" Colin asked.

Stella's gaze clung to his face. It was so vivid. So strong. So alive compared to the ghostly visages of Etienne and Frederic.

"It's very hard to keep track of time. There is a single wind-up clock that still functions. Using that, we've been able to calculate that it must be getting close to the year 2000 now."

"2000!" Stella spurted.

"Yeah, you're close," Colin replied flatly. "Only off by twenty years. It's 2020."

He acknowledged their raised eyebrows and didn't wait for them to comment. "When did your ship sink?"

Etienne and Frederic stared at each other until Frederic finally cleared his throat.

"November," he stated. "1978."

CHAPTER 6

Stella gasped. "Forty years?"

As soon as the initial shock wore off, she frowned. Colin didn't look too happy either.

Contemplating the two men in front of him, his eyebrows dipped in challenge. "How old were you when your ship sank?"

She knew what he was getting at. Yes, Etienne had some gray hair. Yes, Frederic had some silver woven in his pale hair. Yes, their faces were malnourished, which aged their appearance…but they did not look like senior citizens. Heck, they looked like an anemic but younger version of Don Wexler.

"I was thirty-one," Etienne replied, shaking his head with a reminiscing grin. "Fred was twenty-eight. A couple of young Canucks ready to prove ourselves."

"So, you're telling me that you're seventy-three years old?" Colin crossed his arms.

Etienne raised a graying eyebrow. "Based on what you've revealed, I guess so."

His amusement seemed to irk Colin. Stella understood his annoyance. The cavalier attitude of these two oddities was exasperating.

"You don't look seventy-three," Colin observed in a guarded tone.

Etienne and Frederic exchanged another glance.

"Thank you," Etienne chuckled. "Any mirrors down here are tarnished. I haven't seen a clear reflection in quite some time."

The quip did not amuse Colin. Stella could sense his aggravation mounting. It affected her as well. The overwhelming need to fist her hands around the collar of Etienne's wool sweater and shake him, demanding to know how any of this was possible. Answers, dammit. They needed answers.

But they were not in a position to make demands. They needed to find a way to reach the surface, and in order to do so they had to remain civil. They had to accept the help of these two perplexing mariners, and they had to bide their time.

"Tell me more about this canyon," Stella probed, putting on her *interviewer* hat.

Keep them engaged. Broach a subject that will keep them talking. From Frederic's satisfied smile, she gauged that he was pleased with her curiosity.

"A submarine canyon," Frederic explained. "I actually have it charted out in my cabin. I'll have to show you later."

"You can show *us* later," Colin injected with a scowl that Stella couldn't quite decipher.

"Right." Frederic raised his eyebrows. "Well, anyway, a submarine canyon is like a steep valley or chasm in the ocean floor. Very similar to your Grand Canyon. They form for a variety of reasons. Erosion. Currents. Mudslides. Rivers from long ago when the ocean was at a much lower level. They start out as shallow valleys in the continental shelf, and then they are carved deep into the continental slope."

"And we're in one of them? A deep one?"

"Yes."

"How?" Colin inserted. "How could we survive that descent—one that should have caused a stroke or paralysis long before we hit the bottom?"

"I agree. Death was certain." Frederic hooked a finger around his chin in consideration. "It could be a rogue eddy—a black hole in the ocean, so to speak. The current in the funnel was so fast—too fast for the physical effects to occur—as if the natural phenomenon was a protective sheath."

Stella searched Colin's face for a reaction. With his better understanding of the ocean, he still appeared skeptical but held his tongue.

Right. Because, did it really matter how they got down here? The big question—the elephant in this freak netherworld was, *how do we get back?*

Colin's head tipped back as he searched the black expanse above. Shadows obscured the ceiling in this giant arena, a haunting cloak to charge the imagination into overdrive.

"How can this place exist? I mean, with oxygen like this?" His gaze dropped, and he addressed Frederic. "And how have you fed yourselves for forty years?"

Frederic's crisp blue eyes scoped the roof of the cave. "As for the existence of this place, all we can do is speculate. An ancient earthquake— a meteor—something to cause a crack in the continental slope. A gap that was sealed by a similar phenomenon."

"But any oxygen trapped inside would have been temporary," Colin countered. "You've been down here forty years."

Etienne held his hand up. Stella noticed an apparent wedding band around his middle finger. It bounced up to his knuckle as he moved.

"The tunnel system that I pointed out before. It leads to some active underwater vents. Hydrothermal vents, right Fred?"

Frederic nodded. "Right. Think of them as underwater geysers or hot springs. They occur when tectonic plates spread apart, and magma rises, clashing with the cold seawater. The gasses from those vents should not be breathable, but all we can guess is that the high temperature is boiling the water, which is extracting the oxygen from it and channeling it through the cave system. This, of course, is only a theory because we can't get close enough to the vents to understand them."

Colin's throat bobbed slowly. His full lips were pressed tight in consideration. "If you can't get to these vents, how do you know of their existence?"

"By the overwhelming heat and its effects. This oxygen. Some of our food supply—"

On cue, Stella's stomach let loose a growl that had them all turning to look at her. Despite all the trauma, she was feeling hunger pangs. Her last meal was a hot dog on the boat, but she couldn't remember when. She was one of those people who needed to eat something the second she woke up—regardless of the hour. In her opinion, dinner should be the first meal of the day. After that, snacks sufficed.

But here, there would be no big breakfasts. No hot dogs. No snacking on Raisinets.

"There's a host of little creatures living around the vents. Crabs, Mollusks, tube worms—"

Not exactly Raisinets.

All growling ceased in her abdomen.

Etienne read her expression and grinned. "Don't worry. We have a pretty extensive supply of non-perishables. As a matter of fact, why don't you settle into your quarters and meet us in the cafe for dinner? It will give you a chance to get acquainted with the others."

Stella snagged Colin's glance. He raised his eyebrow, as baffled as she.

"The cafe?" he asked, peering down at the avenue of bizarre architecture.

Etienne took a few steps back down the sloped trail and pointed to a spot on the bank of the small stream. An ensemble of benches and chairs flanked four tarnished tables like the twisted version of a Parisian bistro.

"We try to make it a habit to eat together once a day rather than staying reclusive in our cabins."

Sharpen up on the old social skills, huh? Stella thought.

Colin's frown seemed to grow by the

minute. She tried to remember his attractive smile. An image of him on the deck of the STARKISSED with his dark hair ruffled by the wind and his arms bulging as he tried to reel in a giant tuna popped into her mind. His eyes flashed. His white teeth gleamed. Enthusiastic and content were the two traits she witnessed as the sun was setting behind him. Oh yeah, and drop-dead gorgeous.

That Colin was still on the surface, though. As was she. Down here, only somber reflections of themselves remained.

He flicked his wrist. The face of his watch was nicked, and the screen remained black.

"All right," he agreed in a brusque voice. "I'd like some time with my family to discuss what you've told us."

"Of course," Etienne smiled, but the warmth could not thaw his eyes.

"I know how anxious you are," Frederic said. "This—" his pointer finger swirled above his head. "—this is overwhelming. You will be in denial for a long time. Don't fight that. Embrace it. Because when you finally accept this place—"

Then we become ghosts like you.

Stella spared him from completing the sentence. She was anxious to get away.

"We'll see you later," she muttered over her shoulder as she started to negotiate the gritty path down to the cave floor.

Manners ruled her haste just long enough for her to add, "Thank you."

As soon as she and Colin were halfway down the slope, she vowed, "I'm not eating worms."

To her surprise, Colin chuckled. It was brief, and when she swung her head to look, his sober expression had returned.

"Honestly, I have to sit down. I have to digest this before I face Dad. Can we stop in one of our *cabins* for a moment?"

"Sure." She shrugged her shoulders. "It'll give me a chance to unpack."

This time, she caught Colin's grin. He slowed to a halt and regarded her with that haunting smirk.

"You're either taking this remarkably well, or I have to worry about checking you into the *infirmary*."

Stella laughed because, after all, this situation was off the charts.

"You don't have to worry about my state of mind, Col," she assured. "I just—I don't know how to deal with all this."

They reached the bottom of the path, where she noticed a corroded metal box standing waist-high, the screwed panels knocked loose to reveal a series of notched wheels inside. Circling around it, she snorted and pointed.

"Like this."

Colin stepped around and joined her. He shook his head as they stared at the slot machine forever stuck at two cherries and a muddy orange. The arm must have broken off. Seaweed wrapped around the first wheel, nearly obscuring the cherries.

"Did we die, Col?" she asked. "Did we die, and this is it for us?"

"I feel the same way, Stel, but no, we're

very much alive."

She jolted when she felt his hand slide under her hair and his fingertips touched her throat.

"See," he said. "There's a pulse."

Goosebumps dotted her neck, but Colin quickly withdrew his hand and cleared his throat. He even took a step back.

"We have to face facts," he stated huskily. "It's up to us to either find a way out of here or—"

"Or what? Become one of them? Stay down in this obscure hell for forty more years?"

"Stella, we're just taking this all in. When I say it's up to us. I mean you and me. You are strong. I didn't know that about you. Jill, Jill is not." His glance strayed to the ancient aircraft's belly with the red cross hanging in the window.

"And Dad is kind of hysterical at the moment." He turned back to face her and she was locked by soulful dark eyes. "I need you. We need to figure this out logically."

Stella swallowed. Colin needed her. She suddenly felt mature beyond her years.

Deliberating for a second, she said. "Okay, let's go check out these cabins and see if they are something we can get Jill and your dad to for some rest. We'll check on your mom, and then we'll go to Neptune's Bistro and meet the other denizens of this hell hole."

The corner of Colin's mouth hefted up into a grin. "Atta girl." He gave a friendly punch to her shoulder.

Oh bah. Back to the little sister dabs on the shoulder? What about those fingers on my neck only seconds ago?

She searched his eyes for any sign—any glimpse of attraction. Shaking her head, she silently condemned her stupidity. What did it matter down here? What did anything matter?

"What?" Colin asked, concerned.

"Nothing. Let's just get going."

There were more important things to concentrate on than her childish crush. Her earlier assessment that she felt mature beyond her years was dead on, though. Young Stella, the college freshman—the wannabe journalist with chronic curiosity was left behind. Down here was born Stella, the survivalist. And she needed Colin as her ally. Nothing more.

And that was just fine.

Trudging past him without a word, Stella started towards the orange cargo trailer. She sensed him hesitate but soon heard the crunch of his sneakers against limestone.

"Whoa."

Stella halted at Colin's outburst. She looked over her shoulder to find him staring into the shadows beneath the basketball pole. A volleyball rolled across the flat sandy surface towards them. Colin stopped it with his foot, still searching the man-made court.

"I saw someone here before," she whispered. "Or, at least, I think I did."

Colin lingered a moment, gazing into the shadows.

"Come on," she encouraged. "If there *is* someone here, I'm sure we'll meet them soon."

"Why would they wait? Are they spying on us? Come out!" he challenged.

"Colin, don't rile the natives," she warned. "Let's just see what these accommodations are like."

Colin turned away, and as he did so, Stella stooped to grab the volleyball. With one quick hoist she shot it through the netless ring, and then quickly trotted after him.

The rusty storage container sat around the curve of the peak they had climbed earlier. One side of the container was closed by a large plank of plywood. The other side was serrated, but the sharp edges were secured by the circular wheelhouse shoved tight against the metal, creating a whimsical front porch. Shards of tarp hung in the paneless windows.

"Charming," Stella muttered as she reached for the doorknob.

"Hey, hold on." Colin moved in beside her.

She gaped up at him, aware of his body so close.

"You think something is going to jump out at me?" she asked with forced humor.

"You don't?" he countered.

She could have argued that she could handle it herself, but she wasn't going to turn down his support.

Colin cautiously tugged on the door, not so much for what he feared was behind it, but rather that it seemed fragile enough to break. A musty stench assaulted them.

"I'd suggest opening the windows, but—" Stella poked her hand through the glassless frame.

It was dark inside. Of course, no lights, but no candles either. The ambient light came from a torch lit just outside the window—one of many lining the carved lane.

Within the rounded pilot house sat a chrome-legged chair with a torn red vinyl seat. It faced the bank of window frames, enabling someone to sit and enjoy the peculiar view. Further in was a simple desk with a shattered mirror resting atop it.

Stella stepped up to it and jolted. The segmented reflection was the first she had seen of herself since looking in a mirror after a hasty shower before meeting up with the Wexlers. There had been no time to dry her hair, and makeup was pointless on the ocean. Saltwater stripped it away.

That image in her bathroom was much more vibrant than what she witnessed now. Now, long dark hair clung to her high cheekbones, the ends frizzing amidst the humidity. Eyes that were normally a deep brown looked nearly black without any light to ignite them. Friends at school used to challenge, *if you're Swedish, why aren't you blonde and blue-eyed?* She could have argued that half the Swedish population bore dark features. She could have argued that she was only half Swedish. She didn't argue, though. It was never worth it.

Pink lips were dissected by a crack in the reflection as if they were scarred. Her red tank top was nearly dry, but her shorts were still uncomfortably damp. There was a trace of the summer tan in her slim arms and long legs. She was tall and thin, which always made her feel gangly next to her petite best friend. Total opposites, she and Jill. One tall and dark. One small and fair. But there was a link in the personalities that rang true.

A shadow formed behind her reflection. Colin's chest emerged as he stepped up behind her. Here was someone taller than her. Here was someone who made her feel petite. Their eyes met in the mirror. There were no platitudes offered this time—no false assurances that everything would be all right.

Now, there was just this sobering connection. Stella's lip trembled. For the first time since surfacing in the cave, she felt tears inch up behind her eyes.

Colin read her face. He raised his hand and it hovered over her arm. She closed her eyes, took a deep breath and then broke away to inspect the rest of the cabin.

"Well, isn't this just charming," she declared in a thick voice.

On the earthen floor lay a mattress with a blanket folded atop it. Beside it was another pile of blankets.

"No way." She stumbled backward. "There is no way I am sleeping on that thing."

Colin crouched down and jabbed the mattress. No dust erupted. He stooped further and sniffed.

"A little musty," he remarked.

"Ya think?"

He rose and swiped his hands. "Let's go check out the next one."

The inverted hull of a fishing boat sat next door. It had a port hole and a gaping tear in the facade that served as the doorway. The interior was dark and stuffy. It was more modest. No sunroom. It had a chair that didn't look too stable and a couple of tarps piled to serve as sleeping quarters. Stella knelt to inspect them. They were relatively clean. The vinyl must have been washed in the stream.

Outside were the two *lawn* chairs positioned to watch passersby.

"Do you have a preference?" she asked politely.

Colin shrugged. "No. In a little while, I'm going to pass out, and I'm not going to care what I pass out on top of."

That declaration flushed Stella's neck. She swept her hair up to allow some damp air to cool it.

"I guess Jill and I will take the storage container," she decided. "It has more room for your mom when she gets better. And it kind of reminds me of a fort I built when I was a kid."

"How so? Did a hurricane drop a cargo ship in your backyard?" Colin smirked.

He was trying to keep things light, and she appreciated it. She *needed* it. One slip on the tightrope and she'd drop into insanity.

"No, my dad had a few big planks of plywood left over from a shed project. He let me use them. It was kind of a lean-to thing. I sat in it and read."

"What?"

"What?"

"What did you read?"

"Oh." The question startled her. "My mom's magazines. I loved magazines. All the glossy pictures. She had a subscription to TIME."

"Is that the one that started the journalist bug?"

His curiosity seemed genuine. It warmed her.

"Absolutely," she said. "Can you even imagine if I had my camera down here?"

Colin moved up to the doorway, raising his arm and planting his hand on the jagged frame. He peered out at the mystical underground village and, after a lengthy pause, said, "Your photos would be in TIME, no doubt."

When he turned back there was the hint of a smile toying with his lips.

"Thank you," Stella whispered.

Colin frowned. "For what?"

"For being nice to me. I—I really could use it right now."

"Was I ever not nice to you?" He looked wounded.

Stella suddenly felt awkward and wished she hadn't mentioned anything. She had no choice but to answer him, though. All six-plus feet of him filled the doorway, the flicker of torchlight dancing across his arms.

"You never really noticed me," she stated, "so, no, I can't say you were ever not nice to me."

In an attempt to ease the tension, she mustered up a feeble grin.

It was hard to gauge Colin's expression in the dark. His silence didn't help. Trying her best not to fidget, she was relieved when he took a step back, and an opening presented itself.

"Never mind," she rushed. "This place is messing with my head. Let's get going."

Stella slipped past him, her elbow scraping his chest as he gave way.

Outside, she drew in a lungful of rank air and swiped her palms across her face as if she could swipe away the burning in her cheeks.

"Stella," he called quietly from behind her. "I noticed you."

CHAPTER 7

Stella's breath hitched. She was not about to turn around to see if he was mocking her. Instead, she squared her shoulders and kept moving forward. After a brief pause, the crunch of footsteps followed.

The cylindrical body of the infirmary was only steps ahead. The glow from within beckoned. She aimed for it and ducked inside, grateful to find Jill sitting cross-legged on the metal floor.

Jill looked up and managed a brief smile.

"What did you find?" she asked, her gaze slipping past Stella as Colin climbed through the doorway.

Sarah, the nurse, discreetly shuffled sideways to get out of his way and almost tripped on a first aid bag. It was made of canvas, and it was stained and frayed, like pretty much everything else around here. She stepped out of the plane to give them some privacy.

"Well, we found our accommodations for the night," Stella offered feebly once Sarah was out of hearing range.

Don Wexler rose from his crouched position next to his wife. He read Colin's inquisitive gaze and answered, "No change. But her breathing seems a little more regulated, doesn't it, Jilly?"

Jill nodded, but Stella caught the appeasement in that gesture.

Colin briefly examined his mother, shadows of concern and fatigue ringing his eyes. His father watched him expectantly, and Stella felt a jab of sympathy for Col. He had become the man in charge of an impossible situation.

"What did you find?" Don prompted.

"Honestly, Dad, I don't know what to believe down here."

He began to recite the tale that Etienne and Frederic shared. Don listened, shock and disbelief vaulting his graying eyebrows after some of the more absurd aspects.

"We were paralleling Hudson Canyon last night," he observed. "I lost track of it when the storm hit."

"Yeah, I remember seeing it on the depth finder," Colin agreed.

"But I've been sailing out here since I was a kid. There was never any talk of caves—"

"There have been exploratory missions, but nobody ever searched the entire canyon floor," Colin agreed.

His father looked piqued by the observation. "Find that out in finance class, did you?"

Whoa. That sounded like a jab, Stella thought.

Or, like all of them, the predicament and his

wife's health were getting to Don. Regardless, the dig seemed to agitate Col, but only for a second. Running his hand through his hair, he swiped away any sign of annoyance and continued.

"Well, perhaps you'll get more answers at dinner."

"Dinner?" Jill interrupted. "What kind of dinner?"

Stella decided to leave out the tube worms for now.

"It's not so much what we're going to eat," Colin regarded his sister. "It's the company. We're supposedly going to meet the rest of the inhabitants down here."

"The rest—" her lips parted in shock. "How many?"

"How many, indeed?" Don began pacing, stooping to peer out the window.

"We don't know yet."

Colin's father was still hunched over, staring out the window. A perspiration mark stained the green Tommy Bahama shirt at the base of his spine. His salt and pepper hair was drying out slightly shaggy. Normally it was combed back neatly and secured under his baseball hat. He pivoted his head left and right and snapped backward as if seeing some of the spectacles outside for the first time.

"Where and when is this dinner?"

Colin's eyes met Stella's for a second. Her breath hitched again, and she coughed into her fist to relax.

"Tell him, Stel." Colin smiled at her.
Gulp.

"The bistro," she whispered.

"The what?" Jill squinted.

"The cafe," Stella added with more oomph in her voice. "That's actually what they referred to it as."

"Is it next door to the movie theater?" Don scoffed.

Stella stopped herself from saying, *yeah, we've been through the whole comedy skit.*

The humor was fading.

"It's just a little bit down the path here. A grouping of tables near the stream."

The stream they call Styx.

"Water," Jill murmured the word as if it were sacred. "I'm so thirsty."

"The stream must be saltwater," Don tempered her enthusiasm.

"Actually, they claim the stream is clear, distilled by the heat of the very vents that are providing oxygen down here."

"I still find that impossible to believe," Don snickered, "but we are alive, so I'll try to have an open mind."

Stella's eyes sliced towards Colin just in time catch his, *that would be a first* look. There was definitely something brewing between the Wexler men, but Colin was doing his best to moderate it.

Out of habit, Stella glanced at her watch. For a second, she caught a reflection of her mouth on the black screen. "Should we head out there? I mean, it's probably about time."

"If there's something to drink, let's go." Jill encouraged.

On cue, Sarah, Etienne's wife, climbed

back through the doorway. Stella jolted at the sight of her. The woman had a knack for stealth. Her bulky shoes made no sound on the granular surface. Perhaps it was because she was so light.

"Etienne mentioned you would be having dinner with everyone."

Sarah's voice was soft enough that everyone inside had to lean in to catch it.

"I will look after your wife while you go," she assured.

Don seemed unsure. He touched his fingertips to Anne's shoulder and then stroked her hair. There was no response.

"You will be within shouting distance should I need you," Sarah offered quietly.

The idea of this woman shouting at anything was outlandish.

Stella could see that Don was torn. Jill, not so much. The prospect of having something to drink had dug its claws in her.

"Dad, we all need to learn more about this place," Colin said. "That is in Mom's best interest."

Don's jaw muscle twitched. He stared at his wife and slowly nodded.

"How far again?" he asked, stepping up to the doorway.

Colin joined him, hunching over to fit through the hatch.

"Over there," he pointed. "We can take turns coming back to check on her."

That seemed to mollify the elder Wexler. He went back to his wife and kissed her forehead and then looked hard at the unkempt woman now standing in the corner.

"If there is anything—any change—"

"I will notify you immediately," she murmured.

Once they were out of the airplane belly Don shook off his despondency some. His head swerved to inspect the surroundings as the bridge of his nose wrinkled with a quick sniff.

"Sulfur."

"Yeah," Colin agreed. "It's a bit rank in places. I guess a byproduct of the heat down here."

He pointed to the orange storage container and the inverted hull next to it.

"Those are our two cabins. Stel has claimed the orange crate for herself and Jill," he hesitated, "and Mom."

"Why?" Jill took a step towards the barnacled container. "The other seems to have a garden out front."

"Trust me," Stella stood beside Jill. "The sleeping accommodations are better in this one." She pointed at it. "I mean, compared to the other."

Jill looked dubious, but shrugged. "As long as we don't have to stay in it for long."

And that was Jill in a nutshell. Impervious to any shortcomings. Taking the madness of this realm and tossing it aside like it was a temporary inconvenience.

Stella's mood brightened some.

"So, what are your thoughts on tube worms?" she joked.

"Tube worms?" Jill looked horrified.

Their banter ceased at the sight of a shadow approaching from the opposite end of the path.

Two more dark contours trailed behind it. Stella thought she heard muffled whispers. She felt Jill's fingers wrap across her forearm.

"It's going to be okay," Stella whispered. "They're not going to hurt you."

"They may eat us," Jill hissed.

At first it was a funny notion, but under further consideration Stella's heart started to thump. Colin hastened his pace and fell in before her and Jill. Don wrapped an arm around his daughter and tried to give Stella an assuring wink. It looked more like a spasm.

Each group approached the tables from opposite ends. A ring was drawn in the copper-colored dirt to denote the boundaries of the café. It reminded her of childhood, drawing roads with pink chalk in the driveway.

Before she could get a good look at the approaching trio of gloom, a familiar voice called out.

"So glad you could make it," Etienne boomed as he approached with his hand extended.

The extremity was aimed at Don, who seemed uncertain about returning the gesture. Courtesy kicked in, and he reached out for a quick shake.

"Frederic is coming. He's finishing up on some mapping."

"Mapping," Colin was quick to inquire. "Of what?"

"The caves. There are still avenues here that are uncharted…and evolving."

"I'd like to see those maps," Colin said.

Etienne's smile slipped slightly. "He's still

working on them, but he has the previous versions you can review."

Colin would have pushed the matter, but a young woman stepped into the ring of torches. She had straight black hair and a slim build accentuated by torn jeans and a pink polo shirt. Colin's words dropped off, and he followed her with his eyes as she approached one of the tables within the café circle. She pulled back a short pedestal and sat down with her elbows resting on the cracked linoleum table.

Stella watched Colin's reaction before returning her attention to the seated woman. Under the torchlight, heavy shadows scored a narrow face as dark eyes cast furtive glances at the congregation. She slid her fingers through a waterfall of black hair and swiped it off her shoulder.

Stella's inspection was interrupted by the couple approaching just behind her. Middle-aged and a little plump compared to the residents of this cave, a woman in discolored white capris advanced with a broad smile on her clammy face. Flaxen hair was cut into a bob, but judging by the severe angular slices it wasn't a salon job.

"Hello!" she cried out, enthusiastically waving her hand.

Stained white sneakers thumped as the heels slipped off the back of her ankles.

"I'm Margie. Margie Conover."

Stella was rooted by the animated assault and found herself paralyzed as the woman came up and grabbed her arm in both her hands, pumping the limb eagerly. "I'm sorry for the trauma you have been through, but as you can see—" she flashed a beaming smile which revealed a few tarnished teeth, "—I'm so happy to see you!"

Stella smiled politely while carefully extracting her arm.

"I'm Stella," she replied in a voice that was twenty decibels lower.

"Stella!" the woman gushed as if it was the most perfect name in all the world.

Maybe she wasn't so bad after all.

"This is my husband," Margie waved her hand behind her at the slagging man in the yellow button-down shirt and relatively unflawed khakis.

"Jordan," she called, pronouncing the name as *Joy-dan,* "come meet everyone."

As Stella was closest, the man extended his hand to her first. She felt a bunch of knuckles in that grasp, like shaking a handful of rocks. Aside from the skinny fingers, he was tall and possessed a slight girth around the middle. Thinning brown hair was finger-combed back, held in place by the humidity. His face was long and thin, and a gold chain hung around his neck, dipping into the open lapel.

She guessed the couple to be in their forties, but after hearing the baffling caveat on Etienne and Frederic's age, who was she to gauge?

"Welcome to the Underworld," he offered with a strained chuckle.

The moniker made her uncomfortable. This place did not deserve a fancy mythological name. This was just a junkyard under the sea.

"Hi, I'm Donald Wexler," Jill's dad said but

did not offer his hand. "How and when did you get down here?"

Well, so much for tact, Stella thought.

Jordan Conover glanced at Etienne and there was an imperceptible nod. He looked back at Don and said, "We're still waiting on one more to join us. Then we'll go around and all share our tales."

Jordan swept his arm out in invitation, and Don was left with no recourse other than to sit on a sloped bench alongside a Formica table. He patted the rotted wood surface beside him and beckoned Jill to his side. She slid in, hesitating to drop her butt down.

Let it go, Jilly, your white shorts are already stained.

Vanity did not exist down here. Everyone was unkempt, even Margie, although she had a pretentious air about her. Soiled as they were, there were signs that the Conover's attire was pricey, and their jewelry, flamboyant, particularly the diamond ring the size of a football on her left hand.

Well, burglary can't be a popular crime in this netherworld. What good would it do to steal a diamond ring of that size? All five residents would know where you got it, and you couldn't cash it in.

Jill finally sat but looked uncomfortable. Stella slid on the bench across from her and leaned over the table to whisper, "If you think this is bad, wait until you see the sleeping accommodations."

Jill's eyes swept the giant cavern, and she sighed, but she returned to meet Stella's gaze with a smile. It was good to see white teeth again. It wasn't a common sight with these sunken dwellers.

To her dismay, Etienne sat on the bench beside her. Yet, to her relief, Colin slid in on the other side, sandwiching her. Etienne gave off a mild stench, like the smell of a fish market. It was enough to make her lean towards her left, but that caused her to brush arms with Colin. She managed a furtive glimpse to see if he noticed, but he was focused on the adjoining table with the affluent couple and the reclusive young Asian woman.

A rogue stab of jealousy hit Stella in the gut.

Get a grip. Besides, she has her head down. Maybe she's not that good-looking. All you can see is long, glossy black hair.

On cue, the young woman lifted her head and peered at their table.

Oh, just great. Ridiculously gorgeous with her pert little nose and pouty lips. How did this one retain her looks when everyone else around here looks like a ghoul?

Colin's glance lingered a moment, and then he was distracted by the Conovers' chatter as they leaned forward, concealing the view of the young woman at the end of the table. Frederic joined them on the other side, leaving an additional table free. How many more were coming?

"While we're waiting on Daniel, I'll start bringing dinner out." Margie rose. "Loren, will you help me?"

Loren. Of course, she had to have a sexy

name too. Nothing like *Stella*.

Stella's manners kicked in.

"Can I help?"

Margie smiled. A flash of teeth paled in comparison to the diamond studs in her ears.

"Thank you so much, but you are the guests of honor today. Trust me, your chores are coming."

Chores?

Stella watched the woman shuffle off in her sneakers towards a row of basins lined inside the café circle. Some looked like reclined refrigerators, but even from here, she could see that there was nothing chilled about them. They were simply being used for storage.

A shadow encroached on the circle. It startled her enough that she jolted and accidentally jabbed Colin with her elbow. Colin tucked his head in close to hers and whispered, "Daniel, I presume."

Once the torchlight illuminated the figure, she noticed a young man in jeans and a red and white striped shirt. If she was to guess, she'd say he was close to her and Jill in age, but again, that was just conjecture in this ghastly underwater park.

"Daniel," Frederic called out in a booming voice. "Come meet the new arrivals."

Brooding and dark, Daniel looked anything but enthused by their presence. He managed a brief nod and plopped down on the bench, leaving a gap between himself and the hydrographic guy. Stella leaned forward for a better view, but Colin had rested his elbows on the table, obstructing her sight.

"Hi, I'm Jill."

Stella started at Jill's perky voice. She lowered her eyebrows and gave her friend a strong, *what are you doing* glare.

Jill dropped her eyebrows in return. *Chill.*

Regardless of this silent banter, Daniel seemed unaffected. He fisted his hands together atop the Formica and stared straight ahead. His light brown hair was slightly long, curling at the edges. He was thin, but he was also very tall, adding to the overall lanky effect.

Etienne rose and shuffled off of the bench to stand at the end of the table, facing everyone. Stella exhaled her relief at having open space beside her again.

"Well," he started with a wry twist of his greyish lips. "I'm sure everyone here has some questions about each other. As you can imagine, we don't get new visitors often."

"*Visitors* would imply we're just passing through," Stella muttered.

Etienne's grin fell, but he wrangled it back into place.

"Yes, that's what we all wish, but the reality has proven different."

He purposely looked over her head and aimed his next statement toward Jill's father. "Why don't we all introduce ourselves? You can start."

Don's impatience was brewing. His cheeks looked ruddy even in the diffused light. His thumb tapped a rapid staccato on the table.

"Fine," he huffed. "I am Donald Wexler, father of Jill and Colin Wexler," he pointed at his children, "and husband of Anne Wexler, who is currently in your *infirmary* fighting for her life."

"Oh!" Margie gasped as she turned back towards the table with a stack of mismatched bowls in her hands. "I heard about your wife," her eyes rounded in sympathy. "We're all praying for her recovery."

"Isn't that just swell?" Don mumbled before collecting himself and forcing a smile. "Thank you. Please understand I'm a little cranky because I don't know where the hell I am."

The woman set an empty bowl down before each of them.

"That's understandable. When Jordan and I first surfaced here, we remained by the pool and just waited to die."

That statement arrested Don's attention. It piqued Stella's interest as well. She studied the petite but pudgy woman in the dirty capris and pink short-sleeved blouse. The choppy haircut was clearly self-maintained, but under the rough surface, Stella could see signs of a refined woman, one who might have been used to salons and chic clothes stores. Slicing a quick glance at Jordan on the far end of the second table, she envisioned him on a golf course or at a private club, discussing the stock market with his clients. Reining in her wild imagination, Stella refocused her attention once Margie resumed.

"Of course, we thought it was just some freak luck to be dragged into a cave at the bottom of the Atlantic Ocean, but we knew it had to be temporary."

Colin shifted in his seat.

"When Etienne first appeared—" a chill jostled the woman's shoulders. "We were—" she searched for a word, "—startled."

Jordan Conover coughed into his fist. "Startled? He scared the crap out of us."

Frederic laughed. "He has that effect."

Etienne tucked his head down with a slight snicker.

Stella watched them all. Their good-natured camaraderie. It all seemed so out of place— staged for their benefit. These people could smile and joke all they wanted. It didn't make this situation any more acceptable.

"What disaster brought you down here?" Don asked, his hand still drumming nervously.

Margie glanced over her shoulder to make sure the raven-haired woman was following with the food and then scooted onto the bench.

"Do you want to tell them, Jordy?" she asked her husband, when clearly, she was nearly bouncing in her seat at the opportunity to grandstand.

"You go ahead, dear."

Margie smiled enthusiastically, and then her pudgy cheeks tightened in anticipation.

"We were going to see my mother for her sixty-fifth birthday. She lived in Lawng Island."

Ah, Long Island. Stella placed the accent now.

"There is a small airport near our home in Nags Head, and we were able to book a Cessna from Manteo to MacArthur Airport in Islip. It was a bit indulgent, but what an experience…at first. It was just the pilot and two other passengers. A couple from Kitty Hawk. Nice people. It was their five-year anniversary. They had two young kids that they left with their parents."

She looked around and realized she was rambling. Clearing her throat, she continued. "We were about an hour into the flight when the right engine blew."

Jordan nodded. "The pilot tried his hardest, but everything he attempted just overcompensated. We started to tilt, and then it was just a downward spiral." Shadowed eyes replayed the image like a movie. "We never saw the pilot or that couple again. We searched the pools here…waiting…"

Any previous levity was swallowed by the silence. Even the nearby stream seemed stagnant. All Stella could hear was the approach of the young woman and the clinks of silverware hitting Formica as she leaned over each shoulder to place the utensils. She dipped between Stella and Colin, and Stella caught a briny whiff, the same scent that permeated everything here. But there was also a hint of something fresh. Soap?

"When was this accident?" Don broke the stillness.

"November 5th, 1994."

Jill's eyes locked with Stella's over the table. Stella read it all there. Disbelief. Fear. Frenzy. Jill had not been around when the bomb dropped about Etienne and Frederic's ocean mishap and the outlandish amount of time they had spent down here.

Stealing another glimpse at Margie's face, she now detected a gaunt hollowness around the woman's eyes. Jordan's as well. There was no telling what age they were at the time of their accident, but clearly, they were physically older than their current appearance.

People weren't kidding when they warned about the damage the sun could do to your skin. The lack of sun had embalmed Etienne and his wife, along with Frederic. Now Stella was dying to know when the raven-haired woman had encountered her misfortune.

"You look great," Jill raved with her usual lack of propriety.

Margie beamed and patted her hair. "Loren just cut my hair. I was using shoestrings to tie it up. This is so much easier."

At the mention of the woman's name everyone turned expectantly towards the young female looking spooked by their scrutiny.

"Loren," Margie called amiably. "Come over. We'll get the food in a minute."

Grudgingly the young woman stepped up to the far table. She avoided eye contact, instead staring at the empty bench before her.

"This is our newbie, if you will," Margie introduced with a smile. "She landed down here a few years after us."

Under their keen scrutiny, the woman swallowed and fidgeted with the aluminum bowl in her slender hands.

"Hi, I am Loren Hirata." She hesitated, waiting for an acknowledgment, but everyone was silent, anticipating her tale. She began hesitantly. "I—we—had a leak in the head intake valve. We started taking on water." She stopped, clearly hoping that would be enough to satisfy their curiosity.

After an awkward moment of silence, she reluctantly continued. "Forty-five minutes later, and our deck was underwater."

"What type of boat?" Don asked.

Loren seemed startled by the question, but some of the tension lifted from her eyes.

"A Bertram. 28'," she hesitated. "It belonged to my boyfriend."

Don tipped his head. "A reliable boat. What happened after that?"

Still uncomfortable, she kept her gaze averted as she recited in a monotone voice.

"I had a life jacket on, but it wasn't fastened and somehow in my panic it came loose. I could see Toshio, my boyfriend, swimming towards me. He had his vest on. But these jeans, and my shoes, they started to drag me under. It seemed the more I struggled to stay afloat, the less I could. I went under and resurfaced several times, but the last time some sort of current snagged me. It was like being on a waterslide…only underwater."

Solemn nods were unanimous. To this group, the observation was not outlandish.

Loren tipped her head forward so that the veil of black hair could conceal one eye. The other one searched their faces, reading their unvoiced question.

"I never saw Toshio again."

Her voice was flat and she offered no more.

"There have been similar reports," Frederic spoke up. "Victims who had each other in sight, but only one was drawn into the current. The channel is a narrow one."

"And yet my whole family made it down," Don observed.

"But, not your boat," Frederic was quick to respond. "At least we haven't found it yet. All we found was one cooler."

"A cooler," Jill slammed her palms on the table and half rose. "Where?" She sliced a look at Stella. "Sprite!"

Stella's lips lifted at her friend's sudden enthusiasm. Leave it to Jill to find something exciting about this sunken tomb.

"We think it's yours," Frederic smiled, pleased. "We did not open it out of respect. But as you can imagine, we are scavengers down here. If it washes up in our pools, we claim it. Take your dinner, for example," he nodded as Margie rose and headed for the lopsided counter on the edge of the bistro circle. She turned around with two large bowls and beamed at the guests.

"A treat for tonight. Baked beans and corn."

A growl rumbled deep in Stella's core. Colin slanted a glance at her abdomen, and she felt her cheeks heat up. His eyes rose to hers.

"And here I thought you were looking forward to tube worms," he whispered.

Maturity be damned, she stuck her tongue out at him. He chuckled and reached for the spoon at his setting. He picked it up and examined the tarnished surface.

"It's safe," Frederic said. "All our utensils are cleaned immediately after each meal. You'll begin to pick up on the schedule around here. Everyone takes turns with *daily* tasks."

He raised a blonde eyebrow waiting for

someone to challenge the term. No one did.

"We try to establish the length of a given day," he explained. "We adhere to strict meal times, and not too long after dinner is when we sleep. A proper night's rest, if you will, which ends at the ring of the bell." He lifted a long finger and pointed down the rope-lined walkway.

Stella hadn't noticed it on the walk in, but there was a brass bell, its veneer dull and green, hanging from a pole impaled in the side of the copper peak that housed Frederic's quarters and the crow's nest.

"The bell will ring again to signify the start of a new day."

"Who rings it, and how do they determine when to do so?" Stella asked, intrigued.

"It's usually the first person up, but if someone thinks they have slept fitfully or woke unnaturally early they will stay in and await the next person to rise to take on the task."

"Honestly," Etienne reached for the chipped ceramic bowl, "Sarah and I have fallen into such a routine over time, one of us will usually ring the morning bell."

He scooped some beans into his own bowl and handed it to Stella.

"These look—" *normal* "—decent."

"We have a pretty extensive supply of canned goods. Expiration dates are merely suggestions. We've found cans dating back into the forties, and they've still been good," Etienne remarked. "Some might lose a little of their flavor, but our taste buds have tamed over the years."

Stella plopped a spoonful of beans onto her plate and then passed the ceramic bowl on to Colin. His finger touched hers in the process. Such a fleeting contact and yet so grounding.

Stella was about to test the beans, but she noticed everyone sitting with their arms at their sides. She set her spoon down and glanced around expectantly. Once Loren had filled her plate there was a momentary silence and then Etienne's head lifted.

"We would like to wish a warm welcome to our new residents and a speedy recovery to Mrs. Wexler. I know everything is coming as such a shock to you, but soon you will settle in and grow accustomed to the routine. Dig in."

Dig in wouldn't have been the term Stella chose, but she grabbed a single bean on the end of her spoon and tentatively touched it to her lips. There was no odor. A brief flick of her tongue offered very little taste. She watched Jill shovel a mouthful in, satisfied when her friend didn't spew it. Swallowing the single bean whole, there was a tepid semblance of familiarity—a hint of bacon.

"We even have a holiday here," Margie piped in with enthusiasm.

"Christmas?" Jill perked up.

"No," Margie's smile skated, "but close. We celebrate New Year's Day. Our version of a year, at least. At each ring of the night bell, Frederic marks a day in his books, and as we start approaching 365 marks we begin our preparations."

"It's quite an event," Jordan Conover stated. "You know," he leaned in and winked at

Don, "we do have alcohol down here."

Stella focused on her beans. These people were unhinged. But, then again, what else could they do down here? The choices were to either stay in this dungeon or face immediate death if they tried to escape.

"Did anyone ever try to swim out of here?"

The words were out before she could check them. She glanced up from her beans to see the slack-jawed expressions. For a moment, there was nothing but a chilling silence interrupted only by the trickling sound of the waterfall—a chilling weep.

CHAPTER 8

Frederic steepled his fingers together atop the table. He exchanged a look with Etienne and then took a deep breath.

"There have been others here—" he nodded solemnly "—others who felt emboldened."

Stella leaned forward in anticipation.

"We are blessed down here with a rare chemical environment that generates oxygen. The clash of the underwater vents with the cold ocean water—the extensive cave system with minerals that seem to extract the carbon dioxide—the runoff of boiling water from the vent that feeds this freshwater stream. We have learned how to catch our own food when flotsam fails us."

"Yeah, I get it," Don cut in. "You've built a utopia here."

The sarcasm was acknowledged with a twitch of Frederic's eyelid, but he continued. "It *is* a utopia in that it has allowed us to sustain life." He hesitated, his eyes dropping to his hands. "But there were a couple of survivors— they didn't adapt as well, physically. They exhibited signs of hypercapnia—carbon dioxide buildup. Disorientation. Anger."

"What happened to them?" Colin probed.

Frederic glanced at Etienne. It might have been imperceptible, but Stella noticed Etienne's assenting nod.

"There was an entrepreneur whose yacht had capsized. He was irate from the moment he washed up in the cave. The situation here only worsened that. He tried to make demands—demands that we show him the way back to the surface. When we explained there was no such exit, he switched tactics and offered us a huge payout once we made it to the surface. When that didn't work, he charged back to the pool and dove in."

Stella's spoon paused mid-air.

"Did he come back up?" she whispered.

"Part of him," Frederic murmured.

He noticed Stella's raised eyebrow and elaborated in a soft voice. "The next day, a human arm surfaced in the pool. We recognized the Rolex on the wrist."

The spoon lowered. Stella pushed back the beans.

"Shark." Don guessed, still eating.

"Most likely," Etienne agreed amiably. "We've caught a few in here. You'll find some harpoons lying near the cave pool. If you happen to see something edible make an appearance, please give a stab at it."

Jill looked horrified. She dropped her spoon and clutched her arms about her.

Etienne caught Jill's reaction. "We're not desperate for food. We have a huge stockpile."

He shoveled in a mouthful of corn and spoke while chewing, "But if a fish does swim by, it's a nice change of diet."

Oh my! Did Jill think they would harpoon a person if they surfaced?

Stella stared around the table.

Would they?

Another awkward silence ensued until Colin spoke up.

"I understand that all the wreckage we see in here washed up in your cave, but how did you move it? Some of these pieces are exceptionally large. How did you transport the fuselage of that old plane? There is no crane."

Etienne scratched beneath the rim of his knit hat. It dislodged a curly tuft of gray/black hair.

"What you see here didn't happen quickly. Initially, it was just Fred and me. We moved what we could and then started laying out a rope-hauling system. One thing we have plenty of is rope," he added with a grin.

"What about Sarah?" Stella asked.

Etienne frowned. "Well, she's a woman. It was hard work, and she was busy narrowing down the medical and food supplies."

That was all it took for Stella to form her opinion of Etienne. If someone told her she needed to lift a plane in order to survive, she would do it.

"But we eventually had help," Etienne grinned across the table at Jordan.

Jordan Conover crossed his arms, looking smug.

"So, in answer to your question, many

makeshift pulleys and lots of patience," Frederic explained. "We've worked hard as a team to make this place a home. Maybe someday, a miracle will happen. Maybe a reliable deep sea exploration crew will discover us and will be able to extract us safely—but clearly, we can't wait around for that. We've been able to make a comfortable world for ourselves."

"Surely there are risks down here. Life-threatening obstacles." Don tipped his head back and searched the vaulted ceiling.

Etienne's thick eyebrows raised. "Well, of course. We suspect an earthquake created this cave system. And an earthquake can destroy it just as easily."

Jill rose on the other side of the table. She picked up her bowl and spoon and turned towards Margie, mumbling, "Is there somewhere I can wash these up?"

Margie's eyes rounded, and her lips plumped in sympathy.

"Loren and I will take care of all of this for tonight. Maybe we can meet tomorrow and go over some of the chores around here."

"Sounds swell," Jill replied indifferently. "If you'll excuse me, I'd like to go see my mother now." She tucked her chin and added, "It was nice to meet you all."

It was the catalyst to break up the welcome reception. Stella quickly rose, which brought Colin to his feet. They each muttered their good-byes while Don climbed off the bench and mutely accepted their well-wishes for his wife's swift recovery.

As the Wexlers made their way to the

infirmary, Stella hesitated before the storage container that was deemed her cabin. Colin lingered while his sister and father continued on.

"Are you okay?"

The concern in that deep voice comforted her.

"Okay?" she snorted and grinned.

After a quick perusal of their environment, Colin mirrored her smile. "Okay, stupid question."

"I'm fine. I just—well, you guys need some private time with your mom. I'll go try and close my eyes for a few minutes." She shrugged. "Maybe when I open them, we'll all be back on the STARKISSED."

Dark green eyes softened. His wide shoulders relaxed. "Maybe."

Stella was startled when he lifted his hand and dusted under her chin with his knuckle. Surprised himself, Colin dropped his arm. "You call." His voice was husky. "If you need anything—you call."

Stella swallowed down a lump in her throat. "Your cell?"

Under the torchlight, his smile was beguiling.

"Just shout, Stel. I think I'll hear you in this place."

Stella hugged her arms tight about her. "Okay. You'll send Jill into this—" she glanced at the weird building, "—cabin?"

"Yeah, I'll remind her which is hers. Dad and I will be next door shortly."

Stella nodded, grateful that she wasn't in this bizarre drama alone. For a moment they stood side by side silently examining the sunken abyss.

"What have we gotten ourselves into, Col?" she whispered.

"I don't know. But we're going to find out. Dinner was charming, but it felt like a show."

Stella turned, staring up at him. "Right?" She was glad he picked up on it, too. "Something is off here. They're not telling us everything."

"Tomorrow—" he frowned, "—heh, whatever tomorrow is. Anyway, I'm going to search this place. See what else I can find."

"Take me with you. I want to learn more. I saw a notepad and pen on the desk in our cabin. I can write—an article—" Her hand flailed uselessly. "I know it's silly, writing an article that will never go anywhere."

"But it will exercise that mind of yours," Colin said with a hike of his lip.

"Yes." Fortunately, it was too dark for him to see her blush.

"Okay." He hesitated, looking back over his shoulder at the glowing windows of the plane. "I better catch up with them."

"I hope your mom is doing better."

"Thanks," he nodded. "Good night, Stel."

Good night she called after his retreating shadow.

Rooted before the tarnished storage container, Stella felt so incredibly alone. She looked up at the vaulted roof of the cave. The black recessed dome represented an eternal night. A starless crown. Sun would never bathe these peaks. It would never again touch her skin.

She stretched her arm out before her. Her skin held its tan for a long time, while Jill's fair complexion turned rosy at sea and lily white back on land.

Stella turned towards her doorway. A single torch was mounted in the dark patch of copper dust that served as a front yard. Before the wall of corrugated metal sat a deck chair. She considered sitting there, but the cave was now eerily silent. All signs of life, minus the flickering torches, were gone. She could not even hear the hushed conversation of the Wexlers in the nearby infirmary.

Unsettled, she crept into the circular wheelhouse at the front of the container. Light flickered through the empty window frames. Somehow being inside made her feel slightly safer. She stepped up to the desk and pulled back the wobbly chair, expecting the stool to collapse under her weight. It was resilient, though. A shadowy reflection in the mirror caught her attention. With the surge and lapse of the flame outside, her face would be visible for a second and then shift into a stark silhouette.

Stella reached for the notebook sitting on the corner of the desk. She flipped it open and found no written text, just virgin sheets of paper—a temptation too powerful to resist. Beside it was a ballpoint pen. A traditional BIC with a blue plastic cap. She held the clear plastic tube up towards the window and saw a black line running halfway up it. Pulling off the cap, she tried a couple of test marks on the very last page of the notebook. It took several attempts before the ink started to flow.

The seat groaned as her weight shifted. Outside came the distant sound of water falling. It was as intrusive as a trickling faucet.

Drip. Drip. Drip.

That was the first sound to wake her on the STARKISSED. A persistent series of drops landing on the small galley counter. A few minutes later, she emerged into a maelstrom.

Closing her eyes, she sought to block everything out. It wasn't much darker behind her eyelids.

Drip. Drip. Drip.

She opened the hardbound notebook to the first page, picked up the pen, and wrote one word.

BENEATH

Stella jolted and nearly fell on her head as she struggled out of the hammock she had rigged.

"What the hell?" Jill sat up on the ground beneath her.

Stumbling through the dark trailer, her blonde hair mussed into a cyclone, Jill thrust her hands up over her ears. Stooping to peer through the pilothouse windows, she cast an appalled look back at Stella.

"It's that damn bell. That tall freak is ringing it."

Stella took a quick inventory of the denizens of this cave and concluded that the *tall freak* had to be Frederic. Standing on one leg, she untangled her other from the twisted hammock and joined Jill. Frederic released the rope, and the bell fell silent, but echoes reverberated for a few seconds.

"Damn, I had just fallen asleep," Jill griped as she tried to finger-comb her hair.

"Me too."

Once Jill returned last night, Stella asked about her mother. The situation there was unchanged and sounded grim. Jill cried. A torrent of tears that finally ended with her scrubbing her eyes and cheeks and glaring at the cave. Jill tended to get cranky when things fell out of her control. Even now, Stella could read the agitation on her friend's heart-shaped face.

"Do you buy any of this?" she asked. "I mean, come on. This place is ridonk."

That it is.

"It's a mystery, all right."

Jill cocked her head and noticed the open notepad. "Working on your essay already?"

It sounded like an accusation.

Yeah, Jill wanted to lash out.

"Not much else to do."

Riled, Jill moved back to the window. "Well, I'm not staying down here. There has to be a way out."

That was the major difference between them. Jill demanded resolutions. Stella usually worked to achieve them. It was probably a 50/50 ratio on who was more successful. Jill's looks got her a lot of things in life that Stella had to work a little harder for, but Stella rather enjoyed the lack of attention. It left her time to do what she wanted to. Jill's time was always consumed by everyone else's agenda.

Still, they blended. Somehow, the formula worked. Even now, Jill was tossing one of those silly grins at Stella, the tension short-lived. For as cranky as Jill could get—it *never* lasted.

"Hey," she said.

Jill hunched over, and then realizing that she could stick her head through the window, hooked her hands around the wood frame and leaned forward.

"Do you see that?" she whispered.

Stella stepped up behind her. It was Jill's whisper more than anything that caught her attention. Discretion wasn't one of Jill's strong suits.

"What?"

"Over there, by the basketball net."

Stella squinted into the shadows and felt a chill creep up her spine. A male figure stood with his shoulder hitched against the slanted pole.

"I thought I saw him there yesterday when we walked in."

The silhouette was lanky, but the face was lost in shadow.

"I'm going to go introduce myself," Jill declared, hefting off the window frame.

"Hey, wait. You know nothing about him. I don't trust the people down here yet."

Jill pursed her lips. "You never trust anyone. You have to open yourself up, Stel, if you're going to go places in life."

Where was she going to go? The next cave?

"I'll go get Colin."

"Oh God," Jill rolled her eyes. "I don't need my brother. I'm just going to say hi. I'm sure you'll be right behind me."

It was true. Stella would trail after her for damage control if it was necessary. She was the ultimate wing girl.

Jill ran her fingers through her hair and spun to gaze in the cracked mirror. She wrinkled her nose at the image and swiped at her moist eyes again. She adjusted the collar of her blouse and, without a word, stalked out into the dank Underworld. Stella lagged behind, shaking her head. This was how Jill dealt with grief.

A rectangular patch of ground had been leveled to serve as a basketball court. There was a torch at the opposite end of the basket, making the idea of playing the game a challenge. Under the heavy shadows of the basket, a young man stood watching them. Every now and then, his eyes would flash as the flames reached them, reminiscent of the glimpse she had seen in the cave. Was this who had been watching her?

"Hi!" Jill called out boldly. "We didn't get to meet really last night. I'm Jill. This is my friend, Stella." She flashed a smile and took an exaggerated look around. "We're the new people."

For a moment, the shadow continued to study them until it finally budged from its roost and stepped into the glow of the torch.

Stella sucked in her breath at the sight of him. Choppy brown hair capped a dour expression. It was hard to distinguish an eye color in the limited light, but she guessed them to be brown. A long, narrow nose, full lips, and high cheekbones gave him a haunting semblance. For some reason, the character of

Heathcliff in Wuthering Heights came to mind.
A man who had left youth behind but had not
fully reached maturity.

"Daniel," he stated in a gruff voice.

Something about his cold, level look made
Stella uneasy. That flat stare was trained on Jill,
though. He studied her with wideset eyes as she
forced on her perky smile.

"Daniel," Jill repeated. "It's nice to meet
someone our age—I mean, you look around our
age, but—"

Her awkward confusion didn't draw a smile
from the sullen figure. When he said nothing,
Jill verbally stumbled forward.

"How long have you been down here?"

Daniel was still dressed in his pullover shirt
with red and white horizontal stripes, giving him
a tainted, *Where Is Waldo* look. His jeans were
slashed into shorts at the knees, and they hung
low on his hips. The outfit might have looked
juvenile, but his somber expression removed
anything amusing from the image.

"A while," he answered evasively.

Stella wasn't in the mood for games.

"Five minutes or five years?" she sought
clarification.

Jill threw her a *just chill* look, but she
ignored it.

Daniel stepped forward, and Stella
struggled to hold her ground. She was not about
to be intimidated by some creature who had
been living under the Atlantic Ocean for untold
years.

"I have no clue how long," he declared. "I
was a kid. But if you have to know. It was

August of 1997." He shrugged. "I think."

The uncertainty revealed a momentary chink in the hostile armor.

"How old were you at the time?" she pursued.

"What the hell does it matter to you?"

"Stel, we just met Daniel," Jill pleaded. She turned towards the guy. "Forgive my friend, she's studying journalism and conversations with her tend to come across as interrogations."

Daniel scowled. "Then I'll be sure not to have many conversations with her."

And just like that, Stella was excluded as Jill prattled on about her scary journey down to the cave, a journey that was mostly spent unconscious, although that was not relayed in this enhanced version.

Stella lingered to see if Daniel offered up his tale, but he kept mum on the subject, warily eyeing her the whole time. Jill cleared her throat and crossed her slim arms. It was a signal for Stella to leave them alone. Concerned about leaving her friend with this glum stranger, Stella saw Margie emerge from her maritime bungalow, giving them a hearty wave and smile. She seemed unfazed by the young man's presence or interaction, so perhaps he was innocent.

When body signals had not succeeded, Jill finally uttered, "Didn't you have something you wanted to do?"

Some might take offense by the pointed dismissal, but Stella knew Jill well enough. This was not personal. If one of them could obtain more information from this Daniel, then the other would have to back off.

"I'm going to go check on your mom," Stella murmured.

A flash of pain darkened Jill's eyes, but she pasted on a smile for her company. She nodded and just said, "I'll join you in a while."

Stella turned her back, but heard muted conversation behind her followed by one of Jill's nervous giggles.

Ducking her head into the infirmary hatch, she was surprised to find only Sarah inside. She was seated on a wooden crate next to an unresponsive Anne Wexler.

Sarah waved Stella closer with a congenial look on her gaunt face.

"Come. Donald and Colin just left for breakfast."

"How—how is she?"

Sarah glanced down at the prone figure. There was a tightening around Sarah's lips that revealed more than her words. "It's hard to tell. We don't know how long she went without oxygen. There could be brain damage—"

Her lips clamped shut as if she had revealed too much.

"You can tell me," Stella assured. "If it's bad, I won't share with her family."

The rumpled nurse gave a weak smile. She reached out and touched Anne's limp arm. "If the brain damage was extensive enough, she could be in an unresponsive coma right now. The brain simply can't send the signals, and soon organs will begin to fail."

Stella's breath hitched.

Sarah read her face and hastened to add,

"Or, she could just be sleeping and will wake on her own accord."

Stella's head dropped forward. She stared down at her sandals. A pair of soiled white nurse shoes stepped up alongside them, followed by a light brush of fingers on her shoulder.

"I'll leave you alone with her."

All Stella could do was nod. This ghostly nurse was the only person who seemed sincere down in this pit of despair.

"Thank you," she muttered, but when she looked up, she was alone.

Stella sat down on the crate Sarah had just occupied. From that spot, she was even with Anne Wexler's head on the flimsy pillow. Staring at the face in repose, Stella saw a wan version of the attractive middle-aged woman. Dark roots provided a stark contrast with the matted blonde hair. The ocean had stripped all traces of makeup. Stella didn't think she'd ever seen Jill's mom without makeup. There were tiny blue veins scoring the closed eyelids, some pooling beneath the eyes. Glowing pink cheeks now looked ashen.

"Wake up, Mrs. Wexler," she commanded softly. "When my mom is not around, you always fill in."

Tears filled Stella's eyes. She reached for Anne's hand. It was so cold. She clasped it in both of hers, hoping to infuse warmth.

"And my mom is not here now." Emotion clogged her throat. "I *need* you," she emphasized.

Stella stared at Anne's face. There was no sign of acknowledgment, no flicker of an eyelid, no twitch of a muscle. Anne was somewhere far away from this cave…and Stella wished she was with her.

CHAPTER 9

Feeling more alone than ever, Stella slipped from the infirmary and paused outside, searching for Jill. There she was, still chatting with the lanky guy, his shoulders hunched forward as if trying to minimize his presence. Jill's hands fluttered about like birds stuck in the mud, a sure indication she was flirting.

Stella glanced at the upside-down boat but saw no trace of Colin or his father. In fact, with the exception of the light pulsing from Frederic's office up on the hillside, the cave seemed empty.

Just beyond the central walkway, she eyed the tiny stream snaking past the cafe. The River Styx, she thought with a wry snort. Stepping up to its edge, she observed a shallow red bed with a ribcage pattern carved in the dirt beneath the clear water.

A hasty glance over her shoulder confirmed that she was alone. Resolved, she began to follow the water's meandering track.

Torches wedged in the ground lit her way, but as she moved beyond the developed area, the flares grew sparse, and the shadows encroached. Ahead, the maddening spill of water grew louder. Nearly three stories above, water was spattering over the edge of a jagged ledge. It fell into a broad section of the stream, which she approached, kneeling beside the widening pool. Brine and dankness filled her nose, but it was a pervasive scent and not from this water. Cupping her hand below the surface, she was surprised at how warm the water was. After a quick sniff, she touched her tongue to the liquid. No salt. Frederic mentioned that this stream was their water supply. Now, she almost believed him.

Stella spread her fingers and let the water slip through them. Ahead, deeper shadows lurked beyond the slim waterfall. Shadows weren't going to scare her, though. They were just a means to cloak answers, and answers were what she sought.

Determined, she grabbed a warped plank wedged in the clay. Its tip was wrapped in burning cloth. When she finally yanked it free, the jerking motion nearly brushed the flame to her face. Perspiration beaded up on her forehead.

A quick glance behind her assured that no one was watching. Holding the torch aloft, she slipped around the wide pool, feeling a spattering of drops from the waterfall douse her cheeks. Continuing around the base of the furthest pinnacle, she advanced until the village was no longer visible.

As Styx narrowed back into a slim band, Stella hugged its edge, knowing it was her proverbial popcorn path back to civilization.

Civilization. Hah.

Delving deeper into the darkness, she felt the heat intensify. It had to compare to trudging through the Amazon on the most humid of days. Holding the torch above her she saw moisture clinging to the cave walls. The reflection of the light made the cave seem animated.

A quick check of the torch assured that it had plenty of life remaining. If she lost the flame, it would be tough to negotiate the return trip. The turf on the banks of the stream was eroded as if the level of the water was once higher. It made for an easier trek as she delved deeper into nature's passageway. There were no offshoots visible. No nooks to conceal demons of the deep. Ahead, she could hear a hissing sound similar to the steam escaping from her mom's iron. The channel turned misty. The haze clung to her skin, pasting her shirt to her back.

Through the mist, something moved. There was no shape—no form—just the sense of motion. A slight scrape. A brush of pebbles.

For as hot as it was, chills began to charge across her damp skin. Inching forward, she swung the torch in hopes of catching the source. As she shifted the flare to the right, a pair of glistening eyes peered out from the fog.

Stella gasped and nearly dropped the torch. When she looked again, the haze had congealed into a thick cloud. Nothing was staring back at her. Had she really seen eyes or was it just the reflection of the flames off of a shiny rock?

A grating sound came from her left, and she jerked in that direction. Her body trembled as she stood in a silent face-off with the glaring gaze. The eyes were much more vibrant than those of a human. Pulsing and green, like a broken glow stick—wideset like an animal. Before she could even assess what she was seeing, she felt a rush of air and a hard limb crash into her, knocking her off balance. The torch slipped from her hand and rolled down the embankment, extinguished as soon as it hit the water. In an instant, Stella was engulfed in darkness.

Panic pumped her chest into overdrive. She tried to draw in a deep breath. It was pungent with the smell of sulfur and fear. Trembling fingers fisted against the clay, searching for a rock or even a handful of loose pebbles—anything to use as a weapon.

In this obscurity, the acoustics were heightened. The hiss of steam from a faraway vent. The raspy motion of her knee scraping dirt as she began a tremulous crawl in what she hoped was the direction she came from. The echo of her pounding heart. And the scratch of something shifting nearby.

Stella held her breath, hoping to temporarily pause the pulse in her ears. The sloth-like movement drew closer. With it came a new scent. Something foul. Something fetid. Roadkill. That was the first thought it evoked. Memories stuck in your nose forever, and she could clearly remember the scent of a dead deer that she and Jill had stumbled across taking a shortcut through the woods.

Stella had lowered her eyelids to focus on more lucrative senses. It seemed pointless to open them when sight was impossible. But a shift in the air had her peeking out. Phosphorescent eyes glimmered back at her from only a foot away. Foul breath brushed over her face. It smelled like death, and the soulless orbs were pulsing gateways of mortality.

A scream rushed from her throat as she bolted blindly, stumbling into the stream and tramping through the thigh-high water. She dared not look back. In fact, she closed her eyes again, concentrating on every rigorous step through the tepid creek. At one point, she stumbled, her toe hooking on a rock, sending her face forward into the water. She sputtered to the surface and became disoriented, unsure whether she was heading back towards the village or deeper into despair.

At that moment, a light filled the cave. Stella whimpered, certain that the dead-eyed creature had caught up with her. Throwing her forearm over her eyes, she tripped backward.

"Stella!"

Stumbling out of the water, she cried out, "Colin! Colin, is that you?"

What if it wasn't? What if it was a cruel acoustical hoax? What if the green-eyed creature was a ventriloquist? Right now, no theory seemed too outlandish.

"Stella!"

The light bobbed closer. Close enough to realize it was a torch similar to hers, which now lay useless at the bottom of the stream. When she saw Colin's concerned face in the flames, she started towards him on legs as supportive as seaweed.

He dropped the torch on a bolder and caught her before she could stumble again.

"Stel, what happened?" His voice was husky. "Are you okay?"

A trembling fit overcame her, as if this was the coldest place in the world, when in fact, it was only a few feet above Hell. She stared up into heavily shadowed eyes and caught brief hues of caramel-flecked warmth as the flames danced over his face. In them, she found shelter. That's what eyes were supposed to look like. Not the radiance of death.

Before answering, she cast a quick glimpse over her shoulder. His torch illuminated the damp walls and the narrow stream, which she had just discovered was deceivingly deep. Styx was a good name for it. Other than these geological features, the cave was empty.

"I—I—"

Hallucinations? Carbon dioxide poisoning? No. Not this time.

There was no denying the stench of that breath.

"No," she declared breathlessly. "Let's get out of here, Col."

Colin searched her face and then looked past her, deep into the channel.

"Is there something back there?"

There was no condemnation in the question—no leading assumption that she was losing her mind. His assurance bolstered her confidence.

"Yes." She swallowed and grabbed his arm, tugging him away from the unknown. "Some*thing*," she emphasized.

With each step of retreat, she regained control of her limbs. Colin's wide hand on her back helped a lot.

"Something charged at me, Col. It knocked me over. I lost the torch—in the stream."

"Go on," he urged quietly, although she could feel his step hesitate as he glanced behind them.

"It was pitch black, but when I looked up, I was looking into these glowing green eyes. I swear—I swear it was what I saw back by the pool when you and I first entered the cave. The eyes weren't normal. An animal, maybe. But it was upright, and just before I lost the torch, I caught a glimpse of it. Large, dark. It walked on two legs I think, and it slammed me with its arm. And—"

Colin stopped, holding the torch up so he could read her face.

"And?" he prompted.

"It had the foulest breath imaginable. I swear when I looked into those eyes—I swear I was looking at death."

"It won't be the first time that the Grim Reaper came looking for us."

There was no sarcasm in his tone. The blunt acceptance of her tale comforted her.

"Why, Stell? Why did you come back here alone? I was looking for you. We were supposed to do this together."

The sound of the waterfall filled the chamber. They were approaching the village, and as the cavern widened, the heat of the narrow channel and the deep-sea vents was left behind. The comparatively cool air made

Stella's skin feel clammy under her wet clothes. She clasped her arms about herself.

"I looked for you," she muttered. "I couldn't find you. Jill was busy talking to that new guy, so I just—I just went."

Light from the village torches finally reached them. Colin stopped her by cupping her upper arms in his hands. She was grateful for the heat.

"Did it hurt you?"

She shook her chin from side to side, feeling her throat close and tears bubble behind her eyes.

"Hey—"

He pulled her into his arms as her cheek rested against his t-shirt. The warmth of his embrace was the first touch of humanity she felt in this godforsaken hole in the earth. She closed her eyes and reveled in an embrace she had often fantasized about. But this hug was not a passionate declaration. This hug stemmed from need and camaraderie.

"Foolish," he whispered.

She couldn't deny the accusation, yet he didn't seem to be reprimanding her.

"You scared me," he uttered thickly.

Stella trembled. Whether it was from a chill or the hoarse declaration, she couldn't tell.

Colin set her back and for a moment she searched his gaze. Was there an intensity to those forest-colored eyes that possibly relayed more than feelings of protection and companionship? He stared at her for a long time, with his hands still cupping her shoulders, and then finally, he let go.

"Okay, tell me everything." Colin cleared his throat. "How far did you make it into the tunnel?"

Still shaken Stella shared the few details she could. "All I can say is that the deeper you go into that tunnel, the hotter it becomes. I was sweating …now I'm just drenched from the water, and this cavern feels about twenty—thirty degrees cooler."

Colin wrenched his head back the way they came.

"Those vents seem to be the life source of this place. I want to try and get back there. And I want—" he hesitated and regarded her thoughtfully, "—I want to find what attacked you. Maybe it was another survivor. We'll have to check with Etienne."

There was no point in correcting him that it did not seem human. But, in retrospect, what did she really see?

Those eyes.

They were savage.

"You've got to get out of those clothes," Colin ordered. "You're shaking."

Stella felt a laugh rumble in her chest. It bubbled over her lips.

"What's so funny?" Colin frowned.

"We've been in wet clothes more than we've been dry lately."

To her surprise, Colin's sober expression cracked into a grin. It was so attractive, right down to the tiny dimple on the left side of his lips.

"Yeah," he glanced up at the waterfall, "I guess it's something we're going to have to get used to."

"I always wanted to be a mermaid."

Colin's smile grew. He swept his arm out and executed a half bow. "My dear, Miss Gullaksen. Down here, you can be whatever you want."

Can I be your girlfriend?

Stella flinched at the rogue notion. She was eighteen years old. There was no need to act like a gangly teenager with a crush.

"The world's first mermaid journalist," she rushed. "I can fan myself with my tail as I'm conducting interviews."

Colin laughed and it was good to see him relax. Even before the accident, he had seemed distant from everyone on board, as if the weight of the world was on his shoulders.

"I wouldn't mind seeing that," he murmured.

Heat bloomed in Stella's cheeks. It helped battle the chill of the wet fabric.

"Goodness! What happened?"

Colin and Stella jerked at the unexpected invasion.

Margie waddled up to them, lugging a basket of clothes. She was short and had to support the basket against an ample hip, which threw her step off balance.

Stella and Colin exchanged a glance before Stella called out, "I was trying to clean off—and lost my balance."

Margie's loud guffaw was infectious. The woman set the basket down and rested her hands on her thighs, looking up at them, still chuckling.

"I can't tell you how many times I've done that." Her glance dropped to Stella's knees scored with abrasions. "Oh dear, you did take quite a tumble. We'll get you cleaned up proper. I actually have some clean clothes here if you want to try something on while we wash yours."

The woman must have read Stella's skeptical face.

"Seriously, they're clean. Take a whiff." She hoisted the rubber basket, a composite that surely wouldn't break down in the sea.

Stella leaned over for a timid sniff and was surprised at the fresh scent. She expected mildew, when in fact it was something more like soap.

"How do you—"

"Wash them? In water from the stream. There's a basin behind that boulder." She nodded in that direction where Stella caught a glimpse of a porcelain pot jutting out behind the rock.

"And we have accrued quite a bit of detergent over the years," Margie added. "And we've managed to make soap bars with oils and perfumes that find their way down here."

Soap.

The thought of it nearly made her swoon. Suddenly, everything felt grimy. Her skin. Her clothes. It wasn't that she had been in them for over two days, or that she had swam to the bottom of the ocean in them. It was the contact in the tunnel. She needed to cleanse herself of that fetid smell. But no amount of detergent or soap would cleanse her soul.

"I'll need to borrow her for a few minutes,"

133

Margie said to Colin with a wink.

Some color flashed in Colin's cheekbones. But his lips thinned, and he nodded perfunctorily. "Sure. No problem." He backed away.

"Colin, we need to—"

She didn't want to say out loud that they needed to talk to Etienne about what they found. Colin understood, though, and his expression softened some.

"I'll wait for you. *Find me* this time."

Stella's lips curled up. "I will."

Colin walked away, his long back damp from the waterfall.

"Your boyfriend?" Margie whispered with a slight jab of her elbow.

"No, no." Stella's face ignited. "He—he's like an older brother. He's got a girlfriend—or he did."

Margie followed the retreating figure with her eyes.

"Fine-looking *older brother*." She winked. "And his girlfriend sure didn't follow him down here."

Stella ducked her face and followed Margie towards the basin. It was an antique white cast-iron tub with clawed feet. It was empty and had surprisingly few stains. Next to it was a wooden pail.

"You can wash up here," Margie said. "We take the bucket over to the stream and pour it into the tub. Nobody really sits in this tub. They use it more for a hand bath."

Stella saw that the bathtub was strategically placed several yards away from a bend in the stream. Walking up to the water's edge with the bucket, she knelt and let the heavy pail fill.

"Sorry, no hot water faucets, though," Margie apologized with a grin. "Of course, the temperature of the water isn't too bad in here."

"It was actually *hot* where I—"

The woman's gold eyebrow hiked up.

"Where I fell in," Stella quickly added.

"You made it pretty deep into the tunnel if the water was hot." Margie's expression darkened. "Don't wander off too far on your own."

Was that a threat or a cordial suggestion? Best guess was the former, but Margie's affable banter was back in full swing.

"Now, I have just the dress in mind for you while we wash your clothes. Go ahead and take them off back there and hand them out to me."

Uncomfortable, Stella glanced at the boulder she was to undress behind. Technically, the tub and dressing area was discreetly tucked away from view of the village, but it was still awkward. She tipped her head back to inspect the arched ceiling several stories above, half expecting a host of green eyes to be glaring down at her.

Stella's gaze dropped back to the woman in tan capris and baggy blue blouse. Her arms and calves were pale, with some purple veins shooting upwards from her ankles. She wore a pearl bracelet and a costume pearl necklace, bangles that seemed ill placed for here.

"I'll stand outside the boulder as guard, if that will make you feel more at ease, and I'll lay something for you to wear right here." She smacked the smooth rock face.

Stella eyed the laundry basket warily.

"These are clean. I promise. I washed them myself, and I have far more hang-ups than you do about putting stranger's clothes on."

That was plausible. This woman wore affluence as if it were a cape. The jewelry was a symbol of her life above.

"Is there someplace you use as a bathroom?"

This morning Stella had waited until she was behind the waterfall where she finally felt safe enough to relieve herself.

"On the other side of the stream. Further down. There are a number of private spots we take turns using. The waste is later gathered up and stored in a cave to help regulate the carbon dioxide." Margie rolled her eyes. "Frederic's idea. Trust me, you don't want to get cave-dung duty."

Wrinkling her nose at the thought, Stella slowly stepped behind the boulder. She peeked around the corner, waiting until Margie turned her back and crossed her arms, warding off any unwanted visitors.

Stella filled the tub with two buckets of water, enough to do a hasty hand cleansing. She grabbed the distorted bar of soap and took a sniff. It sure didn't look pretty. Brown marble swirls through a grayish-lopsided block. But it had a faint floral scent that wasn't too bad. She dipped it in the water and washed it off before using it.

Confirming that Margie was still stationed as a guard, Stella began to strip. She hastily scrubbed her arms, grateful for this one act of indulgence.

"Oh, this will look lovely on you. Way too small for my hips," Margie mentioned as Stella saw her flip a white cloth atop the boulder.

Stella reached for it, surprised to find a white cotton dress barely stained and smelling surprisingly clean.

"Where did this come from?" she asked.

"A couple of suitcases and satchels have washed up down here. This one held no identification, so I have no idea who it belonged to. We do get several nice clothing items from time to time, so there is always something to change into whenever you want to wash up."

"You'll show me where I can clean my clothes?"

"Of course! Remember about the chores down here."

"Yes," Stella replied automatically. "I remember. And I'm willing to help."

Margie inclined her head enough for Stella to see the approving smile on her profile. The woman had ruddy, plump cheeks. She wasn't fat. Could anyone really be fat down here? But she was curvy, that was for sure.

"Jill—my friend," Stella began, "she was talking to that Daniel."

Margie's smile fell as her cheeks settled into pools beside her chin. "Daniel Schmidt."

"Are there others down here that we didn't meet at dinner?"

As Stella hastily donned the dress, she saw some of the tension leave Margie's shoulders.

"No. You've met everyone. Daniel wasn't

too social at dinner. He is a bit of a recluse. I'm surprised he talked to you. It usually takes a few years to get a 'hi' out of that boy."

"Well, he didn't really talk to me. He has been talking to Jill. And it seems like it's been longer than just *hi*."

The rounded shoulders behind the rock shook slightly as the woman laughed. "Yes, well I imagine a blue-eyed blonde could drag him from his brooding."

Stella rolled her eyes and then asked, "How did he end up down here?"

Margie crooked her head in each direction, checking to see if they were alone. Stella felt a little less vulnerable now that she was cleansed and clothed. The white dress fit her perfectly. Maybe it was a little long, but her biggest fear had been that it was thin enough to see through. That wasn't the case, however. She held her hand under the material and didn't even see an outline. Once upon a time, this dress might have belonged to someone affluent. It evoked a beachy look while still seemingly elegant.

"Would you believe he fell off the QE2?"

QE2. QE2. Oh yes, the Queen Elizabeth 2 cruise ship. She had heard of it.

"Wow? So, he's rich?" she asked.

Margie snorted. "You don't have to be rich to take the QE2. You need some money, but not that much."

Stella figured Margie's perception was skewed by her own wealth. This was a woman who still clung to her above-sea arrogance, yet she did so cheerfully.

"I can't even imagine falling off a cruise

ship," Stella marveled. "It's amazing he survived the fall."

Margie craned her neck, searching for the subject of their conversation. "I think the fact that he did is the root of his displeasure."

Before Stella could mull that over, Margie startled her by smacking her palms around her plump cheeks.

"Look at you!" she exclaimed. "Just beautiful. You look divine."

Stella stepped from behind the boulder, her fingers drawing the skirt out as she executed a slow spin.

"It fits. No one has worn it?" An image of the exotic Loren clouded her thoughts.

"No. I just found this," Margie said. "I was in the process of washing everything from a footlocker that washed up in the main pool. Like I said, I can't tell anything about the ID, but the contents seemed dated. I'm surprised it's in such good condition."

Stella was about to retort, *I could say the same about all of you*, but she clamped her lips shut.

Instead, she asked, "Is Jill okay with him? This Daniel. Is she safe with him?"

Margie crossed her arms. "He is antisocial, not a demon."

Surprised by Margie's vehemence, Stella cleared her throat and fidgeted with the waistline of the dress. In half a second, that congenial smile was back on Margie's coral lips. "You have nothing to worry about from any of us, Stella. You can't even imagine how much we welcome your company. We all look out for each other…even Daniel."

Trust was something earned as far as Stella was concerned, and down here, she was sorely lacking in that department. There was one person she trusted, though. She searched for him now, scanning the row of flickering torches leading to their quarters. There was no one there, but further down she saw Donald Wexler step down from the infirmary. A shadow filled the hatch, and Colin appeared, climbing down behind him.

The two men walked away from the airplane, the deep undertone of their voices muffled. Stella stood rooted, unsure whether she should interrupt. She wanted to go talk to Etienne or Frederic about what happened to her, but having Colin at her side would give her a boost of confidence.

Just as she contemplated turning away, Colin looked up. His tread hesitated for a split second before falling back in alongside his father. Still, his eyes remained on hers.

The men continued to their rustic structure, but Colin did not follow his father inside. Don's wavy crown popped back out of the doorway as he looked up at his son. A hasty conversation took place before he disappeared back into the shadows of the inverted boat.

Colin remained outside until finally he turned to face Stella. Dark eyes roamed over her dress and back up to meet her gaze. She stood rooted, immobilized by the intensity of his stare. When he started towards her, she felt her breath hitch. She knew she was being ridiculous. Just the sight of this tall, rugged figure walking towards her turned her into a statue.

"Hi," he said as he stopped a few feet away.

"Hi." She swallowed.

Colin took in the dress again, and his mouth curled up appealingly.

"Go shopping?" he asked.

"Umm, no." She nervously toyed with the fabric. "I had to clean my clothes. The silt in that stream was all over them. And Margie—" Flipping her hand back towards the boulder, Stella turned to see that Margie was gone. "Well, Margie had this dress. It—believe it or not, it smells clean." She tipped her head to her shoulder to take a quick sniff.

Colin took a few steps towards her. He held his nose up in the air. It was a straight nose with a little bump at the top. Maybe a childhood brush with a football or a tumble on the pavement. He had that bump for as long as she knew him, so it wasn't from a college brawl.

"You don't reek."

Stella's mouth dropped open.

Colin chuckled. "Just kidding, Stel. You look good in that."

Why did such a simple comment make her feel like she had a fever? Even now, chill bumps popped up on her arms. She crossed them over her chest and muttered, "Thanks."

Colin stuck his hands in the pockets of his shorts as he craned his neck.

"Did you see Etienne yet?"

"No. I was—" she cleared the tickle in her throat, "—I was waiting for you."

A quick nod of his square chin, and then one of those hands was out, reaching towards her as it gently touched her elbow.

"Good. Let's go chat with the man, shall we?"

CHAPTER 10

It took a quick stop at the infirmary to learn where to locate Etienne. Sarah pointed them to the path that led to their shared dwelling, a yurt-looking cottage crafted from planks of a wooden hull. Light poked out of cracks in the walls, and a burlap bag hung unfurled as a door.

"Do we knock or call out?" Stella whispered.

"I'm afraid if we knock, the whole structure will collapse," Colin murmured.

"Mr. Fournier," he called. "Could we see you for a moment?"

There was no response. Stella was about to turn around, but Colin captured her arm and mouthed the word, *wait*.

Motion was detected inside the hut. A shadow crossed past those illuminated cracks. The flap was thrown back, and Etienne's curly hair poked out.

"Hello," he stated. The welcoming smile took a moment to accompany the salutation. "Come on in. The place is a bit of a mess, but that's because Sarah has been busy."

Stella felt Colin's hand on her arm stiffen, and then he released her. Of course, Sarah was busy. She was busy trying to save Anne Wexler's life.

Classifying the interior as a *mess* was a stretch, considering everything was basically junk. It was organized junk, however. There were two twin mattresses elevated by mounds of dirt. Atop them were some blankets that bore a hint of the same floral scent as her dress. A small wooden crate labeled COFFEE sat before a much larger shipping container, which had a candle burning inside a porcelain bowl.

"Candles are a luxury down here." Etienne looked sheepish as if he had been caught with contraband. "But I had some work to do. I needed the light."

"What are you working on?" Stella asked.

Steely eyes locked onto her. They were so piercing she felt like he was sucking out her soul. He blinked, and the effect was gone.

"Inventory." He shook his head and scratched his hair. "Always tracking inventory."

"Is there a warehouse or something?"

Colin snorted at her innocent question. Well, maybe it wasn't so naive. Everything down here seemed peculiar.

"In a manner of speaking, yes, there is." Etienne nodded. "We stockpile all items we find in a nearby cave. You passed it on your way in. From there they are divvied up and moved to their designated zones as needed. All food is shared, so there is no fear of someone stealing, but we do have to ration when supplies get low. Of course, then we just fish."

"Can I go with you the next time you fish?" Colin asked.

"Certainly," Etienne beamed.

The gesture improved his gaunt face, but to Stella, everything about the man just seemed gray. His hair, his skin. Even his attire.

"Now, what was it you needed to talk about?"

Suddenly, she didn't want to tell her tale. Colin sensed her reluctance and tapped her elbow for encouragement.

"Stell, it's best to just ask."

Fidgeting with the dress material, she didn't know where to begin. Was this man going to yell at her for going beyond the waterfall? Probably.

"That's a lovely dress," Etienne remarked in an attempt to put her at ease. "Have you started laundry duty?"

"Tomorrow," she mumbled, her eyes combing the inside of the hut.

A pile of clothes sat in one corner. A stack of stained bookbinders was piled up next to the makeshift desk. Atop the desk was an open notebook and what looked like a No. 2 pencil.

"Stella had a run-in with something," Colin stated, sparing her the awkward segue.

Gray-man's face tightened. Sinewy lines connected his cheeks to his jaw.

"What type of run-in?" he asked warily.

Ready to say, *just forget about it*, her sandaled foot tipped backward. She felt Colin's eyes on her and looked up. The warm gaze was such a contradiction to Etienne's bleak stare.

Col nodded. *It's okay.*

That support encouraged her.

"I took a walk," she began. "I ended up behind the waterfall. I was looking for—" heat pricked the back of her head "—a place to go to the bathroom. No one showed us where the designated spots were."

Etienne's lips thinned. "You could have asked. It's dangerous exploring around here without someone to guide you. Certain caves and channels are very close to the underwater vents and can reach hazardous temperatures. We know how to navigate these spots and use them to our advantage. That has come after many years of experience."

Aggravated by the censure, Stella was ready to leave her *run-in* as just that—an encounter with the hazardous heat beyond the waterfall.

"Are there any other dangers down here besides the heat?"

Stella executed a mental backflip. Colin had deflected the target back on Etienne's forehead.

Gray-man snorted. "Look at this place. This is a geological aberration. We discussed the threats. Every day, we fear an earthquake like the one that most likely created this cavern. Every day, we fear the hydrothermal vents that sustain us will somehow cease to function. Every day, we light the torches and pray that the flame doesn't go out."

"Why would it go out?" Stella asked.

"If the flame goes out there is too much carbon dioxide in the air, and we will all die." He paused for effect. "So, *yes*, there are dangers down here."

Stella's gaze swung to gauge Colin's

reaction. He was poised, indifferent to Etienne's menacing tone.

"What about creatures?" he asked evenly.

A slight flare in Etienne's eyes was the only sign of angst, but his composure returned.

"Creatures?"

"Stella was attacked by something behind the waterfall. She said it wasn't human."

Explosions went off in her heart that this man would champion her defense without ever having witnessed the creature himself. She could have made the whole thing up, but Colin believed her. His trust spurred her into action.

"I know this is the second time I've seen something. I couldn't really see skin, but the creature was dark to blend with the shadows. What gave it away were the eyes. Large, green, glowing—"

With each word, Etienne's bushy gray eyebrow hiked higher.

"I will need Sarah to check on you. The atmospheric change could have been too drastic."

"The atmospheric change didn't charge at me and toss me into the water," she retaliated. "The atmospheric change didn't do this!"

Stella tugged the collar of her dress over her shoulder, exposing a contusion that was blossoming in blue and purple shades.

Shock registered on Colin's face while Etienne remained indifferent.

"You took a tumble in the stream," he said. "There are no torches back there. You got spooked by the darkness. We all do. You fell in the water, and portions of the bed are rocky.

You should have Sarah check on that."

Stella glanced down at the bruise, remembering the feel of impact. "A rock did not cause this. Something *hit* me."

It was the pity on Etienne's face that set her off.

"What are you hiding?" she demanded. "What happened to the, *we're all in this together* spirit?

"We *are* all in this together. I take your welfare very seriously. We don't want to lose anyone down here. My wife is working tirelessly to try and save your loved one."

Ouch. A strong counterpunch. She could see the reference bring pain to Colin's eyes. That glimpse of vulnerability took the fight out of her.

"You're right," she yielded. "I was probably just freaked out."

Hastily drawing her dress back over her shoulder, she forced a smile. It felt strained on her lips. "But the good news is that Margie showed me where all the bathrooms are and explained how the recycling works. For the record, I'd like to put in for anything other than *that* duty."

A grin was slow to form on Etienne's face. It looked as forced as her own, but he managed to inflect some good nature into his soft accent. "I'll see what I can do about that."

"What duty?" Colin looked back and forth between them.

"Come on." She grabbed Colin's arm. "We're sorry to have bothered you," she said to Etienne.

"Nonsense. You are welcome anytime. And please," he nodded at her shoulder, "have Sarah check that."

"Oh, it's fine. Thanks. We'll see you at dinner."

Before any further conversation could take place, Stella bowed out of the hut, her hand still clutched around Colin's forearm. He followed and stopped once they were alone outside. His glance fell to her hand, which she quickly dropped.

"What just happened in there?" he asked quietly.

"I don't trust him."

"Well, we agree on that. Come on, let's get further away."

As they left the hut behind them, Stella looked back over her shoulder. Etienne was hiking up the trail towards the crow's nest.

"Look at that," she whispered, "he's running right up there to tell Frederic about me."

Colin frowned. "Whatever. We tried to play the game and go to him for advice. It got us nothing. Tomorrow, I'm going behind that waterfall."

Stella stopped walking. "Col, not alone. I don't want you to go back there alone."

He looked down at her with a faint grin. Half his face glowed from a nearby torch.

"Why? Are you worried about me?"

Being this close. Hearing that soft goading and seeing that tempting smile—they would have all been valid reasons to reach up and link her arms around his neck. But the strongest impulse stemmed from something else.

"You believed me," she whispered. "I could have been scared, disoriented in the dark. I could have imagined it all."

Pensive, he studied her face and then hesitantly reached for the loose collar of her dress.

"May I?" he asked in a husky tone.

Stella nodded mutely, following his eyes while his fingers gently hauled the fabric off her shoulder. The touch brought another bout of goosebumps.

"If it's all in your imagination," he said, "then why does this bruise look like a hand imprint?"

The bell tolled.

A single haunting peal to mark the end of the day.

Everyone was already settled in their lodgings. Dinner had been a quiet affair, with only Margie and Jordan talking about a few of their more adventurous vacations. Swimming with the dolphins in Hawaii, and a safari trip to Kenya. From the glazed-over look in Loren's eyes, she guessed the young woman had heard about the safari a million times.

"It's good to see you back in your shorts," Jill remarked from her darkened corner. "The dress was kinda freaking me out."

"Well, how did you wash your clothes?"

"How do you think?" Jill's white teeth flashed from the dark.

"You just stood there naked until they

dried?" Stella guessed, horrified. "And was your friend there waiting, too?"

"Whatevs. I washed them after I talked to him." She plucked the cotton from her skin. "They're still wet."

"Bet you'd like to borrow my freakish dress right now."

"I'm too tired to care. When I wake up, they'll be dry."

Jill claimed the hammock for the night and now rocked gently in it.

"So, what was your day like?" she asked.

Stella's eyebrows rose. She didn't want to share the scare she'd had today. There was no sense worrying her friend.

"Uneventful. I took a walk. Washed clothes. Took a bath. Pretty rudimentary, not like you. You had all the excitement today. Tell me about him," she prodded. "This Daniel."

Jill sighed. "It's no big deal, Stel. He was just someone to talk to in this godforsaken dungeon."

"You guys *talked* a long time. What's his story? How'd he get down here?"

Although she knew the answer already, Stella wondered if he had elaborated with Jill.

"The dude fell off a freaking cruise ship." Jill propped herself up on an elbow. "He said that he fell off the bow and that when he hit, the force of the hull actually pushed him away from the ship. He broke his arm in the fall and was having a tough time treading water, but he stayed up long enough to watch the ship sail away. It was the cold that finally got him, and he couldn't move his legs anymore. He just gave up and went under."

"And got tugged into the same current that brought us down?" Stella finished.

"Yep, what he described was exactly the same—only he didn't pass out like I did. Or so he claims." She winked.

"So why doesn't this current suck the whole damn cruise ship down here?"

"I asked the same thing. He said Frederic thinks it's a very narrow channel. The odds of getting caught in it—"

"Yeah, yeah, judging by the residents down here, maybe once a decade or less."

"We have crap luck." Jill moped. She was quiet for a moment, and then her voice changed. "Stel, do you think Mom is going to make it?"

The pleading tone tugged at Stella's heart. "I truly hope so."

There was no response from the shadows. Stella presumed Jill had laid back down. Then she heard her pained whisper. *"Maybe she's the lucky one."*

It was futile to offer false assurances. Maybe Jill was right. Stella sensed a sinister outcome for them all, and perhaps Mrs. Wexler was going to be spared that grim fate.

After a few moments, Stella heard Jill's breathing fade into the even rhythm of slumber. Unable to sleep herself, Stella sat cross-legged on the floor, close enough to the window to bask in the light of a nearby torch.

There was no activity outside, but the positioning of this little sunroom restricted her view to only the path, the café, and the darkness beyond it.

She had changed back into her shorts and tank top only because she knew it was too dark for Jill to get a good look at her bruise. In the limited light, she now studied it and could make out the individual marks, like purple bands around her upper arm. The mark of fingers or digits of some variety.

Stella closed her eyes and reviewed the memory. She felt the grip. She felt the shove. It was a raw and powerful force. She smelled the wicked stench of death…and she saw those eyes. Those sinister, luminous eyes.

Straining to search the far end of the path out her window, Stella knew she'd never be able to sleep. She turned towards her notepad and began writing with a pen that poured out sporadic ink.

Time started to fade into a routine of bells chiming and assorted duties. Clean the clothes. Stock food in the café. Search the shores of the cave pools for usable flotsam.

Stella learned the whereabouts of the supply cave. It was a narrow nook off the route to the grotto that she washed up in. The nook opened into a decent-sized chamber stocked with canned goods, clothes, oils, personal items, small furnishings, liquor, books, coiled ropes, and luggage.

"How do you control these things?" She turned to Margie, who was orienting her on the tasks. "Can anyone just come in this cave and take what they want?"

"Everything is doled out as a community," Margie explained, grabbing a stack of canned beans. Some of the labels looked vintage. "If everyone is well-supplied as a whole, there is no need to take anything." She glanced around. "But if you do see something in particular that you would like—it is best to ask Etienne or Frederic."

Stella concealed her frown. She didn't want to go to gray-man for any reason. She found him to be condescending and deceitful and just downright creepy.

"I just thought it'd be nice to browse through some of these books.

"There is a library by the café. These books will be sorted and make their way out there soon."

Stella grabbed a plastic bottle of vegetable oil. Today, she had torch duty and was given a list of potential oils and combustible liquids that she could use. Margie had ingrained the importance of torch duty, but there was no need to explain. Without light down here, madness would quickly ensue.

"I've read all the books out there," she remarked sullenly.

Margie crossed her short arms. "Already? How long have you been down here, a week?"

Stella shrugged. "I don't sleep much down here."

"*Tsk. Tsk.* We sleep a lot here. Sleeping requires less oxygen."

Stella had the feeling she was being lectured, as if her restlessness was somehow tainting their air supply.

"I suppose I'll settle in soon." She forced a smile. "It has just been such an adjustment."

Margie's cheeks plumped up, and she sighed in relief. "You're absolutely right. I guess I can't even remember how I reacted when I first got here. I'm sure I was the same as you."

The woman was quiet for a moment and then added, "It's good to see your bruise is clearing up. That was a nasty tumble you took in the stream You've kept away from there now, right?"

"Right," Stella replied automatically.

That was it. She was an automaton for the time being. Doing their chores. Listening to their rules. Obeying their invisible fences. She used this obedience to grow less and less noticeable. Invisibility would allow her to pass boundaries.

"All right," Margie clapped her hands. "I think we have everything we need. Let's get to work."

Before she slipped from the cave, the woman with the hacked blonde bob sighed. "I just wish your friend was as helpful as you."

Jill hadn't been so accommodating with chore duty. She used visiting her mother as an excuse to get out of several obligations. It would all even out in the end. Stella wasn't worried about the work. It kept her mind engaged. It also allowed her to study the environment. Torch duty would take her from just outside the lagoon they surfaced in, all the way to the waterfall.

"I think I have everything I need," she assured Margie.

"Remember what I taught you? Do you need me to go with you one more time?"

It had been odd to be schooled by this exuberant woman who was more familiar with lighting a candelabra atop a piano than setting a torch ablaze.

"No, I got it. I have torn pieces of cloth and oil. I'll use the existing flames to ignite the new torches."

Margie nodded her approval.

Stella stepped out of the supply cave and commenced her task. The torches lasted a long time. Sometimes, she only had to evaluate and not replace. It sped up the process. Today she finished rather quickly and began her hike up the pinnacle to monitor the string of flares up the spiraling path.

Stopping to survey the five-foot burning Q-tip next to the crow's nest, Stella had an excellent perspective of the village. Jill and Don had just ducked into the infirmary. Colin was on the basketball court talking to Loren. Margie and Jordan were preparing dinner in the café. Etienne was stringing rope—

Wait. What?

Stella's eyes swung back to the basketball court. Loren was sitting with her back against the crooked basketball pole. Her arms were looped around her knees, and her long black hair slid over her shoulders, concealing half her face. Colin stood a few feet away, looking down at her. Occasionally, his hand would move to emphasize whatever he was saying.

What were the odds that there was a young hottie down in this vault? Could she ever catch a break?

Well, technically, Loren wasn't young. When did she come down here, twenty years ago? *Eww*, she was not young at all. But there was no denying the appearance. What did she look like—maybe in her twenties? No one seemed to age too much.

A nearby sound distracted her from the display below.

Humming?

It came from further up the path. The only dwelling perched on this pinnacle was Frederic Nichols' office.

Stella cast one last look below and then approached the barnacled wall, pausing just outside the wooden door. A glow poured through the slits in the wooden plank.

Interview.

Interview.

Interviewing bizarre characters was part of the job for a journalist. There was no room for fear in this occupation.

Stella lifted her hand and rapped on the wood. It felt spongy under the touch and barely made a muffled sound. It was enough, though. A shadow passed before the light and the wood was sliding away in jerky motions as Frederic grabbed it from inside and dragged the huge plank out of the way.

"Stella." He seemed surprised, but a sincere smile lifted his lips. "I'm happy you stopped by."

Stella clutched the bottle of vegetable oil. "I was checking on the torches, and I saw your light on—" she shrugged. "You said I could see your maps sometime."

"Of course. Of course. Come on in." He bent over and grabbed a pile of paperwork off of a crate, and nodded at it. "Have a seat."

Stella sat down, feeling the bite of the wood scrape beneath her thighs. She stared at the painting of the clipper ship on the wall—such a mundane touch.

Frederic was bent over his desk, which was actually two barrels with a slab of wood resting atop them. His pale blonde hair curled above the collar of his uniform jacket. From this perspective, it was hard to believe his age.

Some of the scrolls he had retrieved were now scattered across that weathered surface. He unfurled two and jabbed his finger at the one on top.

"This is crude—based on the data I saw coming in on the punch tape before the accident. But this is more or less where I'm guessing we are."

It was hand drawn—a penciled etching of the ocean floor and its relationship to the surface. The Atlantic shoreline dipped into a plateau that formed a long shelf before plummeting to the abyssal plains at the bottom of the ocean. Several narrow trenches were carved into that shelf, their ominous depth emphasized by the heavy use of lead.

"Here." He pointed to one of those carvings, its base reaching into the abyss. His finger hovered above the bottom. "This is my most educated guess at our location."

The wavy line that represented the surface seemed nearly off the scroll in comparison.

Overall, it was a concise depiction, enabling her to easily envision their demise.

"Yes, that looks very thorough, but you mentioned maps of the caves down here. I'm still confused about what caves are safe and which ones—"

Frederic stood upright. His blue eyes roved over her shoulder. "Looks like that is healing."

Stella absently grabbed her upper arm, concealing the mark.

"Just a testimony to the fact that I need maps to learn my way around here." Her grin was weak.

For an uncomfortably long time, those blue eyes bore into hers. "It's very easy to determine which caves are safe. If you feel the temperature rising, you probably shouldn't advance any further."

Does he think I'm an idiot?

Stella returned his stare. She was surprised at what she saw. It was not condescension like she got from his gray counterpart. It was appreciation—maybe even respect?

"I'm aware of that," she replied drolly.

Playing the role of a twit might allow her some liberties, but it was hard for her to play dumb. And by the look on Frederic's face, he saw through the portrayal.

"What were you looking for back there?" He cut to the chase.

"Certainly not what I found."

Frederic's pale eyebrow rose and an amused smile toyed with his lips. "I imagine not. Etienne tells me you claim to have run into some sort of creature."

Twit or me?

Me.

"I did. It bulldozed me. That's how I got the bruise. And before you all start telling me I'm affected by the atmosphere down here—"

"I'll check it out."

Stella frowned. "You believe me?"

Frederic shrugged. "I believe you saw something. I don't believe it's an evil creature out to do you harm. Either way. I will investigate."

Was he pacifying her? She crossed her arms, not sure how to gauge him. They stared each other down for a few more seconds.

"Am I the first person to see *something*? Have you had run-ins in the dark?"

Frederic tapped his fingers on the desktop. "We have plenty of little creatures we've stumbled upon. A variety of crustaceans living off the vents. Most of them are the size of a golf ball or smaller. And they end up on our dinner plates."

Stella clutched her stomach.

"If you like seafood, you'll enjoy them."

"I'm a hamburger kind of chick."

"If you're hungry enough, you'll eat them."

"Point taken." She dipped her head. "So, how do you get these little creatures if the vents are too hot to approach?"

Frederic regarded her a moment more and then reached for a rolled-up piece of vinyl and expanded it atop the desk. Stella feasted on the detailed cave system, recognizing spots as the great chamber with its twin peaks and the channel to the lagoon—the pool designated by a small rippling line. It was the rest of the schematic that drew her attention. She committed as much as possible to memory before he folded over a flap and used that folded line to point toward the waterfall.

"You were close when you traveled behind the waterfall, but you went straight, which is very dangerous due to the temperature and leaked steam. There is a chute here," he pointed to a tunnel that she clearly missed, "it will take you to another chamber that offers safer water access to the vents. Not safe enough to jump into, but we've crafted some sophisticated nets and baskets that get weighted down and lowered. When we retrieve them, we're often lucky to find the bottoms lined with creatures."

"What made you even try something like that?"

"The edge of that pool is sometimes padded with dead crustaceans."

"And why are they dead?"

Frederic quirked his lip. "Just as you would not expect to find a ventilated cave down at the bottom of the sea, neither would they. They get sucked up into that pool sometimes, and the exposure kills them."

With Frederic being so responsive, Stella began to feel more at ease. She leaned forward, her elbows on her knees and asked, "Why isn't fishing for little sea creatures on my chore list?"

The blonde man laughed. "It takes great skill, hey?"

"Show me once, and I will master it."

"I have no doubt about that, Stella. You seem like a woman who will do whatever she sets her mind to. Sometimes, that determination can get you in trouble." He cautioned, eyeing her shoulder.

Stella reached up again to cover it.

"I'd rather chance getting hurt than die of boredom down here."

The levity left the Canadian's face. "I don't believe that. I see you as a much more calculating individual."

It troubled her that her passive act did not work on this man. Time to change tactics. "Not calculating. Just curious." She leaned forward to view the map. "So, what is behind the waterfall? I mean if you kept going the direction I was headed instead of taking the turn to the pool where you fish for worms and crabs?"

Frederic did not unfold the vinyl as she had hoped.

"It would take you too close to the vents. If you went much further, at a minimum, you might get singed on approach. The further you traveled, the more damage. We had—" he hesitated and glanced toward the gap in his doorway. "—We had someone who did go back there. A survivor of a cargo shipwreck. A young man who ventured back there despite the warning. He didn't return. We eventually found him. Sarah's best guess at the cause of death was akin to excessive smoke inhalation."

Was the story true or fabricated to frighten her? She would heed the caution. But she would also be mindful of what Frederic and Etienne seemed keen on hiding.

"Well," she shrugged. "I guess I'll stick to torch duty for now."

Under that blue-eyed scrutiny, she felt exposed. A chill wormed into her arms, and she rose unsteadily from the crate.

"I better get back to it," she hastened.

Frederic looked down at her. It wasn't often that people were tall enough to look down at her. Again, she felt like she was being analyzed on a microscope slab.

Eventually, he smiled.

"Yes, you better. We don't want to be without light, hey?" He hesitated and added, "You're welcome here any time if you have questions, Stella."

If you are so generous with the answers, why is that map still folded up at the corner?

"Thanks." She reached for the door plank, but Frederic's arm rose above hers to hoist the door to the side.

Clutching her supplies, Stella hurried from the cabin. She hiked back down the path, slipping several times on the granular surface. When she reached the bottom, she swung toward the supply cave.

The only other man in this underworld who was tall enough to look down at her now barred her path.

CHAPTER 11

"Hi," Colin said.

Stella looked up and swallowed.

Colin seemed riled, his full lips tensed into a thin line.

"Hi," she muttered.

"You were up there a long time." He observed, glancing up the path before sliding his eyes back down to hers.

"You were busy," she countered, searching the empty basketball court behind him.

A pleased glint sharpened his gaze.

"Jealous?" he probed with a soft grin.

"Uh—*no*."

The grin faded. "Maybe I am," he added softly.

Butterflies swatted around inside her stomach. Was he teasing her?

"Jealous of a man that is probably older than my grandfather?"

"He doesn't look it. And I've seen him. He doesn't look at you like a granddaughter. He watches you."

Stella was still trying to process Colin's

innuendo. He couldn't be jealous? Could he?

"Frederic knows I'm interested in learning more. He let me see his maps."

"I bet he did." Colin snorted.

"Seriously? Just a few minutes ago, you were *watching* Loren. So much so that I couldn't even catch your attention before I went up there."

A flare in his eyes suggested she'd hit her mark. She decided to dig in.

"And speaking of jealous. Don't you have a girlfriend back in college who you're cheating on with Loren?"

Colin sighed, but instead of looking angry, he seemed amused. That swagger on him was damn fine.

"First," he began, "I have no girlfriend. I *had* one—sort of. She said I was too busy. I've got two degrees I'm working towards. I have zero social life right now. I can't afford the distraction. Second," he reached up and rubbed the back of his neck. "How am I cheating? I was just talking to Loren. She seems nice."

"I'm sure she's charming."

"Stel." He grinned. "I was looking for *you*. I was looking for you when I ran into her. I—"

Suddenly, Mr. Composure seemed unsettled. He reached out to touch her arm, but his hand dropped back down.

"Ah, forget it. I—"

"You what?" she prodded, calmer now.

"So, what did the maps reveal?"

The obvious segue amused her. She actually smiled, which Colin slowly reflected. The tension dissolved.

"It's what they didn't reveal." She began explaining that Frederic had folded over the map to hide the section behind the waterfall.

"Well, you know what that means?"

Stella tried to quell her nerves. "That means we're going behind the waterfall?"

"You don't have to go. I'd rather you stay safe back here."

"And who is going to keep you safe?" she countered. "Of course, I'm going with you."

Colin looked conflicted. "All right, but if we see any creatures, I'm hiking you right back out of there."

"If we see one of those things, you'll be chasing my heels. No need to hike me out."

He grinned. "We'll have to wait until after the evening bell—after everyone is asleep. Will Jill hear you? She doesn't know what happened to you, right?"

Why hadn't she shared what happened behind the waterfall with her best friend? Jill was already worried about her mother. It would be selfish to add to that. And Jill was struggling so hard to remain upbeat. Why pummel her with more troubling news? Jill's optimism countered Stella's pessimism. She needed to keep that balance.

"No, I didn't want to upset her. And I'll wait until she falls asleep."

Colin nodded his approval. "For now, I've got to deal with my father."

"*Deal*? What do you mean?" She frowned.

"Maybe that wasn't the right word to use. He's upset, naturally. He spends all his time with Mom. But—"

"But?"

"There's some tension between Dad and me. Down here—well, everything is amplified. He is spiraling into a depression, and it's hard to communicate with him. I pray Mom pulls through. He needs her. We all need her."

Stella's chest twisted at the pain in his eyes. She wanted to touch him. To offer some form of comfort, but felt self-conscious about it.

"She'll be okay," she assured feebly.

Colin looked back over his shoulder. "I better go to her."

"If—if you want company—I can come with you."

His gaze swung back. "I'd like that."

"I don't want to be invasive. I mean, I'll wait outside while you talk."

"Stel, you are family. You don't have to wait outside."

And there it was. The words to shoot down any fantasies she had been entertaining. *Family.* As she suspected, Colin thought of her as nothing more than a sister. It was a delusion to think otherwise.

What was she doing, even considering it? They were all stuck in a subterranean Hell. Romance didn't belong here—only the steady drip of time slipping away belonged here.

Stella hung her head and trailed after him.

Colin's summation of his father was pretty accurate, Stella thought. He was reticent at times and combative at others. They took him from the infirmary to the evening dinner, but he remained sullen, his eyes fixed on the bowl of white lumps that were supposedly crab meat. Stella ate it. She needed strength to negotiate the erratic terrain of the caves.

Don just shoved his spoon around in the bowl. Already, she could see signs of weight loss. The man was muscular by virtue of the rugged demands of his favorite sport—deep sea fishing, but now his shoulder bones protruded under his t-shirt. She glanced at the younger reflection beside him. Colin was slightly taller than his father and carried the same athletic physique the elder Wexler once possessed.

Stella shoveled another spoonful in her mouth, trying not to breath as she swallowed. It helped avoid the taste.

"How is Anne doing?" Margie asked to break the silence. As soon as she voiced the question it was apparent she regretted it.

Don did not look up. He did not acknowledge her in any way. His dark graying hair was matted and unwashed. He had not used the cleaning facilities yet. A quick whiff of the air confirmed that.

Beside him, Colin looked clean with the exception of the shadow of stubble that clung to his jawline. He had told her earlier that Jordan gave him a razor and he intended to try it. The last thing he wanted was the heat of a beard down here. Stella looked at the bristles on his chin and imagined what that texture would feel like under her fingertips.

She jammed the spoon in the bowl again.

As soon as Jordan rose from the table,

Stella grabbed his bowl and her own and mumbled something about *washing the dishes*. Jill appeared at her side with two more plates.

"I'll help with that."

Some of the tension left Stella at the sound of Jill's voice. It was melodically mundane in a world filled with tinny chaos.

"Thanks. I'm going to turn in after this." Stella rolled her eyes. "Long day."

Jill giggled. She grabbed a pail and filled it with water from the stream. When she returned, she said, "I'm sorry you had to see my dad that way today. He's really depressed." She scrubbed a bowl with a wiry cloth. "I mean, every time I look at Mom, I want to cry. I hate seeing her like this."

"So do I," Stella murmured in sympathy.

"But Dad—Dad gets so angry. He doesn't deal with grief well. He's not thinking about her. He's thinking about being alone."

"All you can do is be there for him. You and Colin are doing a great job at that."

"Poor Col," Jill shook her head. "He takes the brunt of it all. You know, they've been fighting since the end of last semester when Col announced he wanted to switch his major."

"I thought he was all in for finance."

"He was. But it was really *Dad's* dream for him to get an MBA and follow the finance career path. Colin stuck with it, but it wasn't what he really wanted. He wants an electrical engineering degree, but if he switches now, it means at least two additional years of school. He told Dad he would pay for it. He'd take out loans—"

"Wow, he had mentioned something about two majors, but I had no idea."

"Yeah, it's not something that comes up in conversation because we don't want to rile Dad."

"So, what's he going to do? Is he switching?"

"Yeah," Jill nodded and looked up to make sure they were alone. "He announced that before we got on the boat."

"Whoa. I knew I felt tension when we pulled out. Usually, Col and your Dad are all excited about fishing trips."

"Yeah. Well, unless we get back up to the surface, their argument seems pretty lame now. There's no Underworld University down here." She glanced around and smiled wryly. "Or maybe there is."

They finished up, and soon the bell rang. Jill searched for Daniel but finally ducked her head and crawled into the back of their dwelling. She whispered a soft *good night,* and Stella waited for the even sound of her friend's breathing before attempting to move.

Stella rose from the desk chair and peered out into the empty common area. Behind her, Jill emitted a soft snore.

Stella studied the men's bungalow next door but all was idle. Finally, a shadow emerged from the pointed hull. It hugged the base of the peak and stayed off the main path. She followed its trek until it slipped behind a boulder just outside the café area.

Glancing over her shoulder, she confirmed that Jill was sound asleep in the hammock with an arm flung over her forehead. Stella watched her for a second and then slipped out of the wheelhouse. When she reached the café, there was no sign of Colin. The nearby torches cast dancing phantoms across the compacted ground. The wide cavern trapped enough of a breeze to stoke the flames into animation.

"*Over here.*"

Stella swirled towards the hushed call and spotted Colin's silhouette ahead on the path. He had circled around the base of the pinnacle and was now out of sight of the village.

Stella jogged a few steps to catch up with him.

"Everything okay?" he whispered.

"Yeah. Jill's asleep. Your Dad?"

"Yeah." He stepped away to yank a torch from the ground.

"Where are we going exactly?"

Colin held the torch up so that his face glowed. "You're going to show me where you saw that thing, and *I'm* going to go investigate."

Stella stalked to the nearest torch and used both hands to pull it from the ground. She spun around. "*We* are."

Before he could respond, she led the way, losing the sound of his trailing steps in the soft hiss of the waterfall. Once past it, she clutched the splintery staff. No one was going to knock this from her grip.

No one.

No *thing*.

The cascading water grew muffled, and the sound of Colin's steps resumed. She paused until he fell in alongside her and pointed to the darkness clinging to the arched walls.

"That's where I saw him," she whispered.

Colin leaned in to hear her. "Then that is where I am going." Half of his face was cast in shadow. "Are you sure I can't convince you to stay behind?"

A twist of her lips was his answer.

"Fine. Then stay close."

"That's a command I'll obey."

Shoulder to shoulder, they crept deeper into the darkness. Perspiration beaded her forehead and her torch revealed that Colin's t-shirt was stained by sweat as well. Strain as she might to find them, no luminous eyes were glowering back at her.

As she and Colin advanced, Stella began to question her sanity. Had she imagined it? Did the band of bruises on her arm look less like deformed fingers and more like the linear formation of rocks under the water she had fallen into?

"Careful," Colin cautioned, "we've gone off the path."

Stella lowered her torch to view the spongy-looking rocks.

"Did we reach the end of the trail?"

"No." He stretched back and held out his hand to help her negotiate the uneven terrain. "I thought I saw a gap in the wall. We should check it out."

Stella grabbed onto his forearm as her toe clipped a boulder. Stable again, she looked up and searched the jagged black wall. Under the torch's glow, the wall wasn't really black but rather deep ginger with rusty rivulets of ancient water tracks—weeping lines from long-forgotten tears.

The barrier had an opening, a black scar wide enough to fit your shoulders through.

Colin stopped before it, jabbing his torch into the gap.

"Let me get a quick look," he suggested. "It may be impassible in a few feet."

They had traveled deep enough into the abyss to talk above a whisper.

"No." Her fingers stiffened around his arm. "If anything happens to you—"

With the torch extended away from him, it was hard to see Colin's eyes, but she could feel the weight of his stare.

"Careful, Stel. I'll start to believe that you care about me," he teased.

Stella dropped her hand and tucked her head. "Too much carbon dioxide," she muttered.

There was enough light to catch Colin's quick grin before he turned into the void.

Stella switched her torch into her left hand and concentrated on Colin's back as they advanced deeper into the narrow channel. Gravel crunched beneath their feet, but aside from that, all sound was severed. There were no echoes of vast space. This chasm was only a few feet wide, and the ceiling was low, swallowing the resonation from the cave. In this tight space, her eyes welled from the flames.

Colin halted.

Stella was so close on his heel that she stumbled into his back, pushing him forward.

"Whoa, sorry," she whispered. "Have we reached the end?"

"No," he hesitated, "but there is something ahead."

He splayed his free hand behind him, holding her at bay.

"What is it?" she hissed, hiking up onto her toes to try to see over his shoulder.

"A gate?" he murmured. "No, a cage." He stepped forward, swinging his torch from side to side.

"No," he corrected. "A cell. *Cells*."

Another step, and she glimpsed what he saw. A gap in the wall to the left. The hole was about four feet wide, barricaded by a stockade of wooden posts.

Colin swung his torch to reveal another barred cell on the other side.

"These aren't really cells, Col."

Colin ran his hand along the posts, all impaled into the cave wall with crudely formed spikes.

"You're right. There are no gates."

"Whatever was inside was not supposed to get out." She stuck her nose between the posts. "Unless there is another exit."

Holding the torch as close as possible to the barricade, Stella gasped.

Colin was at her side immediately.

"What?"

"On the wall." She pointed. "What does that look like?"

With the flickering light from both torches filling the vault, the craggy walls came into view. She wasn't a geologist. She didn't know the rock composition down here. However, the slashes carved in the bedrock were not a natural phenomenon. Four parallel gashes, like the mark of bear claws. This grouping was found in multiple spots, the focus mostly towards the front of the cell—the area where the posts were embedded into the bedrock.

"Whatever—*whoever* was in here tried to claw their way out," Colin murmured.

Stella trembled but forced herself to look past the frenzied scratches and deeper into the shadows.

"I don't see another way out." Her voice wavered.

"Me either, but—"

Col spared stating the obvious. There were no skeletal remains or anything so macabre. Yet those claw marks reached out and tore at her soul. There was desperation to them. Madness.

He wrapped his fist around one of the posts and tugged. It didn't yield. He tested another with the same results.

"Come on," he said. "We better get back before anyone notices us missing."

It was a wonderful suggestion. Suddenly, her perpetual curiosity was tempered. She had a sick feeling that she didn't want to learn more about these cells or their captives.

"Are you going to ask Etienne about these?" she probed.

"Not yet. I doubt we'd get the truth from him. He wants us to believe this is paradise."

"People don't claw their way out of paradise."

The Underworld was still sleeping when they returned. Preparing to slip back into their respective bungalows, Colin and Stella were startled to see his father emerge from his dwelling. He snapped to attention at their approach. A hasty head-to-toe scan of their dirty clothes produced a dour look on his pale face.

"Where have you two been?"

The suggestive question brought heat to Stella's cheeks and a deep frown from Colin.

"We were investigating," he whispered, patting the air with his hand, instructing his father to keep it down.

"Yeah, right." Don rebuked in full volume.

"Dad, quiet." Colin hastily glanced up the trail, but there was no sign of activity. He leaned in so that his mouth was closer to his father's ear. "We found something," he declared quietly.

Don's eyebrow rose. He looked from Colin to Stella and back again. With a jerk of his head, he motioned them into the inverted boat.

Stella climbed in behind the two men and caught a pungent whiff. She realized the foul scent came from Don. He hadn't been too concerned with hygiene lately.

Colin stood just inside the doorway, his arms crossed, his face lost in heavy shadows. He bowed his head to peer back outside, and their eyes connected for a second. He gave her an assuring nod.

Don turned around, his hands on his hips. His shirt, once taut, now hung loosely over a thin waistline.

"What are you two up to? I know you're both adults, but—"

"Dad, come on." Colin shook his head. "I'm serious. We found something. There were cells, like a man-made dungeon, far back behind the waterfall. And we saw signs that they were once occupied."

"Dungeon cells?" Don repeated. "Take a look at this place. If one of the handful of people acts up, I'm pretty sure they'll just get a strong lecture—not a jail sentence. They don't seem like barbarians—"

Even as he made the declaration, Stella could see the wheels of doubt spinning on the elder Wexler's face. He reached up and scratched the back of his head. "You probably just found more storage facilities. I'm sure things wash up down here that these utilitarians want to regulate. Might as well put the good stuff behind bars."

"There was no door, Dad. It was a chamber barricaded with the intent to keep whatever was inside from getting out."

Don wiggled his fingers and waved his arm. "Ooooh, scary." He snorted. "Nothing surprises me down here. We are screwed. Is that what you want to hear from me? We are screwed, and we're all going to die, so what does it matter if you think you found Alcatraz or you two sneak away for a grope fest?"

"Dad," Colin warned in a gruff voice. "We're not all going to die. Stella and I are looking for a way out of here. We're not staying."

Don's lips twisted. "Bravo. Great performance. But the only way out of here is to swim. So help me God, if anything happens to

Anne, I am going straight to that pool."

"You can't swim to the surface," Colin argued. "You know that."

The glow from the outdoor torches reached through the windows and captured Don Wexler's eyes. Stella witnessed the first signs of gravity in them. For a moment, he was not overcome by grief. Carbon dioxide wasn't affecting his decision-making. Those eyes were lucid. And they were sad. In that moment, he was the surrogate dad she had spent so much time with—the man who picked her up from school when her mother was working late hours—the man who taught her how to parallel park.

Outside, the bell announced a new morning.

Don's eyelids dropped closed and pressed deep into his cheeks as if he was in great pain. When they opened again, the clarity was gone. The man she knew was gone.

"I'll make it," he vowed. "Whether you come with me or not."

"We're all sticking together. We're a family." Colin's eyes slid to hers. "*All* of us."

Stella swallowed and nodded.

"Good. Then, as a family, we can all swim to the surface."

The bitterness in his tone was disturbing. This environment was proving toxic to Don, and Stella saw the toll it was taking on Colin as he swung away, placed his hand against the wall, and hung his head.

"I'm going to check on Mom," he announced.

He looked at her questioningly. Yes, she

would join him. There was no way she was staying here.

Inside the infirmary, they saw Sarah hunched over Anne's inert figure. The nurse was humming an unrecognizable tune.

"We've got to find a way out of here," Colin vowed in a whisper before they ducked through the doorway. "Tomorrow night we'll go past the cells."

"Yes," Stella agreed.

Yes, she repeated in her mind as she watched Sarah Fournier rocking back and forth as she hummed her tune and fingered Anne's blonde hair.

Finally sensing their presence, Sarah jerked her head in their direction. Her pale eyes were rounded, and the circles beneath them were etched in black. Her thin lips sagged, and her narrow chin dropped in contrition.

"I'm sorry," was all she said.

CHAPTER 12

JILL

Jill woke abruptly, vaulting into a seated position with her palms splayed flat on the blanket. Disoriented, she glanced around at the heavy shadows, which only increased her fear. Finally, her lethargic gaze landed on something familiar—the desk. Before she fell asleep, Stella was sitting at it. Now, it was empty, and the pad that her best friend dawdled on was tucked away from view.

"Stel?"

For the past few nights, it was always the same schedule: fall asleep with Stella sitting there, wake up alone. Today, that fact bothered her. It was probably a byproduct of the nightmare that she could barely remember.

She rose, wiping imaginary dirt off her arms. In her mind, everything was dirty, but in reality, the blanket she slept on was relatively clean. At the window, she saw people stirring from their dwellings.

Loren, with the shiny black hair, was

already sitting at the café, reading a book. Jill scanned the basketball court but saw no sign of Daniel. She looked forward to talking to him again. He was everything she wasn't. Quiet. Dark. Angry. In contrast, she was the one who had to keep the peace during any family arguments. Recently, the arguments between her brother and father had escalated. She understood her brother's frustrations. He wasn't wrapped up in finance and the stock market like his father. He had a keen mind for detail and design. As kids, he had constructed their backyard treehouse himself and even rigged a pulley system strong enough to act as an elevator.

Jill often played the role of the joker at family dinners, anything to lighten the tension and make them laugh. That was her goal. Stella often said she should be a stand-up comedian. Hah. If her father wasn't happy about Colin's engineering ambitions, what would he do with a stand-up comedian for a daughter?

Jill glanced towards the infirmary. Maybe her mom would wake up today. She missed her terribly. She was the other peacekeeper in the house.

Combing her fingers through her long hair and applying a fingertip full of ancient toothpaste to her teeth, Jill stared into the tarnished mirror above the desk. The once glossy hair looked matted now. The whites of her eyes looked yellow in the tarnished reflection. There was no blush to enhance her cheeks. No gloss to brighten her lips. No mascara to make her blue eyes pop.

Make them laugh.

Arms crossed despite the heat and humidity, Jill started towards the infirmary. A hushed call stopped her. She hesitated, listening.

"Hey."

There, in the shadows at the foot of the spiraling peak, stood a familiar long-limbed profile. She started towards him, still a little uncertain about this brooding stranger.

"Hi," she said quietly as she came to a stop a few feet away.

Daniel inched his chin up, nodding towards the infirmary.

"You going to see your mom?"

"Yeah." She glanced over her shoulder. "But I have a few minutes. I think my father and brother are in there now."

"I saw them go in. How is she doing?"

Jill glanced down at her toes. A tiny trace of red nail polish remained on the center of the big toes.

"The same."

Daniel crammed his hands into the pockets of his loose jeans and murmured, "I hope she gets better." He hesitated and added, "If you have a minute, do you want to see something?"

She looked up eagerly. "Sure."

Yes. Anything. Anything that was a diversion from desperation.

A thin but strong shoulder hitched beneath the red and white-striped shirt, and she followed Daniel's lead. Watching his long back, she guessed him to be at least six inches taller than her. Of course, she was considered pint-sized by many, particularly Stella, the Amazon woman. How she envied her friend's statuesque good looks. Stella's legs were endless, while hers were like little pistons, always working harder to catch up. Even now, she jogged a few steps to keep up with Daniel's long stride.

"We're heading back towards the grotto?" she asked, recognizing the tunnel at the end of the great chamber.

"Yeah, but not all the way."

Their initial approach through this tunnel had been little more than a foggy memory. Nothing had been perceptible outside the scope of the torch. Now that she searched harder, she could see formations in the arched shadows. Mineral daggers. Dark fissures in the walls like scars. If her life depended on it, she doubted she could find her way back to the cavern where they emerged from the sea. In some ways, she was grateful when Daniel said it, *but not all the way*. In some ways, she never wanted to see that black pool again.

"Here." He stopped and pointed to a black aperture, a thick gash in the cave wall.

"There are many chambers down here. Some are tiny nooks. Some are pretty decent-sized caves. It's really like a maze, but this little prize is a bit eerie."

"Eerie?" She shied away from the opening.

A rare grin clashed with Daniel's dark looks.

"Don't worry, I'll protect you."

That she would *need* protecting is what worried her, but she had arrested this reclusive man's attention. She wasn't about to dissuade him.

Jill followed, at one point having to turn sideways to shimmy through the tight channel.

"How did you find this place?"

"Boredom," he replied. "There are some places down here you shouldn't go exploring when you're bored, but this end of the cave system is pretty safe."

"What's unsafe about the other end?" she asked. A rogue image of Stella's arm with the lined bruises across it flashed in her mind. "Cave-ins?"

Daniel shrugged as he emerged into a narrow cave. Jill stepped out of the chasm, grateful for the room to breathe, but this wasn't much larger. The chamber was maybe ten feet wide and Daniel had to tuck his head to avoid the low ceiling.

"Here, you're better off sitting down to enjoy the view."

He crouched down, resting his back against the slate rock. The torch filled the snug chamber with an orange glow. It fought off the humidity too.

Jill concentrated on finding a spot to sit that wasn't too close to Daniel, but there were limited options. She finally collapsed into a cross-legged position and just stared at him. In this warm atmosphere, he didn't look so dark. What she thought was near-black hair actually was mostly brown with even a few strands of red woven in. Eyes that she thought were black were really a deep hazel. As the flames reduced his pupils, she noticed a ring of jade around them. His jawline was sharp, but that rare smile she had caught before reminded her that his expression wasn't so severe. He looked mysterious.

"So—" A dark eyebrow raised. "What do you think?"

I think I like what I see.

"About what?" she stuttered.

Daniel cocked his head and looked up. She followed his gaze, and her mouth dropped open.

One wall was scarred with handmade drawings. Images carved into the rock took a moment for her to decipher.

"That's a boat." She pointed. "And that's a—a cow?"

"I'm guessing it's someone's dog," he chuckled. "It's probably hard to draw your dog with a rock."

Jill climbed up onto her knees to inspect the wall better.

"There's a flower—*flowers*," she corrected enthusiastically.

She looked at him, watching her. "Did you draw this?"

Daniel snorted. "Do I look like someone who draws flowers?"

Jill laughed. A full, real laugh and it felt so good.

"No, I guess not. So then, who? Margie? Sarah?"

He shook his head. "When I first found this place, I asked who drew the images. Frederic said that these were here before he and Etienne arrived."

"But I thought Etienne and Frederic were

the first—"

Her comment died at the *seriously?* look on his face.

"Well, yeah, I guess this all has been down here a long time. But then, who drew this, and where are they? Where are the people that were here before Etienne?"

"Etienne claims that they searched and found no signs of previous inhabitants."

"*Hello.*" She pointed at the wall. "I'd say this was a sign."

Daniel smiled. It was short-lived. "I guess he was saying that they have not located any remains of previous residents."

Jill hugged her arms about herself. "Oh."

She stood fully now, running her fingers along each image. Some so innocent. There was a circle with two holes and a concave line inside. A frowny face. Her palm spanned outward, locating a few more images lost in the shadows.

"What is this?"

Daniel rose and brought the torch closer.

A stick figure was hunched, its exaggerated hands reaching forward. Two large circles on the head represented eyes.

"A self-portrait of the guy doing the drawing?"

Jill rolled her eyes. "Come on."

"I don't know. Somebody was bored out of his skull and doodling." He stepped back and pointed at an image close to the ground.

She stooped and frowned until she guessed what it was. "A skull and crossbones?"

"Very good." He nodded his approval. "I

added that a few years ago. I figured I should contribute to our predecessor's artwork. I thought maybe he was a pirate."

Jill clapped her hands at the thought. "Yes! If Etienne and Sarah came down here in the 70s, and if you have cans of corn from the 40s, God knows who could have been down here before."

Daniel looked pleased with her enthusiasm.

"What happened to you guys?" he asked, sobering slightly. "Your boat sank in a storm?"

"Ummm." She nodded. "It all happened so fast. When we went to sleep, everything was normal. Then, all of a sudden, I was rolling around the cabin. When my mom opened the hatch, I thought we were in a tornado. I didn't even have time to grasp what was happening. Next thing I knew, I was in the water, and the next thing after that, Stella was pulling me out of your pool."

Daniel pondered that quietly. "Must have been pretty scary."

"Hell, not as scary as falling off a cruise ship," she countered. Catching his gaze, she blushed. "I mean, seriously, you're damn lucky to have even survived the fall. How high up were you?"

"Lucky?" he remarked, focusing on the ground.

"Right. Poor choice of words."

She didn't know what to say, so she pretended to focus on the illustrations. Stella would have a better command of the English language. She was the one with all the words.

Lost in her introspection, Jill jumped when Daniel cleared his throat.

"I think it was about 150 feet," he murmured. "I don't remember hitting the water. I must have been knocked out by the impact."

Jill made a sympathetic sound. "How did it happen? Were you sitting on the rail? Were you taking a selfie?"

"Selfie?"

"Oh, right. You don't know what that is. It's so weird to think this happened to you, what, twenty years ago?" She studied his face, mature but with the glow of youth still clinging to it. "How is it that you look so young? How old were you at the time?"

Daniel shrugged. "Thirteen."

"Wow. Seriously?"

Sometimes, she didn't think. Sometimes, she just plowed on. "Can you read? You didn't get through much school then?"

He rose and glared down at her.

"Yeah, I can read."

"I'm sorry," she rushed to her feet. "I—I'm just trying to understand. You look—"

His eyes narrowed. "I look *what*?" There was an edge to his tone.

Jill stared for a second and finally admitted, "You look smart."

Daniel hitched his shoulders back as if he'd been slapped. He averted his gaze, staring hard at the skull and crossbones. Jill fisted her hands at her sides and cursed her loose mouth. She quickly rehearsed several plausible phrases to back out of the awkward moment when she heard a strange sound coming from Daniel. At first, she thought he was going to be sick, but then she caught a glimpse of half a smile on the side of his face.

He was laughing.

"I've been called many things," he muttered, "but *smart* was not one of them. Especially from a girl like you."

"Like me?" She frowned.

He turned to look at her and saw her piqued expression.

"I mean—" Suddenly, Mr. Cool looked off balance. "You're pretty. You are friendly. You look like a cheerleader. Someone like you wouldn't have given me the time of day up there." He pointed to the cave ceiling.

"I'm not a cheerleader," she said, sullen. Mechanically, she drew a smile to her lips. *Make them laugh.* "But I am friendly."

Daniel flashed a quick grin and then hid it behind a swipe of his hand. "Yeah, well, I don't talk much down here, so thanks for spending some time with me."

Jill frowned. "You don't have to *thank* me. It's crazy to thank someone for spending time with you. You should talk more."

"Because I'm so smart?" he quipped. "You thought I couldn't read."

"Come on. I'm just saying you didn't get to finish your education. That's a shame."

She thought he'd grow angry, but he just stared at the drawings.

"I *was* pretty smart when I was in school." He rolled his eyes towards her. "I had nothing else to do but study. When I got down here— after a long period of being a recluse, I started to read the books Margie and Sarah gave me. If I didn't know something, I would ask them about it. Eventually, I read everything down here. Heck, I probably am a greater scholar than anyone on the surface at this point."

Jill smiled at that. "So, you're saying you're not a recluse anymore?"

He smirked at her good-natured taunt.

"I look at you," she continued, "and I just can't get over it. You only look maybe a few years older than me. Seriously, how is that possible?"

"Look around you," Daniel splayed his arms. "There's no sun to age the skin. I saw my father drink too much from the stress of his job. People down here don't have jobs. They don't have stress."

"No stress?" she countered with a squeak. "I am extremely stressed. I don't know how long my mother will live. I don't know how long I will live. I'm afraid of the dark. I want to go home. I have *stress*."

Daniel's face softened. He took a step towards her in the tight chamber. Jill held her ground, but her trembling betrayed her.

"Don't be afraid of the dark," he soothed. "I'll be here. I will always hold a torch for you."

Jill's throat caught at the declaration. Her lower lip trembled slightly, and she felt tears building up behind her eyes.

To spare her from the awkward moment, Daniel cleared his throat and added, "What I'm saying is that without the physical stress of our atmosphere and the mental stress of life's interactions, there is little down here to age us. Everything seems to move so slowly, including our maturity." He shrugged. "Or, at least, that is what Etienne tells everyone."

Jill hugged herself again and stared at the torch.

"Are you cold?" he asked.

"No."

He regarded her for a lengthy minute and finally asked, "How old are you?"

"I—I'm eighteen. My birthday was three weeks ago."

Lame. Why did she add that?

Daniel smiled. She was growing to like his smile.

"Happy Birthday, then."

Her lips fumbled upwards.

"I better get back." She glanced over her shoulder, wanting no part of heading back into the black tunnel.

This small cave filled with the luster and warmth of the torch and all the interesting images carved from hands long gone was the only bit of comfort she had experienced since the shipwreck.

Maybe it had nothing to do with the glow, or heat, or pictures. Maybe it had to do with a seemingly young man with dark hazel eyes who offered to light her way.

"Sure," he said, raising his arm towards the exit to guide her.

She grudgingly turned in that direction and felt his hand settle on her arm for guidance. She completely tuned everything out and focused on that touch. It warmed her skin and bolstered her confidence.

In silence, they made their way back to the village, but Daniel's light touch was always there to keep her steady. She needed it the moment she saw Stella walking towards them. Stella stopped, and Jill recognized the stance. Long legs spread slightly, hands at her sides, shoulders back, and soulful eyes that could not hide their message.

"No," Jill whimpered, feeling the sustaining grip on her arm as her legs failed her.

CHAPTER 13

Stella stroked Jill's golden hair, soothing her as she mumbled in her sleep. Across from them, Colin stared down at his sister, his face solemn and his shoulders struggling to sustain an unimaginable burden. In the corner, Don sat with his knees tucked under his chin, his arms wrapped around his legs. He rocked slightly.

"They say they're going to hold a service."

Don's voice sounded dispassionate. He spoke mechanically.

"Dad," Colin tried to soothe.

"But your mother won't be present. They told me it would be too difficult for me. They let me say my goodbyes in person, though, before they took her away."

Jill sobbed, and Stella tried to quell her shaking.

"Took her where?" Colin frowned.

"They're going to let her go. Back into the sea that should have claimed her to begin with. The ground here cannot be dug for an adequate burial."

Jill clamped her hands over her ears, and

Stella guided her so that she reclined against her chest, where she could hug her. Stella felt each quiver and imagined how devastated she would be at the loss of her mother. Knowing that her mother was alive and safe in the world above gave her some peace.

Colin's expression was stark as he studied his father. Stella agreed with his concerns. Grief was an all-consuming beast, but this air of submission was unexpected. Even now, Donald Wexler seemed disconnected. After all, shouldn't he be holding his daughter? Consoling her?

Stella shook her head to toss her doubts aside. There was no defined etiquette down here. There was just survival. Physical …and mental.

"We'll be there," she vowed quietly.

It was a somber event, made bizarre by the attire of the inhabitants in this macabre mythological world. Sarah in her grey nurse's uniform, Margie in her tan Capri pants and a tight royal blue blouse. Loren in her snug jeans and a black tank top. She was the only one wearing black to the funeral.

Stella's thoughts were chaotic. She needed to get out of here. Across the way, Jill was comforted by Daniel, the dour-looking guy from the cruise ship. He made Stella nervous, but Jill assured her that he was just shy. Donald stood between Etienne and Frederic as if the two men were there to catch him should he fall in grief…or run.

She cast a desperate glance towards Colin, who looked stoic in his shorts and t-shirt. He met her eyes and tipped his head. Tonight. When this was all over, they would resume their search. The urgency for answers had increased. So much so that when the sad event broke up, Stella followed Etienne, cornering the sailor after he parted with his wife in front of the infirmary.

"Sarah stays in the infirmary?" Stella asked boldly. "Even when there are no patients?"

Etienne stopped and regarded her with a tolerant smile.

"She works on inventory. She is sorting through the latest haul to see what can be useful for our continued health."

A very practical response, but Stella hated the sanctimonious delivery.

"An icepack would be handy. I could have used that for my bruised arm."

Stella knew she was challenging the man. She didn't care. She was hurting, and there was nothing in Sarah's haul that could fix this kind of pain.

"Alas," Etienne shook his head. "Ice is one thing we can't preserve down here. And your injury—" he nodded at her now healthy arm, "could have been prevented if you didn't stray past the waterfall. The terrain is not stable there. Stay away from it, and perhaps Sarah will not have to work so hard."

Was he counseling her, or was it a threat?

"Then tell me what's back there," she challenged.

She was curious to hear his interpretation. She had a feeling he would spew out Frederic's depiction identically.

"You're too close to the vents back there. The further you progress, the more danger it holds."

"Yet, it's safe enough for *you* to go back there and fish?"

"It is not safe," he corrected, his lips thinning. They barely formed a white stripe across his mouth. "But we need to eat. By the grace of God, we found a food source back there. We take great care to preserve it and ourselves. We can't have anyone jeopardizing that."

Stella decided to drop the battle. Etienne would be watching out for her now. That kind of scrutiny would hurt their nighttime surveillance.

"You're right," she conceded. "I was just curious. I'm studying for journalism," she added lamely.

Etienne continued to stare, unconvinced. Finally, his white lips angled up. "Perhaps you can do a paper for here. Local news. Girl goes missing behind the waterfall."

It was a sad attempt at a joke, heavily laced with menace, but she forced herself to smile.

"Sure, the Underworld Post," she suggested.

Etienne nodded. "If you want to see the fishing process. I will take you back there myself."

Was that a peace offering? Stella decided to treat it as such.

"I'd like that," she replied sincerely. "Just

let me know when."

Etienne glanced up the trail towards the crow's nest. "All right. For now," he added, "we best keep an eye on your friend's father. I know he is grieving, but I also see signs of the atmosphere disagreeing with him. *That* is why Sarah is busy preparing."

Stella shut her notebook and stowed it beneath the folded blanket that served as her pillow. Today's entry was somber and poignant. She squeezed her eyes shut and thought of her mother.

"Mom, I think the garage door is coming down."

Caroline pressed her face against the driver's side window as she backed out of their garage.

"I don't see it."

"I hear it. It doesn't sound right." Stella reached to turn off the radio.

As soon as the music stopped, they heard and felt the thunk.

"What the hell?" Caroline frowned.

She tapped the gas to continue in reverse, but the car would not budge. She switched gears and tried to roll forward. Nothing.

Now, they could see the garage door suspended above them.

Caroline got out, careful to duck her head. Stella did the same. The roof of the red Corolla was pinned beneath the garage door, the mechanical gate now making a sickly whirring sound.

Their eyes met over the dented aluminum roof. Caroline looked fraught for a minute, and then a snort escaped her nose. It was followed by gushing laughter. One thing her mom could do was laugh. Loud. Hard. Embarrassing.

Stella glanced down the street to see if anyone heard, but even though the houses on this lane were built on top of each other, miraculously, no one was out and about.

Looking up at the vise that clutched the Corolla like a mouse in an eagle's talons, Stella heard her mother claim, "Well, this sucks."

Stella burst into loud, hard, embarrassing laughter too.

Grounding her palms into her eyes, Stella tried to quell the burning inside them. She crawled over to where Jill was sleeping, worried about the shadows ringing her friend's closed eyelids. Seeing Jill like this strengthened Stella's resolve. She rose quietly and approached the window, gazing out on the empty walkways of the Underworld. No sign of Colin, but that was not surprising. He wasn't likely to stand in the middle of the café, blaring on a trumpet. Their rendezvous were discreet.

From this perspective, she could not see Etienne and Sarah's shack. The infirmary was dark. No sign of the nurse there. Stella crouched and crept out into the eternal night.

Colin emerged from the shadows, startling her.

"Is she okay?" he asked quietly.

Stella nodded, glancing back towards the wheelhouse. "She was exhausted. How about you? I didn't really get to say it to you yet—but Col—I'm so so very sorry." Her throat caught.

His dark gaze fled to the ground. "I haven't really come to terms with it yet. It's all still surreal."

Encouraging words were on the edge of her tongue when Colin's head snapped up.

"Someone is out here," he warned in a low tone.

Stella's skin prickled. She strained to see any movement. There was a faint scuff of a shoe on dirt nearby.

Colin bent to whisper near her ear. "It's okay. I see who it is."

Who?

The question remained mute as she saw a slim shadow approach. Long black hair perpetuated the mystique.

"Colin," Loren's voice was quiet as she advanced. She gave Stella a brief nod. "Stella."

Stella dipped her head in acknowledgment but worried that this intrusion would ruin their search plans for the night. Not to mention the rogue pang of jealousy the young woman stirred.

"Colin," Loren kept her tone low, "I need to see you for a moment."

Colin looked startled. "Okay. What's up?"

Running a pale hand up into her inky hair, Loren looked up at him from under her bangs. "I mean when you have a minute alone."

He glanced sideways at Stella.

Stella raised her hands and started backing up. "No worries," she whispered and hooked her thumb behind her. "I'm just going to head back—"

Loren watched her with dark sloe eyes but said nothing.

"Stel, don't—" Colin stopped himself. "I'll be over shortly."

"Yeah, cool." She waved him off, turning back towards her wheelhouse.

She could feel his eyes on her back, but she had her pride. She didn't look back. Let him have his chat with Felicia—oh, Loren.

When she reached her bungalow, Stella finally peered over her shoulder. Colin and Loren were retreating in the other direction.

Ducking into the wheelhouse, confirming that Jill was still fast asleep, Stella stood with her hands fisted at her sides and sighed.

Now what?

Where were they going? Did she wait for him? Would there be enough time to explore before the bell rang?

Pacing in a tight circle, she poked her head out the door but could no longer see the couple. Her gaze swung in the opposite direction—the trail leading towards the waterfall. It was empty. Everything was quiet. To waste this opportunity would be a shame and an exercise of patience that she would fail.

Stella checked on Jill one more time and then headed outside, dodging into shadows to keep from view. They were running out of time, she was sure of it. They had lost one person today—a woman who Stella had come to love. There was no time to wait until another was gone. She had to find a way out of the Underworld, and it looked like she had to do it alone.

If there was any advantage to the time they had spent down here, it was her growing experience with the snaking caverns. Each foray past the waterfall inspired more confidence. The fact that she had no more encounters with freaky shadow figures was beginning to convince her that maybe she had suffered from a bit of CO_2 acclimation.

According to the calendar that Frederic maintained, they had been down here for over three weeks. That same calendar marked the Underworld's New Year celebration as only a week away.

Well, there would be no midnight kisses for her. There would *never* be any kisses if she was damned to this eternity.

Anger motivated her. Her steps became more nimble as she ventured beyond the point she and Colin had last traveled. Her agility was short-lived once the trail grew rugged. If she lost her balance on the slick surface, any attempt to right herself would meet with a sharp rock or serrated slab. Already, she had drawn blood when she tripped over a rut in the path. It could hardly be considered a path now. Only instinct guided her in this direction, following the natural channel and the increasing heat.

Somewhere around here was the fishing pool. She was fascinated by the pools as they seemed the only viable source of escape. To keep the darkness at bay and her sanity intact, she began to recite them.

There was the grotto where she had first surfaced. Further down that same tunnel was a smaller pool in which Anne Wexler had washed up.

Stella's throat twisted at the thought.

Forcing her mind forward, she calculated the fishing pool location, which she was supposedly very close to. Conversations with Etienne and Frederic indicated there was an additional pool or pools responsible for providing oxygen throughout this cave system, but were in areas too hot to be reached.

A loud clatter sounded to her right.

Stella swung the torch in that direction to find a collapsed stalactite, its column broken into pieces on the dirt floor. She tipped her head back and located the severed post on the low ceiling. The circumference of the channel narrowed in this wing of the caves. The stalactites dangled precariously close over her head. If she had been standing one foot to the right—

Brushing aside that disturbing thought, she shifted the torch again to confirm her path. Debris now riddled much of the ground. The trail she thought she was following all but disappeared. She inched forward with the flames casting rippling sparks across a moon-like terrain. Although the ground she stood on was level, she seemed to be barricaded on all sides by large boulders.

The first twinge of panic clutched her lungs. Towards her left, there was no defined avenue. Disoriented, she pivoted around, still unsure which way she had come. Spotting the only viable gap in the stones, she aimed for it and trod gingerly through the narrow breach. Abrasions stung her toes. Sandals weren't the type of gear for hiking like this.

Continuing towards the cave wall, she felt it would act as a constant—a guide to get back. The river Styx would have been the best escort, but she lost sight of it a while ago. Trailing her fingertips along the mottled limestone, she felt the warm mist that clung to it. When her fingers met air, she halted. Unsettled, she didn't know if this gap represented a new corridor or the way back.

She thrust the torch into the black chasm and knew it was foreign. Somewhere she had never traveled. The ceiling was conical, almost like a pyramid. It was void of any limestone daggers, and the floor, what she could see of it, seemed clear—just packed earth. It wasn't a large chamber. The alcove had about a twenty-foot circumference. From what she could tell, there was no alternative exit.

One way in. One way out.

Something rested against the wall in the near corner. With a hasty glimpse over her shoulder, Stella swung the torch forward and took a few cautious steps inside the chamber. A long shadow sliced through the center of the alcove—a pit or a hole that she circled to avoid. Approaching the pile of rocks she saw stacked against the wall, she stooped to get a closer look and choked on fear.

On the ground, propped against the wall, was nearly a complete human skeleton. The skull was missing and one leg, but the ribcage was clearly defined, as well as the hip bones and a relatively long femur. Stumbling back from the carcass, her right foot caught the edge of the pit behind her. She dropped the torch and flailed her arms to regain her balance, falling backward into the hole.

It wasn't deep, thank God. Even now, she was sitting up, her eyes even with the torch abandoned on the floor. Her fall was cushioned by gravel or twigs.

Twigs?

Stella scrambled onto her knees and reached for the torch. She held it above her and squealed in terror.

They weren't twigs.

She had fallen into a pit of bones.

CHAPTER 14

In a frenzy, Stella clawed at the rim of the tomb. She struggled for stable footing so that she could climb out, but the splintered sound beneath each attempt was a rattle that would forever haunt her soul. A keening wail bubbled from her lips as she stepped on an exceptionally tough bone and used her elbows to hike up onto the cave floor. She crab-walked a few feet and grabbed the torch again.

Breathe in through the nose and out through the mouth. Wasn't that the mantra they always taught?

She was far enough away now that the deep shadows cloaked the contents of the pit. That didn't help with the headless skeleton sitting next to her. There was a tiny shard of cloth stuck to a shoulder, but she didn't stick around to analyze it any further. She climbed to her feet and prepared to bolt.

A glow outside the tight chamber halted her. It bobbed in approach.

Stella searched frantically for a weapon and tossed aside the notion of grabbing a bone.

Instead, she held the torch like a baseball bat and assumed a battle stance.

She nearly sobbed with relief when Colin's familiar frame filled the entrance.

"Stel, why didn't you—?"

Colin jerked to a halt. He saw the skeleton sitting on the floor.

"What the hell?"

Stella shook her head. "Oh, that's nothing." She swept the end of the torch towards the ground to reveal the quarry of bones.

Colin staggered a step, but he didn't say anything. His lips parted, and deep shadows rooted across his face. Curling his free hand into a fist, he stepped forward and surveyed the hole that appeared to be man-made based on its rectangular shape.

"The ground cannot be dug here for an adequate burial," he quoted. "Isn't that what Dad was told?"

Stella jerked her head up and down, unable to speak. The grim finality of what she was looking at settled in.

"Who are they?" she whispered.

Colin dragged in a deep breath. "Others like my mother? The survivors who didn't make it. Maybe the ones who succumbed to carbon dioxide poisoning."

The morbid thought that she could easily end up in this pile tortured Stella.

"What do we do?" she probed hoarsely.

Colin looked angry. "We'll mention it, but I doubt there is any great mystery to what we have here." His eyes met hers, and she saw the flames dancing there. "The truth is that people are going to die down here. Maybe they don't want to release them all to the ocean. Maybe it will encourage too many sharks." He shrugged. "I just—"

As if he was going to be ill, Colin stooped over, his hand on his knee for support.

"Col!" She came to his side immediately.

He raised his hand to keep her away.

"I just—" he whispered, "—am glad we didn't find her here. I'm glad for that one small favor."

Stella ignored his protest and went to him, resting her palm on his hunched shoulder. He accepted the touch momentarily and then slowly rose until her hand slid down his arm and finally off.

"Let's not tell Dad or Jill about this," he suggested in a husky voice. "Not today. Maybe someday, but not today."

"No," she agreed.

"Come on." This time, he touched her, his fingers cupping gently around her arm.

He caught a glimpse of her soiled clothes. "Are you okay?"

Concerned, his hand roamed up her arm as he reached to turn her for an inspection.

"I'm okay, Col."

"You, you're filthy. What happened?"

Stella glanced down into the pit, and her body trembled.

"I—I fell in there."

Shock registered on his face. There was no vocal outburst, no hollow words of solace. He crouched to set the torch on the ground and then took her into his arms.

Stella stiffened at first, but the comfort of his embrace was what she needed the most. Her torch slipped from her hand and landed beside his. Pressing her cheek against his collarbone, she sagged until she felt him support her. Adrenaline had kept her going, but this one act of kindness tore down her defenses. Tears welled in her eyes and she didn't bother to hold them back. She sobbed openly against his chest, and he just held her tighter.

It was all too much. The loss of Mrs. Wexler. The sight of these poor souls who had survived death in the ocean only to end up in this common grave. No respect. No sorrow.

What scared her the most was having little fear of joining them. Their sentence in the Underworld, or Hell, was over.

Amidst her whimpering, she swore she felt Colin kiss the top of her head. She tried to tilt her chin back to look up at him, but his thumbs brushed at her tears, and with a long look, he finally set her back, holding her upper arms.

"Can you walk?" he asked thickly.

She nodded.

"Let's get away from here," he uttered. "Let's get back."

Back to civilization.

"Yes," she murmured.

They traveled in silence, Colin's hand linked with hers no matter the obstacle. When they reached the dark side of the waterfall, he stopped.

"Why did you go back there on your own? Why didn't you wait for me?"

There was little fight left in her at the

moment. She sighed and replied honestly. "Because you were busy."

Dark eyes studied her for a long time.

"Because I was with Loren?"

She avoided his stare and nodded.

"She wanted to give her condolences," he stated. "She felt uncomfortable doing that in front of you."

Stella kept her gaze locked on the ground. Her toes were all scraped up.

"I was about five minutes behind you. You could have waited five minutes," he reprimanded, but the soft concern took the edge from his voice.

"I was fine. I was on my way back," she mumbled. "You don't have to be the big brother all the time."

"Dammit." His hand clenched. "Is that what you think I am? Your big brother?"

Something in his tone caused her eyes to swing up. What she saw there stole her breath.

Colin closed in, his hand weaving into her hair as his mouth descended on hers. He kissed her. At first it was intense, but his lips softened and the kisses lingered until Stella felt weightless.

He drew back enough that only his breath caressed her lips.

"I am *not* your big brother."

"But—"

"Stella," he kissed her again, and she whimpered deep in her throat at how good it felt.

"I always thought you looked at me like the big brother type." His deep voice mingled with the chimes of water falling. "And I admit, I felt that way—until—"

"Until?"

"Until that time you landed on top of me on the boat. I touched you. I had my hands all over you, and you didn't feel like my little sister's friend anymore. You didn't feel young. I wanted to kiss the hell out of you right there in the dark."

Stella swallowed.

"But—but—Loren. I thought maybe you liked her," she murmured, still confused—still excited.

Colin's eyebrow inched up. "I like it when you're jealous."

His smile tantalized her, but it disappeared all too soon. "I am worried about Loren. Something is not right with her. I can't tell you exactly what, but maybe you'll catch it next time we see her. She wants to show us something."

"Us?"

Colin chuckled. "Yeah, believe it or not, she's not interested in me."

His teasing elicited a quick grin from her. "No, I don't believe it," she kidded.

And I don't believe you wanted to touch me.

As if he read her mind, his hand slid down behind her neck, and he kissed her softly. "I wanted to do that for a long time, Gullaksen," he whispered against her lips. "If you think I'm out of line—if you're not interested—you better tell me."

Stella reached out and fisted her hand in his t-shirt. "I'm interested," she smiled and tucked her head, folding against his chest.

With both of them holding torches, it was an awkward embrace, but she cherished every second, knowing that they were about to go back and face their grim reality.

The bell rang in the distance. Stella jerked back.

"They'll see us."

Colin glanced at the waterfall. "Do you think I care? Hey," he added softly. "It might get intense, but we've got a few things we need to accomplish."

She frowned and cocked her head.

"Such as?"

"Ask about the pit. Check on Dad and Jill. Find out what it was Loren wanted to show us."

"Why didn't she just show you?" Stella interrupted.

Colin's lips quirked. "Because I told her I needed to find you."

"Oh." She hesitated. "Those are all important tasks." She searched his face. "Was there more?"

"Yeah," his eyes traveled over her face. "There's more."

He reached for her hand as they started towards the waterfall. She felt him tense. The grip on her hand turned into a vice, but when she was about to ask what was wrong, she saw his gaze had shifted past her shoulder.

Anxious, she followed that stunned stare. At first nothing was evident. Beyond the reach of their torches lay the abyss they had just traveled from—a blackened confluence of tunnels and caverns. One avenue led to life-sustaining food and oxygen, another led to extinction. In that shadowed junction two eyes glared out at them.

Ghostly—floating—unblinking. Those pulsing green orbs stalked them. The shadowy figure advanced to the furthest reach of their torchlight. Stella's gasp was trapped in her throat, and her feet became numb, useless for any means of flight.

What had simply been a pair of luminous eyes now took on mass under the ambient light. Black shadows congealed to form an upright figure, tall but hunched. Its neck hung low so that its head was even with the sloped shoulders. Maybe there was the hint of a mouth or nose, but those features were lost on the charred face—lost to the gleaming eyes.

It took another awkward step forward, an imbalanced stride as if it didn't know how to handle its own weight. The legs were long and defined but seemingly soiled. Likewise, was the long torso and dangling arms. The creature had human elements, but it was naked, every inch of it covered in what now appeared to be blackened scales.

When Stella took a step backward, its eyes latched onto the movement. It had the predatory instincts of an animal.

"Get behind me," Colin whispered.

Stella stuck beside him. Colin reached forward and brandished his torch. Green orbs followed the motion. He took another step, thrusting the flames forward. The creature grew agitated and aggressive as it lumbered headfirst towards Colin.

"Col," she cautioned with a yelp.

The creature reacted to her cry. It lurched towards them, but Colin waved the torch, and it held its ground, swaying side to side. Its arms extended, and Stella could make out scaly hands with squat fingers. The palms were exceptionally large, reaching to mid-knuckle.

Stella raised her torch and edged closer, standing shoulder-to-shoulder with Colin. The motion pressed the beast back. It lifted one of its arms to deflect the flames.

"It doesn't like the fire," she mumbled through tight lips.

The sound of her voice made the sullied head snap in her direction. It freaked her, but she jabbed the torch in the air again, forcing it to retreat.

"Okay," Colin urged quietly. "Let's start backing up. Keep waving the torches. I don't think it will follow us past the waterfall."

Stella swung her flare. The sound of falling water filled her ears, but over it, she heard a keening pitch. The creature was moaning, torn with the desire to give chase but wary of the flames. As Colin and Stella reached the waterfall, the beast dropped its arms in apparent resignation. It swung around with its head hunched and its charcoal legs plodding stiffly away.

As it disappeared into the shadows, Stella broke into a cold sweat. The hand that gripped the torch trembled.

"Come on," Colin encouraged, his fingers on her arm.

She followed him. Trauma was setting in,

and she could feel the blood pounding in her head.

Boom. Boom. Boom.

"Stel?"

Boom. Boom. Boom.

"Stella?"

She blinked hard and saw the path to the Underworld ahead, the waterfall fading behind her. Colin's hand was steady and strong around hers. The memory of his kiss startled her. Had that really happened, or was everything on the other side of the waterfall a bizarre illusion?

"We're almost there," he assured.

Stella forced one foot in front of the other, some of her aches and pains flaring into focus now. Ahead, Margie's boisterous voice was heard before she even came into view. As they wound around the curve of the footpath, Stella saw the curvy woman stooped over a footlocker, pulling scarves out like a magician would do with his hat.

"Will this work?" she asked her husband, who was busy tying drab-colored ribbons to the rope railing along the path.

Jordan glanced up at the matted furry boa wrapped around his wife's neck. He raised an eyebrow and smirked. "Is there a tiara in there to accompany it?"

Margie's rear made a giant heart as she stooped over and searched the box. When she rose with a victorious smile, she held up a sequined hair comb in triumph. Her smile suddenly fell, and she dropped the comb. Jordan followed her gaze and frowned.

"Oh my," Margie exclaimed. "Have you

fallen in the stream again?"

Glancing down at her clothes, which were covered in a blend of soot and grime, Stella drew her shoulders back and inched her chin up.

"Something like that."

"Tsk tsk," Margie turned to Colin. "You don't look much better."

Colin remained silent.

"Well then," she plopped her hands on her hips, the ends of the faded pink boa dangling beneath her waist. "Go get cleaned up. Stella, do you still have that dress?"

In fact, she had just cleaned the dress yesterday. It was sitting folded on her desk.

"Yes, ma'am," she replied automatically.

"And you," Margie frowned at Colin. "Jordan, do you have something he can wear while he's cleaning up?"

"Thanks," Col muttered, "but Frederic gave my father and me some clothes. I'll be fine."

Relief washed over Margie's face as if the ultimate crisis had just been averted.

"Great. After you clean up, come join Jordan and me. We're sorting through our supplies, looking for decorations for the New Year's party next week."

Stella forced a smile. "That sounds swell."

Colin's elbow poked her, and she rubbed a hand over her mouth to conceal her smirk.

"We're hoping to make the event a special one." Wrinkles folded around Margie's blue eyes as she focused on Colin. "We want you and your family to know that even though you've lost someone—" she hesitated, "—there are others here to care for you. And we will do our best."

Jordan cleared his throat. "Let them go change, Margie."

Stella offered him a grateful smile. The man gave her a quick wink and settled back to decorating.

As she and Colin walked away from them, he tilted his head towards the infirmary. "Are you okay," he whispered. "Your toe and your palm—those are two pretty nasty cuts."

Stella flipped her hand over, remembering the slice from the sharp rock. The blood had clotted.

"I think I just really need to soak in the water. I'll be fine."

The concern in his eyes warmed her. She suddenly felt shy in front of him.

"Go soak," he ordered softly. "Clean up, and then we'll find Etienne and Frederic and tell them about what we saw."

Staring down at the scratches on her toes, she nodded. When there was nothing more from him, she glanced up and caught the slow grin that caught the corner of his lips.

"And then," he murmured, "we will revisit what happened between us."

CHAPTER 15

"No more. You can't tell me I'm imagining things. We both saw it," Stella stressed, swinging her arm towards Colin who was beside her in a plain white t-shirt and his freshly cleaned shorts.

Frederic stood with his arms crossed, his slate eyes pensive. He was much more composed than his counterpart, Etienne, the agitated sailor who now paced the infirmary.

Only moments ago, Colin and Stella had gathered Etienne and Frederic just outside of the airplane as they sought a bandage for Stella's palm.

Sarah had adeptly applied clean gauze and then ducked through the hatch after a dismissing nod from her husband. Once she was gone, Etienne's pacing halted. He stared at Stella with eyes the color of ice-covered cement.

"If you had listened to my *advice*," he uttered, "you wouldn't have had any encounters. They stay on that side of the waterfall." He pointed over her shoulder. "They do not bother us here."

"*They?*" Colin probed.

Etienne's eyes shot to Frederic, who just shrugged.

Moving up to a cracked window, Etienne peered out. His head swiveled back and forth, furtively scanning the courtyard. He glanced back to them with his lips pressed thin.

"We came across the first one not long after we were stranded down here."

"The *first?*" Stella repeated in a whisper.

"They are rarely seen," Etienne resumed his short march. Each step elicited a creak from the warped floor. "They shun the light. They stay away from torches, that's why you won't see them on this side of the waterfall."

"What are they?" Colin asked, stepping into Etienne's path to halt his progress. "Some sort of prehistoric creature?"

The man reached up and scratched beneath his hat. His lips twisted into a sardonic grin.

"Prehistoric creature," he repeated as if it were some private joke. He even rolled his eyes at Frederic, who didn't look amused.

"To presume that we were the first survivors to wash up in this cave would be very arrogant and naïve," Etienne explained. "We've seen signs of others that came before us. We've watched people die down here from the high levels of $CO2$. We've watched people die down here from the trauma of the rapid descent—from the trauma of their injuries—from all sorts of acclimation illnesses."

"The pit of skeletons," Stella murmured. "You didn't toss those victims back into the pools. You just threw them into a mass grave."

The corner of Etienne's eye twitched. "Goodness, you really *did* travel deep into the caves." He pumped a fist into his open palm. "Yes, you found our burial pit. If we started throwing bodies into the pools, it would entice unwanted visitors. There are sharks at this depth—rare, but we like to keep it that way. If they start hanging out down here, it will be harder for us to get to our food source."

"Those creatures—" a horrifying thought occurred to her, "—were you feeding them?"

Etienne laughed. His head tipped back, and a loud cackle poured out. Frosty eyes glared at her.

Stella shot Colin a glance, and he nodded in agreement. Etienne was succumbing to toxicity, or maybe just madness from civilization deprivation.

"No, we aren't *feeding* them," he spat. "There aren't enough corpses down here to sustain the Chimaera," he rationalized, not noticing Colin wince. "And there have been very few Chimaeras spotted, anyway."

"*Ky mere-ah,*" Stella repeated his enunciation. "Another mythological reference?"

She had read about the Greek creature made up of more than one animal. It had the head and body of a lion, but it also had a goat's head on its back.

"You're up on your mythology," Etienne nodded in approval. "Although it is pronounced the same, the Chimaera is also a rare breed of shark that inhabits the lower depths of the ocean. It rarely swims any higher than 500 feet below sea level. It is called the Ghost Shark, and that is what we call the creature you saw."

Stella's hackles immediately rose. "That was no shark we saw. It walked. It raised its hand and pointed at us."

She sought Colin's glance for validation.

"It looked human," he confirmed. "A scaly human."

Etienne studied both of them and some of his enthusiasm waned.

"Yes, well, we *call* them Chimaera. I'm not saying they are actual sharks."

"Then what are they?"

Frederic hefted off the cabinet he was leaning against. "The life you find around the hydrothermal vents are called *extremophiles*. Creatures capable of living in extreme conditions. Constant darkness, freezing cold. Just like us, there is enough to support the Chimaera down here for a very long time. We don't know how long they have been here."

Stella's eyes flared. "So, you think they are something prehistoric?"

Frederic exchanged a glance with Etienne. She resented that air of collusion.

"Tell them," Frederic ordered. "Everyone else knows. All they'd have to do is ask."

Etienne frowned. "It's too soon."

"If they're going to go snooping around, it's better for them to be armed with the facts. Something terrible could have happened today."

Colin stepped up. "Yes, the facts would be nice."

Etienne barely acknowledged him. He continued pacing, stopping to run his fingertips along the cot Anne had been sleeping in just yesterday.

"The Chimaera," he began tensely, "are *us*."

Aggravated, Colin looked to Frederic for an explanation.

To his credit, Frederic did not wait for Etienne's approval. He stepped forward, his shoulders eclipsing the gaunt sailor.

"It is our theory," he explained, "that the Chimaera were once human—perhaps some of the first victims to wash up in this cave."

Stella held her hand to her mouth. "What happened to them? How did they live so long?

"After a prolonged period, their bodies simply adapted to the environment. At first, these survivors might not have had the means to make a fire or have any light. They adapted to the dark. Even with the torches, we have learned to live with minimal light. Imagine what it would be like for Etienne or me to see the sun right now?"

Vampires. The word jumped to her mind.

"Their eyes were probably the first to alter," he continued. "The physical changes might have come from their diet. All they had to eat was whatever deep-sea creatures washed up in the caves, or perhaps they sustained themselves with the organisms breeding near the vents. The Chimaera's skin started to transform based on its nourishment. The dark color, perhaps a natural form of camouflage. It depends on the individual and the environment on how long it takes for the *change* to start."

Stella couldn't help herself. She openly gawked at him, searching the skin exposed above the neckline of his undershirt. He seemed amused with her inspection and tilted his neck to the right and then to the left.

"No, the change has not begun in me yet. But we have had people down here who showed symptoms—"

His Adam's Apple bobbed as he hesitated. Etienne sulked in the background, occasionally turning his head to search the window.

"The eyes," Stella prompted. "You said it starts in the eyes. I swear, sometimes when I look at people down here, I see a flash there, similar to what I saw on that creature, that Chimaera. But when I look closer, it is gone."

Frederic nodded. "It takes such a long time to evolve into what you witnessed. To have reached that stage—"

"You would have had to survive madness," she whispered.

"Perhaps."

"But these Chimaera are not human," she stated. "Not anymore. And, they are hostile. They have attacked me. You stated that the torch line keeps them away. You tell me you travel beyond the waterfall to get food. Haven't you had run-ins? Haven't you had to protect yourself? Have you ever had to kill one?"

Stella caught Etienne's flinch. He brushed Frederic aside and stepped up close to sneer at her. "You don't kill your own kind."

Foul breath washed over her face, and she caught another cryptic flare in his otherwise pale eyes.

"We must study them. We must be prepared. We must understand what may happen to us. They need to be treated with respect," he bristled.

It was impossible to debate with this man, so she chose a less volatile route rather than rile him.

"How many do you think there are?"

Etienne eyed her warily but muttered, "It's hard to tell. We know of at least five or six. We can distinguish them from each other by shape, height, coloring."

"And still, you don't search for a way up to the surface when you know that is going to be your fate?" Colin challenged.

"Did they find a way to the surface?" Etienne fired back. "There is none."

Stella read Colin's dark expression. He also knew this was pointless.

"All right—look," he said. "If we're all going to live down here together, we'd just appreciate you being a little more upfront with us. We're not fragile. If there is anything else like the Chimaera out there, please let us know. If you have any other secrets, it's a small place. We will find them. So, do the wise thing and share them now."

Etienne's pale face darkened. Perhaps on a healthy man, it would have appeared as the red flush of anger. On this man, it was as if ash filled his veins.

Frederic hooked his hand across the man's shoulder, restraining him.

"That's fair," Frederic agreed. "But you now know everything that we are aware of. We weren't purposely being secretive. We wanted to spare you having to see where our departed have been placed because it is a traumatic sight.

Witnessing something like that—it will play with your mind, thinking that your fate might be close at hand. You only arrived here a few weeks ago and are still acclimating. Mentally, I'm talking." He paused. "Dead bodies. Creatures with glowing eyes." He shook his head and even managed a grin. "That's a little too much to grasp so soon. Understand that Etienne only wanted to spare you from that."

Stella shot a look at Etienne, and from his dark expression, she doubted there was any benevolence behind his motives.

"Great," Colin uttered, unconvinced. "We're going to go now. Thanks for the information." He hesitated. "But, one last question. Did you really release my mother back into the water, or are you planning on bringing her to that pit?"

The rawness of his voice pained Stella. To have to ask such a question—it was inhumane.

Frederic was the first to respond. "I personally took her to the pool." His tone was sincere, and the sympathy in his eyes seemed genuine. "She deserves the peace of the sea. What you saw in that pit—they never had surviving family down here. They were alone."

There was no one to care.

Stella caught the moisture in Colin's eyes as he blinked angrily and tilted his head, prompting her outside. With one final glance at Frederic's forlorn expression, she followed, eager to leave.

Colin was ahead a few steps, marching with

little focus. Stella jogged to catch up to him. She reached for his shoulder and felt the muscles bunch under her touch.

"Are you okay?"

He halted and spun around, allowing her a fleeting glimpse of the storm of emotions raging within him. Under her patient gaze, he settled some, and warmth flickered back into his eyes.

"Another minute, and I was gonna lose it in there," he said.

Stella smiled. "Another minute, and I would have kneed the dude between the legs. I was getting so frustrated."

To her relief, a real laugh poured from Colin's lips, and the edge left his expression.

"That was all bullshit in there." He pointed towards the infirmary. "I'm at the point that I don't really care what his explanations are. Everything is supposition. I'm just going to go by what I see from here on out."

"I agree. At least we know what we're up against inside these caves." She glanced at the empty windows of her wheelhouse. "I want to warn Jill. She needs to know—"

Colin nodded. "And Dad. I'm worried about him."

"They'll be getting up soon."

Intense eyes took her breath. "Come here," he urged softly.

She stepped into his arms. His palm guided her head to rest on his shoulder, and his fingers remained in her hair. She could feel his breath tickle her forehead. For this precious moment, she was anywhere other than this crazy crypt at the bottom of the ocean. She was in his embrace as they stood on a pier overlooking the Atlantic. She was in his embrace as he sat on the bumper of his Jeep, and she stood between his legs. She was in his embrace as they cheered at a football game on his campus. She was in his embrace as he tipped her chin up and touched his lips to hers.

All these fantasy embraces—and none came close to this feeling—to this moment. The beating of his heart tapping against her own. The warmth of his skin. The peace of knowing that it wasn't just her who had fantasies.

"You feel right, Stel."

Maybe she murmured something against his shoulder. She didn't dare move and chance this moment would end.

"Of all the things I've done in the past few years, you're the only thing that feels right."

His arms constricted, and she welcomed the additional heat.

"I could go on trying to be polite—pretending I'm not attracted to you. That's the mature thing for me to do. Right now, you need that big brother to watch out for you. You don't need a guy that's—"

Frustration rumbled out of her throat as she drew her head back and reached up to cup his face in both her hands.

"I need this," she demanded, pulling him down until she could kiss him.

Colin hesitated for a second, and then he kissed her back, his arms closing around her as he murmured her name against her lips.

Maybe the timing wasn't perfect, but as Col had said, it *felt right*.

Finally, his head drew back enough that he could look into her eyes. His pupils were wide and dark, like the black depths of the pools.

"Demanding little wench," he teased.

Stella smiled, resisting the temptation to run her fingertips along his bottom lip. Insecurities surfaced, as they usually did. Colin read the brief shadow that passed over her face.

"What is it?"

She kept her eyes averted, feeling foolish but craving reassurance.

"This isn't—" she hesitated, "—this isn't just convenient, is it? I mean, I'm not just a diversion?"

Colin massaged his forehead. He drew in a deep breath.

"I could ask the same thing, couldn't I?"

Stella stiffened. "Of course, it's not."

"This—" he tapped his hand on his chest and then tapped hers. "—this is new, and we've both got a lot of crap going on around us right now. It's not the way I wanted to—" He stopped, considering his words. "If I hadn't been a coward on land. If I had said something to you sooner—" his hand waved between them again, "this would have been something really special."

"It's not special?"

"It's damn special," he grinned. "But on land, I would have been able to take you out to dinner. I could have walked along the beach and watched the sun set with you."

Stella swallowed, picturing an image that could have been plucked from her own daydreams.

A grating sound nearby yanked them apart. Colin looked alert. *Stay here*, he mouthed. Inching past her, he peered out of their shadowed nook and returned with a somber expression.

"Take a look for yourself," he murmured.

Stella peered out and noticed Donald Wexler stumbling from his boat dwelling. There was a bottle clutched in his hand, and his bleary eyes hinted at the contents.

"Where'd he get that?" Colin asked.

"Margie was stacking up the supplies for the upcoming New Year's party. I saw several bottles on the café shelves."

Her heart broke at the sight of Colin's bleak profile. His shoulders rose and fell as he took a deep breath.

"All right. I'll go talk to Dad. You're going to talk with Jill?"

Stella nodded.

"Then get some rest, Stel." He touched her arm. "You could have been seriously hurt tonight. You're acting so strong, but don't. It's not necessary. It's okay to be scared and to admit that you are exhausted."

This simple acknowledgment made the symptoms manifest. Her body trembled and ached. She feared sleep because if she closed her eyes, the creature would return.

"I'll be right next door," he assured. "Just holler, and I'll be there."

She knew that he would. It was one of the traits that had first attracted her to Jill's older brother. During her sophomore year, she was stuck after school one day, working on the school newspaper. Running through the halls, she threw open the front door just in time to see the late bus ride off. Neither her mother nor Jill's mother answered the phone. She had no cash to hire a ride, and the walk home was about ten miles. Preparing to start that long trek, hoping someone would eventually pick up the phone, she suddenly remembered that Colin had football practice. She stopped along the fence to watch the seniors practicing their running routes and noticed Col launch into the air for a skilled catch. He jogged back to the bench and glimpsed her standing there.

"Hey," he called. "Looking for an interview?" His grin teased her in more ways than she could register.

A few other jersey-clad players looked up and then away in disinterest.

Stella forced herself to wave Colin over. He trotted to the fence, his dark hair stuck to his forehead and his face flush from the workout.

"Uh," she fumbled, "I missed my bus. Is there any way—"

"Yeah, sure. I'm done here. I just need a quick shower. I'll meet you out front in ten minutes?"

No questions asked. No ribbing. Just, *I'll meet you out front in ten minutes.*

"If you need help with your dad—" She returned to the moment. "Same thing. Just holler."

She turned to head to her bungalow when there was a slight tug on her arm. Colin dipped and kissed her, his thumbs brushing her cheeks when he pulled back.

"That's so you can have some sweet dreams tonight," he whispered.

With that, he was gone, and Stella stood, hugging herself, missing his warmth already. She tilted her head and searched the dark recesses of the Underworld. The ceiling gaped overhead, black and mysterious. Twin red pillars of rock, each several stories high, stood like two giant canine teeth in this yawning mouth. In the distance, Margie and Jordan sang Christmas carols, humming unintelligible words when the lyrics failed them. Their rowdy voices tuned out the constant churn of the waterfall in the distance. That liquid curtain was out of view but was still too close for her liking. Just beyond that flowing veil stalked the nocturnal beasts—creatures that were evolving, slowly transitioning into the deep-sea monsters that would one day rule this subterranean land.

CHAPTER 16

"I saw you."

Stella stepped inside the wheelhouse to find Jill sitting on the hammock with her legs dangling off.

"Saw me?" she felt her stomach dip.

"Yeah, I saw you and Col."

Stella crossed over to the desk and sat on the chair, fidgeting with the bandage on her palm.

"Jill, I—"

"Chill, girl." Jill's white teeth gleamed in the dim light. "Like, if you haven't seen the way my brother has looked at you for the past couple of years—well, yeah, you probably haven't seen it."

Stella reeled at the notion.

"But," Stella stuttered, "he was in college. He had college babes."

"So?" Jill shrugged. "Maybe he was waiting for the right time." She stood up and peered outside.

Stella watched her guardedly. "Are you— does it freak you out?"

Jill looked back over her shoulder. "Does it freak you out if I tell you I'm kinda into Daniel?"

Whoa. Okay, yeah, maybe that did freak her a bit, but after a moment's consideration she got over it. As long as the guy was decent. If he hurt Jill in any way, he'd have to face Stella's wrath.

"I don't really know him," she hedged.

"I can talk to him," Jill explained with a frown. "I mean, it's really easy to talk to him."

"You can talk to me." .

Jill hoisted off the hammock and plopped down on the blanket. "I know that."

"So, talk to me, Jilly. I hurt and she wasn't even my mom."

Jill looked up, her eyes red and brimming. "All girls are supposedly *Daddy's Girl*. Not me. I was Mommy's Girl. Mom adored me, Stel. She poured everything of herself into me."

True. And Colin had a father who rode him constantly. He wasn't exactly *Daddy's Boy*. Jill was definitely the chosen one in the family, but it wasn't obnoxious to the point of being sickening.

Stella walked over and dropped to her knees on the blanket. She reached forward and wrapped Jill in her arms and felt each tremor as Jill sobbed. Murmuring words of support, Stella hugged her tight.

Finally, Jill gathered herself and sat back, wiping her eyes with the balls of her hands.

"She's at peace," she sniffled. "I know that. Well, maybe not so much at peace. She's probably worried about us. We could use all the angels looking down on us that we can get."

Stella kept her gaze averted. Troubling images hacked at the inside of her head.

"What?" Jill probed. "What's wrong?"

It didn't seem like the right moment to tell her, but she needed to be warned. She needed to practice caution if she was to strike out on her own. Stella wondered if Daniel was already aware of the Chimaera. Sure. He had to be.

"I need you to be careful," she said. "Promise never to go beyond the waterfall."

Jill sat up cross-legged, pulling her hair back into a ponytail as she used the scrungee from her wrist to cinch it.

"Why, what's back there? Is that where you and Col do the wild thing?" She wiggled her eyebrows and grinned.

"Eh, as if!" Stella couldn't help but laugh. "Seriously, Jill." She sobered. "There are things back there. Things that will hurt you."

"Things?"

Stella began to chronicle the events, leaving out only the mass grave. There was the anticipated disbelief in Jill's blue eyes, and then darker shades of horror. She hugged herself and rocked slightly.

"I saw one," she whispered.

"What! Where?"

"I didn't actually see one, but I saw a drawing of what you're describing. It was in the cave of pictures."

It was Jill's turn to share her escapade with Daniel. When she was done, they both sat quietly contemplating each other's tales. Stella was the first to break the silence.

"Why don't we go grab some lunch?"

She wanted to get some food into her friend. She knew Jill wasn't eating much.

Jill blanched at the thought, but she curled her hands into fists and pushed up off the ground. "You're right," she said quietly. "I *want* my strength."

Stella beamed. "Atta girl!"

The bell rang its solemn chord. The night was felt only by the silence that cloaked the Underworld. Peering out the wheelhouse window, Stella reviewed the progress of Margie and Jordan's decorating. Faded ribbons lined the heavy rope fences. Boxes of baubles sat out, waiting to be strung up. Margie had already crafted a tree of sorts in the café. The center post of a coat rack had strands of frayed rope tied to it. Each strand was lined with shiny bits of metal and exotic shell fragments.

After meeting Colin at lunch, it was agreed that tonight would be a night off to rest. Colin would watch over his father, and she over Jill. Jill was making efforts not to spiral into depression. She helped Margie siphon through some of the boxes and even located a rusted trumpet, which she tested by putting her lips to it. The sound was far from melodic, but it might do for a New Year's celebration.

Once Jill fell asleep, Stella pulled her journal out and began catching up on the events of the past few days. There was plenty to write about. Enough to cramp her hand and strain her eyes in the faint light. She finally closed the binder and slipped it back into its hiding spot beneath her blankets. Settling into a comfortable position on the tattered fabric, fatigue finally claimed her.

There was no telling what the time was, but something woke her. A soft knocking outside the bungalow—a persistent little tap like an annoying woodpecker.

Stella scrambled onto her knees and crawled to the window. A shadow stood outside, and she saw a pale wrist rap faintly against the wood. Poking her head out the window frame, she was startled to see Loren standing there. Just as Loren was in mid-knock, Stella called out softly, "Shh. You'll wake Jill. I'll come out."

Scrambling to think what Loren could possibly want from her, Stella smoothed down her wild hair and tried to sweep some of the wrinkles out of her tank top.

Outside, Loren had backed into the shadows, her black hair and dark attire the perfect camouflage. She beckoned Stella with a haunting wave.

When they were past Colin and Don's shanty, Loren continued around a mound of dirt and stopped when she was out of the range of the closest torch.

"What the hell?" Stella asked in a whisper.

"Sorry for the cloak-and-dagger treatment, but Colin said you were both probably under surveillance from the Brothers Grimm."

English, please.

"Brothers Grimm," Stella tested. "Ah, Etienne and Frederic. Appropriate." She nodded.

"Colin is trying to make a distraction right

now, and he'll meet up with us here when he's sure they're appeased."

Stella scanned the grounds for any sign of a disruption. The torches leading up to Frederic's office revealed nothing. The windows to that enclave glowed, but they always did. The man kept a torch going constantly. Given what she had witnessed last night, could she blame him?

A scrape of rock nearby had her jumping out of her skin. She nearly hiccupped in relief when Colin appeared beside her.

"Done," he nodded at Loren.

"What did you do?" Stella asked.

"A lot of running around." He grinned. "I went back behind the waterfall."

Stella gasped. "By yourself? Colin, don't do that."

"You were worried about me?" He gave her a quick wink.

Uneasy, Stella looked at Loren. "Did you go too?"

"No, I came to get you." Loren fidgeted with the zipper on her pullover.

"It was no big deal," Colin explained. "I just ducked behind the water and waited there for a while. I took a different route back. I don't think they saw me return. Let them think I'm still deep in the caverns again."

"But why?" Stella looked back and forth between them. "What's all this about?"

"That is what Loren is about to tell us, right?" Colin shifted his gaze to her.

The young woman looked uncomfortable under their scrutiny. Her furtive glances made Stella edgy. Loren shoved her fingers into the pockets of her jeans and cleared her throat a few times. When it seemed doubtful that she would speak, she finally uttered a few husky words.

"When your mom—" she tossed a quick glance up at Colin, "when she passed—I don't know—it kind of really hit me. I miss my mother so much." Her breath caught. "And your dad," she hesitated and glanced towards their bungalow even though it was out of view behind this rise. "Your dad is showing signs—they're not positive signs."

"The place is getting to him," Colin kept his voice controlled. "That's all."

Loren looked doubtful but discreetly tucked her head and nodded.

"I'm just saying it would be a good idea to try and get you and your family out of here."

Colin snorted. "Sure, point the way, and I'll get right on that."

A pale hand swept back the dark veil of hair so that one deep brown eye could study him.

"That's what I'm about to do."

Stella and Colin exchanged glances. She could see her own shock mirrored in his expression.

Loren stood taller now as if she was full of purpose. All the body gestures were there. Fingers that had been crammed defensively into her front pockets now hooked the back pockets of her jeans as she took a deep breath and lifted her chin. She really was beautiful and made Stella feel like an awkward oaf. But Colin's interest in her now seemed solely based on curiosity, not attraction.

"I'm not going to lie," Loren uttered in her

husky murmur, "where I'm taking you is very dangerous. If you don't want to go, I understand."

"We're going," Stella asserted before looking to Col for confirmation. He nodded readily.

"Okay." Loren lifted the hood of her black pullover so that only a slice of her face was visible. It seemed an outlandish gesture in this darkened underworld, but from a distance, with her slim frame, she could easily be mistaken for Daniel. Maybe it was calculated.

They followed her, mimicking her elusive maneuvers, ever vigilant that someone was watching them. They were heading opposite the waterfall, back towards the grotto where they first entered the Underworld.

Loren was nimble across the slick path. Her flat-top sneakers were frayed and dirty, but they handled strewn boulders with deft precision. Stella recognized the narrow, windy channel leading to the grotto, but Loren continued past it. Her demeanor seemed to relax as they put the Underworld far behind them.

"Daniel and I know our way around these caves with our eyes closed. Sometimes that has even been necessary."

Stella clutched the torch she had picked up just before they slipped out of the colossal cavern. She didn't want to test the *eyes-closed* theory.

"Etienne knows we come back here. He doesn't like it. He knows what's back here, but he's left us alone. I guess after twenty years, he figures we're going to stay put. Now, you guys, however—"

"You're saying that you've found a way out of this hellhole and chose to stay down here?" Colin propped his hand on the cave wall and climbed over a huge rock. He turned immediately to offer Stella a hand.

"I'm not saying it's a sure way out. Not at all. If it were easier, yes, maybe we would have tried it."

This was sounding more and more like a dead end, Stella thought. But options—even the hint of one—should be explored.

They were in uncharted territory again. Hiking endlessly to the point that she would never be able to find her way back. They had invested a lot of trust in someone they barely knew.

"You've seen the Chimaera, then?" she asked, slightly out of breath.

Loren stopped. The torchlight crept into the gap in the hood where her face hid. There was pure fear there. No mistaking it.

"Yes. It's why I travel to this end of the caverns. They don't usually come this way."

"Why not?" she asked. "Etienne said that the torches kept them away, but there are no torches here."

Colin raised his flare, estimating the length of flame remaining.

Loren tucked her head down so her face was lost in shadow again.

"Etienne keeps them on the other side of the waterfall," she said quietly.

"*Keeps* them?" Stella frowned. "How do you *keep* them anywhere? They're wild animals."

"Are they?" Loren countered quickly.

Too quickly.

"I know that they were once humans," Colin reasoned. "But they are dangerous. Are you serious that he somehow contains them in the back caves?"

Loren nodded, her hood plucking at her hair.

"He's more or less trained them. I've seen him use the torches to keep them back. I swear he communicates with them somehow." She shrugged. "Anyway, they seem to listen."

They traveled silently until Loren held up her hand to stop them.

"There," she pointed.

Stella saw nothing at first. Colin took a few steps forward, kicking loose rocks to clear the path. He plodded forward until Loren yelled, "Stop!"

Colin froze and crouched down, holding the torch out before him.

"Water."

Stella walked up alongside him, and their combined flames revealed a black pool, maybe only ten feet in circumference. Its slate shoreline was elevated a few feet above the rippling surface.

"Another pool," Colin observed. "Is this what you claim is an escape route?"

Loren unzipped her jacket and pulled it off, laying it across a pitted boulder. She wore a black tank top that revealed willowy arms and a neckline that exposed an unsettling number of bones. Other than that, she seemed in good physical condition. As she stooped to take off her sneakers and place them next to the jacket, Stella saw sleek lines of muscles beneath her thin jeans.

"What are you doing?" Stella gasped. "Are you going in there?"

Loren flashed a humorless smile.

"I warned you this was not going to be easy. It could even be deadly. But it's worth it if you make it through."

"Whoa." Colin set his torch down and rubbed the back of his head. "You want us to dive into this? Where exactly are we going?"

"There is an underwater tunnel over there," she pointed to the far end of the pool, "about five feet down. Swim over to the other side of this pool and then just sink until you feel the hole with your hands."

"And swim into it?" he cringed. "You have done this? How did you ever discover it, and *why* did you swim into it?"

Loren's gaze was unblinking, like a fish. For a moment, Stella thought she saw a luminous flash in those dark eyes. She was just spooked, though.

"You get desperate enough down here. You do things that aren't rational," she explained. "I didn't just discover this. Someone died here. He—he kind of lost it. He dove into this pool and didn't return. Danny found his body. That's how he found the underwater tunnel."

Danny. Daniel. The guy that Jill was probably with right now.

"Why would we want to swim into this tunnel if it already killed a man?" Colin asked carefully.

"To have a chance, maybe. I wouldn't be showing it to you if I didn't think it was important."

Colin stared at Loren. Stella could tell he was trying to gauge her sincerity or, more likely, her lucidity. His gaze swerved to Stella.

"Stel, please stay here."

She was shaking her head before he even finished.

"No way. We stay together, remember?"

"What if I don't come back? You need to stay here. You need to watch after my sister— my father."

"Col, no." She grabbed his arm. She was desperate. She couldn't lose him.

In the ring of torches, she saw his eyes soften. Loren discreetly turned away, refolding her jacket.

"Listen to me," Colin stepped in close to her, his hands cupping her face. "I will go check this out. If it's safe, I'll come back and bring you with me."

"If you don't come back—" Tears pooled behind her eyes.

Colin dipped his head and softly pressed his lips to hers. "Well, at least I got to finally kiss you." He grinned.

The tears slipped out of the corners of her eyes. She wrenched her arms around his neck and hugged him tight.

"Five minutes. You get five minutes, Colin Wexler. If you're not back, I'm coming to get you."

"Stel—"

She held up five fingers.

Colin looked troubled, but he stepped back and pulled his t-shirt off. If the situation hadn't been so dire, she would have enjoyed that view, but she was too worried to think straight. She was even too worried to notice that Loren had pulled off her jeans. The black tank was long enough to reach her thighs.

Stooping down to sit on the ledge, Loren dangled her toes in the water. "It's not exactly warm," she peered up from under her bangs.

Colin was in his shorts. Stella could see a few goosebumps dot his forearms. He climbed down to the ledge and plunged into the water, resurfacing and holding onto the rock shelf. He looked up at Stella with water clinging to his long eyelashes.

"I'll be back in five minutes," he vowed.

Loren lowered into the pool and then crept her fingers around the edge.

"Work your way around the rim and then try your best to follow me. It will be dark. Use your hands and arms to find the hole. It's pretty wide, and it's about eight feet until you enter the next cave. If you're smart, it's no big deal. If you panic," she warned, "it can get ugly."

Stella crouched onto her knees to get closer. She touched Colin's hand just as he met her eyes. For a moment, they stared at each other, and then, with a nod, his dark hair slipped under the even darker water.

How quickly that rippling black water consumed him. For a second there was the ghostly white flash of a foot, and then nothing. Stella began to count to occupy her mind. When she hit 300, she was diving in.

Ten.

Eleven.

Twelve.

She stooped lower, trying to get her head down to water level. She could hear nothing but the agitated slap of water against rock and the fuzzy drone of panic inside her ears.

Sixty-two.

Sixty-three.

Stella pulled off her sandals.

At least I finally got to kiss you.

Ninety-five.

Ninety-six.

Someone died in this pool, Loren had said. Yet, still, she and Danny had dived into it voluntarily. They found something. It couldn't be the express elevator to the surface, or they would have taken it, no matter what she argued.

One hundred seventy-one.

One hundred seventy-two.

So, then, what? What was down here that could possibly be worth such a horrible fate?

Two hundred six.

Two hundred seven.

Two hundred eight.

Stella scooted onto her rear and inched close to the edge, her toes gingerly testing out the water. It was cold—far enough away from the vents that it did not benefit from their warmth. It was also murky. An obscure window where she imagined the damned staring up at her from the harrowing abyss.

Two hundred thirty-seven.

As terrifying as the notion of jumping into

this ghostly pool was, the thought of Colin being claimed by it was scarier. She had given him time—too much time. Jill would take care of her father. There were other survivors here—survivors who weren't as deranged as Etienne. There was no one for Colin but her. She had to save him.

Two hundred fifty-two.

Stella jumped before she could talk herself out of it. The frigid water made her gasp, and she nearly gulped in a mouthful of brine. She tested ducking her head and opening her eyes, but the cold was too much on them. She rose and took a couple of rapid breaths to fill her lungs.

Motion on the far side of the pool stopped her. Loren's head cracked the surface, her black hair pasted to her face like a veil of tar.

"Colin!" she implored.

Loren shook her head, but it could have been to toss some of the hair off her eyes.

Stella plummeted beneath the water, attempting again to open her eyes. She saw only her hand clawing through the murk. As she rose for air, she was startled to find Colin staring back at her. His head bobbed as he treaded water.

"Col!" She swam to him, and he smiled.

Grabbing onto the ledge, he swung his free arm around her. "It wasn't that bad. Loren gave great instructions. Do you want to try it?"

She pumped her head up and down, her chin dipping into the water. "What's under there?"

Colin's voice was clipped by the cold and

exertion. "No magical passageway to the surface, but it's interesting enough. Let me show you quickly, and then we'll head back."

"Can you find your way on your own?" Loren asked, pulling herself up onto the ledge. "I'd like to get dressed."

"Yeah, no problem. I've got it now." He hesitated and then added, "Thanks, Loren. Seriously, thank you."

She kept her eyes averted, but she nodded slowly. "I'll wait here and guide you back."

Stella's lips were already trembling, but when Colin asked if she was ready, she stuck her thumb up out of the water.

"Remember Loren's instructions? Feel for the hole down here with your hands and arms. Swim forward about eight feet, and you'll surface on the other side. I'll be right there."

It was easy to nod affirmatively, but as soon as the water closed over Stella's scalp, the memories of that ill-fated night returned.

Down.

Down.

Down.

The futile attempts to swim against the current. The crazed need to breathe. The panic. The fear.

Stella tried to focus. She swept her arms in a wide arc and one connected with the wall, the other touched Colin's leg. That steadied her, and she blindly swam after him. Using one hand to sweep above her, she felt the arched ceiling of rock. It creeped her out. She kicked forward, but her shoulder kept butting up against the rock, spurring her anxiety. The need to scratch and claw was about to consume her when she realized the craggy ceiling was gone. Peering through slits in her eyes, she even caught a faint glimmer of light. Swimming towards it, she surfaced with a quick gasp.

Colin was already hefting his lean torso onto the shore, and as soon as he was up, he quickly turned to assist her.

Stella took his hand and slid up onto the gravelly ledge. She was surprised to find two torches embedded in a pile of rubble, their wicks just now blossoming.

"How?"

Colin held his hands up to one of the flares. "Loren said she and Daniel brought them here, along with a box of matches they kept in an airtight bag when they swam in. The matches didn't work initially, but she finally got them going. We're supposed to douse the flames when we leave. There's a metal bucket over there that we just have to hold over the torches."

Stella drew in a deep breath tinged with salt and sulfur.

"This cave has oxygen," she observed.

"Yeah." Colin tipped his head back. "If you look up, there's a natural chimney above that must connect it with the other tunnels. It's just too high to reach. Swimming is the easier option."

"Not for the dead guy."

"No—" he paused, "—but his sacrifice helped Loren and Daniel discover this place."

Stella hugged her arms about her. "If they know about it, there's no doubt Etienne will search here if he can't find us."

Colin stood up. "Yeah, Loren said we should be quick. He'll come looking soon."

Stella's face scrunched up in anger. Let him come. He didn't own this land. What was he going to do?

An image of the cells she and Colin had discovered came to mind.

"So, what's so special about this place?" she challenged, scrambling up beside him.

Colin grinned and tugged a torch from its moorings.

"Follow me."

The ceiling was high enough that Stella was able to stand upright. She searched its jagged surface. There were no sharp fangs of stalactites here. Instead, it was a crusty canopy of rock that looked like it could pulverize her just as well.

She followed Colin's bare back, crying out when she stepped on a loose rock.

"Are you okay?"

How much abuse had her poor feet taken in the past few days?

"Yeah, fine. Keep going."

As Colin progressed, his torch revealed new portions of the cave. The pool widened and she lost the far end to the shadows. Blunt molars of rock dipped down periodically, but the floor was relatively flat and unobstructed. A large pile of rubble stacked against the walls gave the daunting impression that there was once a cave-in.

Busy taking in these details, she walked right into Colin when he stopped abruptly.

"What—"

Colin turned to steady her and swept the

torch out in front of him.

"Look."

Stella followed the torch.

About fifteen feet ahead, a bulky object rested on the bank of the water. At first she thought it was a boulder, but then she realized it had color. A vivid flash of yellow was visible in the torchlight. With its two elongated feet it looked like some sort of cartoon character. A reclined lion with his two paws splayed out before him.

The seamless spherical shape hinted that it was man-made.

"What is it?"

Colin stepped up alongside the object, which was taller than him. Its bulbous belly looked large enough to consume him—to consume them both. He reached out and knocked on that yellow globe and a dull clang filled the chamber. He moved another foot and knocked again, this time receiving a brief clunk. As Stella circled around it, she saw a steel sphere, rusted in some spots, but remarkably intact. A murky domed window gave a shadowy insight to what the container might be.

"A sub of some sort?" she speculated.

Colin nodded. "It must be a research submersible. It's got a logo." He reached over and rubbed the mud-caked surface.

AHI.

"It had to have been lowered from a ship. There are a few feet of its lifeline still attached."

"Didn't the ship come searching for it?"

"Probably. If we're tucked deep in this canyon, they must have lost all traces of it, though." Colin continued his inspection. "Loren said that the pilot of this sub mentioned investigating a plane crash but that most everyone chalked it up as another loss to the Bermuda Triangle."

"This pilot. What happened to him?"

Colin's eyes moved from the sphere to the threatening water. "Apparently, he was the guy who died down here. He was trying to get back to his sub but got disoriented in the underwater cave."

That notion humbled her. The very cave she just swam through had claimed the life of the man commanding this vessel.

"Is this it? Is this what Loren proposes as our way out? How long has it been down here? How can it be seaworthy?"

"Actually," Colin crawled around behind it, "I've been looking it over, and it appears to be intact. It needs a little work, but—"

"Col, seriously? You think you could make it to the surface in this?"

"*We*," he emphasized. It's clearly a one-man submersible. There's one seat inside. But we could fit two—maybe even three—just to get to the surface."

"Well, that would be you, Jill, and your father." She studied the orb, which looked like it was only eight feet in circumference. They would be plied together like sardines.

Colin's silence drew her attention. He looked down at the ground, but his jaw muscle was pumping in thought.

"Whoever it is," he muttered hoarsely, "we'll get to the surface. We'll get help."

Stella was ready to argue that if anyone from above had searched for this pilot, no one had ever found him. How would they ever be able to locate the Underworld again if they managed to get to the surface? Instead, she approached Colin and placed her hand on his shoulder.

"If you think this could make it to the surface," she glanced dubiously at the cancerous decay, "then I believe in you. You're the engineering student."

Colin looked up with a poignant smile. "This," he slapped the hull, and it echoed hollowly, "is a long shot at best. Whoever goes in here has to accept that they have a 5% chance of making it to the surface. Hell," he added. "A 5% chance of living."

"I'd take those odds," she whispered. "What are our chances down here?"

"They seem to live a long time."

Stella rolled her eyes.

Colin diverted his gaze by stooping down to peer into the domed window. "Of course, there is no power," he related, "but power would have been necessary to maneuver forward or backward. Ascent and descent are controlled solely by buoyancy. There must be a ballast system in there. Fill the ballast tanks up with water and the craft sinks. Fill the ballasts up with air and the craft rises."

He circled more and patted a bulky slab of metal affixed to the submersible with a thick rope. "This apparently used weights to aid its descent."

Stella finished his thoughts, suddenly

catching on. "Remove the weights, and the sub rises."

"Exactly." He frowned. "We would have to try and regulate the ascent."

"Decompression?" she asked. "The bends?"

"Well, not exactly. The bends are caused by breathing compressed air from scuba equipment. Once this hatch closes, we'd have what limited oxygen is trapped in there. There may be some variances as the hull contracts with the outside water pressure, but we should be okay." He sounded unconvinced.

Stella searched his face. "Find that out in finance class?" she quoted his father.

Seeing that she was teasing, his lips inched up at the corner. "No. Acquiring my diving certification helped with some of the physics."

"Ahh." She glanced around. "I still can't believe no one else tried it. I understand the risks, but Loren and Daniel have clearly been here several times. They brought these torches. Why didn't they try to escape?"

"I don't know." He shrugged. "But I think we should go ask."

Climbing up onto the ledge, Colin and Stella found Loren where they left her. Her jeans and jacket were on now, and she was just slipping on her flat tops.

"What do you think?" she asked.

"It's a possibility," Colin replied. "But there must be a reason you and Daniel haven't tried it. Or any of the others."

"I don't think the Conovers know about it. They don't venture out of the Underworld much. They never even knew about the pilot. He died almost as soon as he made it down here. And Etienne isn't sharing the fact that this is here, so me and Daniel—we just keep quiet." She searched the cavern and added quietly, "Danny and me—we've been down here a long time. We've probably spent as much of our life in the Underworld as we did above the ocean. It's what we know."

"So, you just want to stay here?" Stella asked incredulously.

Loren shrugged slim shoulders. She held out her hand, examining her fingers.

"I can't go," she whispered, forlorn.

There was nothing visible in that extended palm, but Stella knew at that moment what was in store for Loren…for all of them. She had already caught glimpses. The flash in their eyes—the precursor for the soulless glowing orbs Stella witnessed in the dark. That was the fate down here.

"I don't see the change in you," she observed in quiet respect. "You have time."

Loren looked up at her with such gravity.

"Time ran out for us."

CHAPTER 17

JILL

"Why haven't you gone?"

Jill sat cross-legged on the earthen floor of the graffiti cave.

Daniel stood with his shoulder hitched against the wall.

"And go to what?" he asked with a stony expression. I was thirteen years old when I came down here. I barely remember the surface, and what memories I do have—" he hesitated and looked away "—they weren't good ones."

Jill felt bad for him. There was a toughness to Daniel that she found attractive, but there had to be a reason for that hardness. Nothing about her felt hard. She felt weak. Even this morning, when Stella explained about the submersible they found in the cave, Jill's first reaction was to cower in the corner.

I don't want to drown in that can.

I'm safe where I am right now.

Why can't I wait until another option comes

along?

Those were the pitiful protests she offered as Stella sat there, sacrificing her spot in the submersible to keep the Wexler family together and offer them a chance at escape.

Well, Jill didn't want it. She was scared.

"So, you don't want to try?" she asked Daniel. "You don't even want to try to make it back?"

Daniel watched her with dark eyes. "No. But you should go. You haven't been tainted by this place yet. You can have a normal life."

Jill glanced around at the murals, and then her gaze landed on him.

"I've been tainted," she muttered.

She curled her toes up, trying to squeeze herself into a ball. It was hard to admit insecurity to a guy who was so cool, who was so mysterious and handsome, who was really much older than her even if he didn't look it. But the words slipped, unbidden.

"I'm afraid," she confessed.

She waited for his laughter. His mocking.

When there was no retort, she finally glanced up. He was watching her with an odd expression. It was a rugged blend of conflict and concern, and it caused her to squeeze herself tighter.

"Fear in general, I understand," he sympathized. "But you don't have to be afraid down here. I won't let anything happen to you."

Heat rose to her cheeks. A pleasant buzzing sounded inside her ears.

"Maybe if I stay down here long enough, I'll have your courage." She tried to joke.

"Courage," he spat. "That's laughable. I'm not one you would pin a courageous label on."

"Why? Look at you. You're the definition of courageous. You're not afraid of this place— or these creatures." She flung her hand at the carved depiction of a hunched figure with wide eyes.

"There's a hell of a lot more up there to be afraid of," he countered. "Don't look at me like I'm some sort of a hero."

He turned away from her. "Do you really want to know what happened the day I ended up here?"

A chill stole over her arms. Something about the desperation in his voice warned her to say, *no, no, I don't want to hear it*.

Instead, her voice cracked as she murmured, "Yes, please tell me." Because suddenly she had to know. She had to know what crafted Daniel into such a puzzling contradiction of hard and soft.

Daniel wouldn't look at her. He faced the wall of murals and traced his finger along the skull and crossbones.

"I didn't fall," he asserted flatly. "I jumped."

The shock she anticipated never registered. Somehow, she had guessed this already. But the words shifted the focus off her anxiety. She concentrated on what he had to say.

"What happened?"

He didn't turn, but she saw his shoulder flinch.

"Did you know I used to be real fat?" A harsh chuckle came out. "I mean *really* fat. I was picked on every day. Other than school, I never left the house. I was afraid of running into someone from school, afraid to hear their words. I know it sounds stupid now, but at the time, it was really awful."

He leaned back against the wall, avoiding her gaze.

"It doesn't sound stupid," she uttered quietly. "Kids are cruel. Too cruel."

His chin jerked slightly. The scuff of his laceless sneaker in the dirt sounded unnaturally loud.

"When my parents planned the cruise, my first thought was of all the food that would be served. Then, the guilt was always quick to follow. I never consciously planned to jump. I mean, I wasn't planning out my great farewell." He paused. "I was standing at that railing, and the ocean was just hypnotic—it beckoned."

Jill didn't speak. She sat, gripped by his tale.

"The moment I let go of that rail, my first thought was, *Oh shit*. But it was too late. I knew I'd made a huge mistake—but it was just too damn late."

This time, she drew her feet up under her and hoisted upright. He eyed her warily, so she gave him his space, but she wanted to be more than a blob on the floor for him.

"Anyway," he continued. "Not many people have the opportunity to survive their mistakes. My hell is in sitting here for years imagining what my parents went through—the pain that I caused them. They loved me so much. Probably fed me too much, but that was just my mother's way. And now, how could I go back there and traumatize them all over? They've put me to rest. Hell, I don't even know if they're alive."

He shook his head in frustration. "I live with my guilt. I grew up—I matured down here. About the only reason I might want to go back is to find those bullies just so I could say, *Really? Look at you now. Are you all that?* But no. I'm content in the Underworld. Hatred hasn't made its way down here."

Jill stepped forward to touch his arm. The muscle jerked under her stroke.

"Don't," he said. "Don't pity me. That's as bad as telling me I'm fat."

Studying him from head to toe, she could barely imagine the awkward boy he described. Daniel was at least six feet tall. He was thin but had a solid frame. He had been climbing around these tunnels for a long time, and his efforts showed in his build.

"I don't pity you," she whispered. "I envy you. You've made peace with yourself. You are comfortable with yourself. You have no need to worry about what the world perceives you as. And I—"

"You what?" Daniel turned to face her.

"I—" Oh God, her face was on fire. "I find that hot."

"Hot?"

Jill did a fast calculation. Was the word *hot* around when he was up top?

"Umm," *Dammit, Wexler, you're embarrassing yourself.* "Attractive."

Daniel's lips hiked up into a damn fine grin. "I know what hot means. It's definitely not something I've been called before."

Jill bit her lip. "Well, people are stupid."

He laughed. "That they are." He stepped up to her and cupped both her shoulders in his hands. The touch sent pleasant currents through her skin.

"And you must be crazy, Jill Wexler," he said, his face close enough that she could feel his soft breath. There was a faint hint of mint in it.

"I'm not crazy," she protested softly.

"I don't know a lot about women," his voice was husky. "But I know what I like. And I like you."

And just like that, his lips were on hers. The kiss was curious, his mouth testing out the feel of hers. The patient exploration heightened her senses as she wrapped her hands over his shoulders for balance. Instinct soon took over, and he knew exactly what he was doing. She never wanted it to stop. She clung to him, needing more of this—more of him.

Slowly, he withdrew, but his mouth was still so frustratingly close. She finally opened her eyes to stare into deep brown waves as tumultuous as anything the ocean could produce.

"Sorry—I—I never did that," he whispered, the words tickling her lips.

"You sure couldn't tell," she murmured back.

She felt him smile, and then he pulled her into a tight hug.

"Well, if you go back up to the surface, I'm going to have something to remember for a long time."

Jill drew back.

"I don't want to go up there," she swore. "I don't want to die in that little coffin that Col and Stel are so excited about. I mean, seriously, you've seen it. Can you tell me it looks safe? That it will make it? No one must think so, or they would have tried it already."

Daniel swiped his hair back from his face and blew out an extended breath.

"What do I know? You tell me your brother is some kind of engineer—that he's been around the water and boats his whole life. I've been on one ship. It didn't go so well."

For such a desolate statement, Jill had to stifle a giggle. Daniel caught her expression and chuckled. "Yeah, so see?"

"It's not just a matter of me being afraid," she said.

He touched her cheek, his palm warm and inviting. She leaned into it.

"I don't want to leave *you*," she added.

Daniel's smile was sad. "Aww, hell, Jill. There are a million guys you can have up there. You didn't have much to pick from here."

Jill swallowed down a clog of emotion.

"Out of a million guys, I would pick you."

His eyes dropped closed, and fine lines of pain formed at their corners.

"You've got your whole life ahead of you," he said. "You owe it to yourself to try and get back to the surface."

"I get it. You don't want me."

"Jill—" He took her face in both palms and drew her mouth up for another kiss. "I want you more than you'll ever know. It's gonna sound really corny, but you've brought sun to my world."

"A little corny," she grinned, "but I like it."

He reached for her hand. "We better get back. Your family will be looking for you."

Jill linked her fingers through his. "Stay with me."

"For as long as I can," he vowed.

CHAPTER 18

Stella was hunched over her desk, writing busily in her journal. Jill's soft snores resonated from the dark. It was such a mundane sound, a din she could hear back in her IKEA-themed room or Jill's white wicker bedroom.

Restless, Stella stood and walked over to the window, but the Underworld was asleep. Even the staple light in Frederic's peak house was doused.

Mindlessly scratching at an itchy patch on her arm, Stella continued her surveillance. The itch intensified until she was raking at it with her short nails. Light from a nearby torch reached into the bungalow. She raised her wrist to it and found black scales wrapping around the limb. They spread like melting tar between her fingers and down her forearm.

Stella screamed.

"Hey," Jill shook her. "It's just a nightmare."

Stella sat up on her blanket, her chest heaving with fear. She crooked her arm and inspected it but found no traces of the blotchy growth.

"You okay?" Jill prompted.

Stella took in a deep breath and tried to steady herself.

"Yeah. Just a nightmare, as you said."

Jill sat down beside her, their shoulders rubbing together.

"Col and Dad should be back now," she remarked, staring at her feet.

"Yeah," Stella agreed.

That had to be the trigger for the nightmare. Worrying about Colin going back into that cave. Worrying about whether his father would be able to make it through.

Stella rushed to her feet to look out their windows at the dwelling next door. She saw a shadow cross past the door.

"I think they're back. Let's go over there."

Joining her at the window, Jill asked, "Should we wait for the bell?"

Stella snorted. "I think they're used to my nocturnal activities by now."

As if on cue, they saw Frederic's tall frame climb down the hill and approach the dangling bell. He tugged the rope, and the haunting clang filled the cavern.

"Come on," Stella beckoned.

Outside, Frederic stared into the distance at them. His gaze lingered for a moment, then he dipped his head and started back up the path to his perch.

Jogging over to the inverted hull, Stella and Jill ducked inside, the musty scent amplified in the tight quarters.

As they entered, Colin looked up, his eyes

locking on Stella. Her anxiety ebbed. He was here. He was safe. He took a step towards her.

"I'm glad you're both here," Donald crowded forward.

He looked nothing like the composed, trendy man she had known for the past four years. Graying hair, still wet from their foray into the submarine cave, was plastered to his forehead and temples. He wore a dry white t-shirt, but it stuck to damp skin. There was a bleak look in his crystalline eyes. It was not the look of imminent salvation. Deep despair had taken root in this man.

"Did you learn anything more about the sub?" Stella asked. "Do you think it's possible?"

She had given up hope for herself, but if this beloved family could escape this torment, she would forever be happy for them. A glance at Colin brought pain to her heart. She fisted her hand and clutched it against her chest.

Col nodded. "It's a little rough in spots, but it appears intact. We've lowered it into the water and tied it to the shore with rope around the boulders. The hull held up. No leaks. The cabin is clear."

"There are stabilizers rigged to the outside and some controlled from inside," Don added. "Once we untie it from its moorings, it will drop like dead weight in that pool. It will need the lines manually cut to release two of the weights so that it can start its ascent, and it will need a gentle nudge out through the cave and into the open ocean."

Stella's eyes widened. Someone was going to have to cut the lines! If the three Wexlers could fit into the submarine, that left her as the one to cut the lines and push the sub out of the cave. Could she do it?

"Don't worry," Don read her fear, and his expression relaxed. "That will be my task."

Everyone turned to gawk at him.

"Dad, what are you talking about?"

Running a hand through his damp hair the elder Wexler looked at his son. Normally there was tension when the two men exchanged glances—now Don looked tolerant. Tired. Patient.

"I'm not going back up there," he announced in quiet resolve. He held his hand up to halt Colin's protest. "My wife is down here. My health has turned to crap. I won't lie and say I haven't been affected by this environment. I'm not a hundred percent, and it's going to take a hundred percent health to survive this ascent. It's going to take youth." His sharp eyes swept the trio. "You three can make it. It will be a real tight fit for you in that small cabin, but less so than if I was one of the passengers."

"But, Daddy—" Jill protested.

"Easy, Princess. I'll be fine down here. Heck, I might outlast all of you based on the longevity of these people."

Jill shook her head, frustrated.

"I want the three of you to make it," he continued. And I think it will be possible if you play it smart." With that last word, he looked at Colin.

Stella fumed slightly. Colin was the smartest man she knew, but his father denied him credit even in this darkest hour.

"No," Jill injected.

This time, she commanded the attention in the tight chamber.

"I'm not going."

Don massaged the bridge of his nose. His eyes were red when he looked up.

"Seriously, Jilly, it will be okay. I think it's worth the risk—"

"It's not about the risk," she interrupted. "I just would prefer to stay here. You go with Stella and Colin."

"What the hell?" Don seemed startled. "Why would you want to stay in this godforsaken pit? You have your whole life ahead of you."

Stella couldn't stop herself. She whispered the word, *Daniel*, but there was no such thing as a whisper in this tight compartment.

Don eyed her until Stella felt uncomfortable.

"Daniel?" he spat. "The loner?" He looked at his daughter now.

Jill squelched under the scrutiny but gathered her strength and raised her head. "It's not just about Daniel. I think Stella and Col should go. If it's just the two of them, there will be enough room. Enough oxygen—"

"There's no gauging the oxygen," Don argued. Once the hatch is secured, you'll have whatever oxygen already exists in the cabin. In theory, that should be enough to make it to the surface. You also have to worry about controlling the ascent—be it two people or three."

Seeing her blank expression, he continued,

"Think about it this way. The submersible should rise at the same rate that an air bubble would rise from the depths." He shook his head. "It's all going to hinge on the timing of the release of the weights."

"And hoping that water doesn't come gushing in some hole you didn't identify," Jill added, then slammed her hand over her mouth.

Stella shuddered. She felt Colin move in closer, his arm brushing against hers. The touch provided moral support.

"There's always that chance," Don agreed sedately. "And there is always a choice. You've apparently made yours. I have made mine. No one is forcing anyone to get in that submarine. Clearly no one from down here has chosen to use it. They must know better. So, maybe you're right, Jill. Maybe it is a terrible idea."

"Sure, there are obstacles. Maybe we'll freeze once we leave the hydrothermal vents," Colin contended. "I'm aware of the odds. I want to try. If I can make it up there, then maybe I can get help down to everyone here."

"Oh, son, I'm starting to grasp the futility of this. Even if you make it to the top…what then? You have no means of communication. You will bob in the water, adrift for who knows how long—what, hoping that someone sees you? You could be—"

Dead before anyone finds you.

Stella hugged herself. Beside her, Colin was frowning. He was determined. And if there was one person out of this group who had the conviction to pull this off, it was him.

"I won't let you go up alone," she vowed

softly. "I will go with you."

Colin reached for her hand. Don caught the gesture and focused on their linked fingers.

"I see," he marveled.

An awkward silence followed, but Colin would not let go. The contact bolstered her. She squeezed back.

"All right," Don said. "This is a very emotional topic, one that deserves additional consideration. Colin and I agree that the best time to attempt this will be during their New Year celebration. Hopefully they are preoccupied, maybe even a tad inebriated. They are less likely to try and stop our plans." He rubbed his temple with his fingertips. "That gives everyone a few days to seriously consider their decisions."

Colin nodded. The fierce grip on Stella's hand eased some.

"I agree. It also gives me a few more opportunities to go over the sub. To understand it better."

Don extended his hand to his son. Colin released his grip on Stella to return the shake. Their clasp lingered with significance. Then Don reached with his free arm and drew Jill into his fold. He released Colin's hand and hauled him into the embrace. He met Stella's gaze over Jill's head and said, "Get in here. You're one of us."

Stella moved into the huddle, tears burning in her eyes. She threw her arms around Colin and Jill and leaned forward, her head resting against Don's shoulder.

"This is my family," Don whispered

thickly. "All I want is for my family to be safe. Can you blame me for that?"

They all muttered, *no*.

"But, in this case, safety requires sacrifice. I have to sacrifice letting some of you go for the greater good. I accept whatever decision you make, but please accept that I am too tired to try. I just want to lie down. I promise you that I will be there to help when you make your move. And if some of you decide to stay," he hugged Jill tighter, "I will be here to support you. I have made mistakes. I am not going to win any *Father of the Year* awards. I had it in my mind what the perfect father should be, and maybe it made me push too hard. Col, I watched you in that submersible today and realized how talented you are. I am trusting in your strength and intelligence. All of you are my hope for the future."

There were sniffles and inarticulate murmurs of encouragement. But it was the feeling of solidarity—of family—that infused Stella with strength. No matter what, she would do everything in her power to protect this clan.

It was dinnertime. Collectively, they felt it best to act normally. They dared not fool themselves that Etienne wasn't aware of their plans. Very little happened in the Underworld that he wasn't aware of. But keeping up pretenses by engaging in the public meal was a good start.

Daniel, who normally shied away from the

community dinners, was seated beside Jill. She bent into him and laughed pleasantly at a shared joke.

"We have such a treat for the party," Margie's voice was unnaturally loud in Stella's ear. She winced but turned to acknowledge her with a bright smile.

"Oh?"

"Yes," Margie clapped her hands together, "It's—"

"Marge, it won't be a surprise if you blab about it now." Jordan leaned in to reprimand with a wide grin.

Margie clamped her lips tight but raised her eyebrows, her eyes twinkling at Stella. Stella couldn't help but giggle. It wasn't all bad down here. There were some fine people. Even Loren, whom she had first held some animosity towards, now chatted with Don Wexler. Stella strained to hear the conversation. It was about boating, of course. Loren regaled some of her and her boyfriend's trips before the accident. Her tone was bittersweet, but she had made peace with the old pain.

Stella felt Colin lean in beside her. He whispered against her ear, the soft wisp of breath stirring her hair.

"I have a surprise for you after this, too."

Her eyes widened. "A surprise?"

Eyes the color of a forest held a grin. An alluring, darker shade lurked in their core. Stella smiled in return. She wanted this dinner to be done. She just wanted to be in his arms.

"So, what did you all do this morning?" Etienne spoke up, the insinuation in his voice obvious to everyone but the Conovers.

Stella watched as Colin's alluring grin faded. In its place was a stony look of conviction. His head swung towards Etienne.

"Explored more caves. We sure could have used Frederic's maps."

Etienne didn't look pleased. Frederic spoke up, though.

"Yes, I have some sketches. I forgot to give those to you. But I don't think there's much you've missed."

Frederic's tone did not seem spiteful. As he set his spoon down, his glance swung from Etienne to Colin and back again.

"Just be careful," Etienne warned. "You've already had several accidents." He looked pointedly at Stella.

Heat rose to her cheeks.

"After all, Sarah can only do so much," he chuckled hollowly.

No one laughed.

Sarah kept her head down. Stella saw more gray hairs poking out of the brown floppy twist. The woman had barely spoken more than ten words in the past few weeks.

"Maybe there wouldn't be so many accidents if you were a little more forthcoming with information about this place," Colin volleyed.

Etienne's bony face tightened. He pushed his bowl back and rose. He was not a tall man, but with everyone seated, he had a moment to tower over them all.

Frederic once again sought to avert a confrontation. "My office is always open. If there's somewhere you need to go, just ask me about it."

Stella had to bite her tongue and avoid asking about the submersible. There was no need to draw their attention to the object.

Don stood now. He stared down the man across from him. "Thank you for dinner. The crab was divine."

Margie smiled proudly, but she struggled to maintain the gesture amidst the obvious tension. "No dessert?" she asked. "We have canned jelly from the Philippines."

Don placed his hand on her shoulder and gave her a congenial wink. "I'll pass tonight." He rubbed his stomach. "I'm saving up for the feast I hear you have planned for the party."

This time, Margie beamed. "Oh yes. You will need to run laps around the Underworld after I am done with you."

Don allowed himself a rare smile and then bowed his head and backed away from the table. Colin and Etienne were still locked in a glaring showdown. Stella tugged on his arm and whispered, "Let's get out of here."

Colin slid his gaze to her and nodded. Soon, the table dispersed, and Etienne took a step in pursuit. Stella caught the motion and reached for Colin's arm. He stopped, ready for an argument, but Sarah spoke softly in her husband's ear. Whatever she said worked and the man backed off towards their bungalow.

"Whew. I hope every dinner isn't going to be like that," Stella said as they walked away. "It won't make for a pleasant eternity down here."

Colin frowned. "Stel—"

"What?"

"Well, wait. Come with me. I told you I had a surprise."

Stella was curious as he took her hand. The sounds of the dinner participants scattering grew distant as Colin kept walking down the path. A torch lit up his face every few feet, but she could tell nothing from the stony expression. He caught her watching him and hiked up the corners of his lips.

"Don't get excited," he muttered as they followed the path back towards the waterfall.

Stella looked up at the cascade with trepidation. *Excited* wasn't the word that came to mind when she considered what lurked behind it.

Colin surprised her, however. Just a few steps ahead and out of the sight of the village sat a boulder with a thick yellow candle on it. It was lopsided, with trails of melted wax rolling down its side, some dribbling over the reservoir of the tin bowl it sat in. The flame flickered from the mist but stayed strong. There were two unopened cans of soda—Coca-Cola—but the logos were ones she didn't recognize.

"Col," she cried, running up to the boulder. "These are like contraband! Frederic said candles were only to be used in emergencies. He said they have a limited supply. And Coke! Where did you find that?"

Colin grinned, plucking open the old-fashioned pull tab. There was no fizzing sound, but Stella marveled at the rare treat nonetheless.

"Well, it turns out that the cooler they found

was indeed from the STARKISSED, but it was the cooler Dad and I used for live bait. Jill was a little ticked that she wasn't getting her Sprite."

Stella chuckled at the thought.

"Margie has been hoarding some special supplies for the New Year's party." He leaned back against the boulder and winked. "I convinced her to share a few of those items."

Stella crossed her arms. "And how did you do that? Your charm, no doubt."

"No one has ever accused me of being charming, that's for sure. But I did explain to her that it was for a good cause." He paused. "Romance."

Stella's eyebrow rose, and her lips tickled with the itch to smile.

"I told her that I wanted to give you a romantic dinner. If we were up above, I would walk you along the beach, take you somewhere nice, and woo you until you couldn't resist me."

The tickling jerked her mouth up at the corner. "Woo? And that's not charming?" she whispered.

"It was the truth, and it worked. She gave me these few items. But—" he looked at them futilely, "—it's not the real thing. I wish I could do those things with you, Stel. I haven't really wanted a relationship with anyone. I've been too busy, and the girls I met at college—I don't know—they all kind of seemed empty to me. It's easy to look pretty on the surface. But you—"

"I what?" she asked softly.

"Maybe it's because I've been around you so long. I *know* you. I have seen you with bizarre creams on your face when you slept over, and I thought you looked so damned cute. I've seen you try to play football at our July 4th cookouts. You're not that coordinated."

Stella snorted. "Everyone always said to me, *You're so tall. Why aren't you into sports*? I guess you know the answer to that."

"It always made me smile watching you. You never stopped trying. And I gotta tell you, I really had to stop myself from tackling you just so I could get my hands on you."

Stella felt a little lightheaded. It was a pleasant sensation. "Maybe you should have."

Colin sobered. His dark eyes flashed.

"I have seen you cry when watching the news. And I've seen you sit alone for hours on a bench by the beach, your notebook in hand."

She lived five blocks from the water, and she always snuck over to the boardwalk to plop herself down on a cement bench, jotting down notes for the school paper. The sound of the water, the laughs and cries from the beach, the seagulls—they faded as her mind was at work.

"When did you see that?" she asked, her voice raw.

"I used to jog along the boardwalk. You never noticed me. You were so focused."

Stella suddenly wished she hadn't been so absorbed and had taken a moment to look up.

"I missed many opportunities to tell you how I felt," Colin declared in a husky tone. "Long before this place." He waved his hand. "I don't want to miss opportunities anymore."

He stood and approached her.

Stella was paralyzed, locked by the frank

look in his eyes and the admissions that left her breathless.

Standing before her, he didn't move. He just looked at her for what seemed like an eternity until finally, he lifted his hand and his finger hooked under her chin.

"I want to kiss you."

Her vocal cords froze. Only the flutter of her eyelashes served as an answer.

Colin leaned in, and tears welled behind her eyes when she felt his lips so tender against hers. He pulled back, but his hand slipped down to the crook between her shoulder and neck. His finger caressed the bare skin there.

"Part of me wants you to stay here. I know it's not the best place, but you will live. If we go up in that submersible and something happens to you—"

Stella followed his eyes as they dipped to her throat and back up to meet hers.

"But the part of me that wanted to tackle that girl playing football—that wanted to tap that girl on the shoulder who was so busy writing—the part of me that is falling in love with you—" he hesitated, "that guy wants you to be there with him inside that sub. To that guy, you are the greatest inspiration. If we make it, he can't think of anyone that he'd rather kiss in victory."

Stella swallowed down the thick clump of emotion. She blinked back the moisture and cleared her throat.

"I think I'm falling in love with that guy," she whispered.

Colin's fingers drifted under her hair and

behind her neck. He pulled her close for a soft kiss.

"Stel, the chances are so slim. We may not even make it out of the cave." He shook his head and added, "I talked to Dad and Jill again. They are adamant about staying. In some ways, I'm relieved. At least I know they'll be safe, and if somehow I make it up there—I'll get help. I will find them again." His hand dropped. "And I should feel that way about you too, but I'm being greedy. I want you with me."

This time, he stepped away altogether. "Tell me not to be so damned selfish."

"Tell *me* not to be so damned selfish," she countered.

Colin looked up, quizzical.

"Basically, we've admitted to being attracted to each other for years, and now finally—finally I am touching you. I am kissing you. I am talking to you the way I always wanted. Tell me how I'm supposed to just let you go—never knowing if you made it to the surface. No." She jabbed her fist against her thigh. "No. I don't want that. I want to be with you."

There was some relief on his face, but he still looked conflicted. He let loose a weary laugh. "You have the pretty face like those college girls, but it doesn't end there. You back it up with one hell of a punch, Stel."

Stella laughed. "And you say you're not charming."

The mood lightened and Colin reached for the other soda, popping it open and handing it to her. With them both holding a can, he raised his and asked, "What shall we toast to?"

Stella considered for a moment.

"To our first glimpse of the sky."

Colin reached for her hand and squeezed it. He tipped back the Coke and took a swig. The squelchy look on his face made her giggle. After a second, he tilted his head to the side. "Not that bad," he remarked and then added, "And I'll drink to that."

As they enjoyed the soda and discussed their covert plan for New Year's night, Colin held up a finger.

"Wait. I have one more surprise."

Curious, Stella set her can down on the boulder and clasped her hands together.

"I can't even imagine. Peanut butter cups, I hope."

"No, not that good." He grinned. He disappeared behind the boulder and reappeared with his hand behind his back.

"Here." He pulled it out and extended a folded paper to her.

It was yellowed and torn, but there was evidence of black text on it. Sensing its age and fragility, she took it carefully and gingerly flipped it over.

Much of the text was blurred, but the header was remarkably intact.

"Boston Evening Globe," she read, tracing her finger over the *1-cent - Evening Edition* note in the top corner. "Oh my God, it is from 1917. How is that possible?"

"Margie said they found it down here a long time ago. It was inside a foot locker, and they have since wrapped it in plastic. She wants it back, but she let me have it for tonight."

Stella gaped at the headline.

LUSITANIA SUNK.

One of her many fascinations was with sunken ships—an irony given her current plight. She thought about it, and even Colin had to have known that she was a Titanic buff. Just a few weeks ago, there was an auction for a handwritten letter from someone aboard the Titanic. She told her mother she wished she had a spare hundred thousand dollars because she wanted to bid on it. Her mother shook her head and laughed.

"Not known how many passengers saved…" she continued to read. She glanced up. "Could you imagine if some of them ended up down here?"

"Yes," Colin nodded. "After all we've seen, I sure could imagine that."

Stella's mouth still hung open in awe.

"Col, this—this- "

"You like?" He winked.

She took great care to set the paper down gently on the boulder. As soon as it was at rest, she lunged at Colin and wrapped her arms around his neck.

"I like," she vowed. "I like."

CHAPTER 19

New Year's Day.

The café was buzzing as everyone gathered for lunch. That energy stemmed from mixed motives, however. Colin and Stella's anxiety mounted with every passing minute. Their plan was to attempt their escape tonight after the festivities.

Donald Wexler seemed tense, undoubtedly preparing for his part in the getaway. Jill chatted with Daniel, but both their heads were ducked, precluding anyone from hearing their conversation. Loren sat at the end of the table with her legs crossed as she scooped a spoonful of small, spongy creatures into her mouth.

Stella's stomach rolled. Whether it was from the cuisine or nerves, she wasn't very hungry. Nonetheless, she, too, spooned in a mouthful of crustaceans. She would need her strength. If they made it to the surface, there was no telling how long or *if* they would be spotted. Their supplies would be limited. She had to eat now. Beside her, Colin seemed to have the same thoughts as he devoured what was left on his plate. His fingers touched her thigh below the table—just a physical contact to say, *I'm here with you.*

"All right, everyone." Margie rose, her ceramic teacup in her hand. "A little early toast, and then I need you all to retire until Jordan and I complete the final preparations. Today we will have a rarely heard extra bell. When you hear the bell next, it will signify the start of the celebration." She beamed.

"For now, though," she raised the cup, "I leave you with a simple Happy New Year message. Another year in the Underworld has come and gone, and though we have lost someone," she dipped her head to acknowledge Don, "we have all kept our health. We continue to thrive—"

Thrive?

"—and we have each other to thank for that." Margie turned towards Etienne on the final comment.

The gaunt, stony face cracked into a rare smile as he lifted his copper cup.

"And to our new residents," she added with tempered animation, "we welcome you and look forward to celebrating many more New Year's with you."

Jill raised her glass hesitantly. Stella followed to keep up pretenses, as did Colin. Don clasped his fingers around his mug, staring at it until everyone grew uncomfortable. Finally, with great exaggeration, he hoisted it into the air and boomed, "Hear, hear!"

Colin dropped his head, avoiding eye contact with everyone. He thanked Margie for her hard work and then excused himself.

Stella uttered a hasty, "I'll see you after the bell." And followed him.

The café cleared out quickly, with everyone retiring to their dwellings.

Jill and her father trailed a few steps behind Colin and Stella. They all returned to the boathouse.

"Well—" Don forced a grin, "—that was awkward. "I just may need one of the cocktails they claim they'll have at this party."

Jill looked at him anxiously.

"Don't worry, Princess. Only one. I know what I have to do tonight."

"Daniel said he will help you," she murmured, keeping her voice low in case there were unwanted ears outside.

Don nodded approvingly. "I got a chance to talk to him today. Seems pretty knowledgeable, and he told me himself that he would help."

Jill smiled, relieved.

"Are you two ready?" His voice was level, his blue eyes intent.

Colin nodded. "Stel and I have been back there several times. We think it's sound, and we're comfortable with the interior weight release. Daniel came with us once, and he's going to help you navigate the submersible out into the water and cut the weights."

Colin walked over to his bedding area and drew two wood-sheathed blades from beneath his blanket.

"We've tried sharpening these as best we could with rocks and sand. We did a test by cutting a thick coil of rope and it went well. Of course, cutting sodden rope underwater under duress is a whole different story."

Don waved that off. "We'll get it. I promise."

The two male Wexlers considered each other for a long time. Don was the first to crack a smile. It burgeoned into a proud beam, and Stella could tell it inspired Col.

"So," Col summarized, "our biggest concern is the rate of ascent. The water resistance alone should slow us down some. It will be in the timing of releasing the second set of weights. There's a handheld radio inside the sub, but of course, no power, so it's useless. We should have enough oxygen to make it to the surface, and if we do make it to the surface, we'll have to throw the hatch open and pray it's not raining."

So many ifs. So many variables. Stella stared down at her fingers. They trembled until Colin folded his hand over hers.

"You don't have to do this," he asserted. "Stel, please, if you're scared, please stay here with my family."

She chewed on her bottom lip but lifted her head high.

"You're going to need help. Even if it's just a fist pump and an *atta boy*."

Colin looked conflicted, but his hand squeezed hers.

Outside, the bell tolled. Two rings. As if the bell was not enough, Margie's boisterous voice could be heard, "Come out, come out!"

Colin searched Stella's eyes. There was so much conveyed in his meaningful gaze. She smiled in return, feeling confident for the first time. This was it. No matter what happened, she wanted to try. She didn't want to be a victim. She wanted to control her fate. She clutched his hand, and her smile grew. Reading her face, he relaxed and managed a swift grin. His glance extended to take in his sister and then his father. Wordlessly, they reached for each other, folding into a group hug.

"This is going to be some New Year's party," Don murmured inside the pack.

A small trickle of laughter sounded.

Jill slipped her arm tight around Stella's waist. "You be safe, Gullaksen. Do you hear me? You take care of my brother, and you both make it. *You make it.*"

Stella released Colin's hand to squeeze her friend tight. It was agreed that Jill and Loren would stay behind later to distract the others from spotting the departure.

"Come on, everyone!" Margie yelled again with a bit of desperation in her summons.

"We better go," Stella murmured. "We have a party to attend."

With one final collusive smile, they all turned to leave the hull. Outside, Stella gasped at the sight. The café was alight with an array of candles. Candles were on the tables along with various centerpieces, such as large ceramic bowls, one filled with fake plastic flowers. The bits of shiny metal hanging from the artificial tree sparkled with the reflection of the flames. More handmade bows littered the tables, and as she got closer, Stella saw bottles of liquor and cans of soda. Every indulgence that was monitored so closely was now free for consumption.

Daniel appeared at Jill's side and looped an arm around her waist. Loren stood at the cabinets in the café, lining up glasses of odd shapes and sizes.

Frederic hiked down the trail, carrying something Stella couldn't identify. As he approached, she recognized a ukulele. It only had two strings, but it looked festive. Even the man himself was in full uniform. The gold pendants on his navy jacket were polished until they shined.

"Happy New Year!" he called out congenially.

Jordan, looking dapper in a stained white long-sleeved shirt and frayed khaki pants, clapped the man on his back.

"Happy New Year, Fred."

Frederic winced at the nickname, but his smile swiftly returned.

All heads turned as Etienne and Sarah made their way down the path, arm in arm. Sarah had replaced her staple uniform with a pale blue dress that fell nearly to her ankles. She still wore her flat nurse's shoes, but everyone focused on her hair, which was down, long, and waving over her shoulders. She still looked painfully thin, but her smile was the best enhancement to her appearance.

Etienne looked formal in his dark blue pea coat. He raised a pipe in salute and called out, "Happy New Year."

Stella glanced down at the white dress she had thrown over her shorts and tank top. It was her attempt to be ceremonious yet maintain an escape outfit.

"Come, come," Margie waved her arms, urging them towards the confluence of lopsided tables in the café.

She looked silly but festive in her pink feathered boa and floppy red beret. She still wore her capri pants and sported a tattered red sweater with a few sizeable holes in it.

"Loren is our bartender tonight. Everyone grab a drink as I get the surprise ready."

Stella grabbed a 7-Up, trying to keep her mind as sharp as possible. Don reached for what appeared to be a can of beer. There was a tall black bottle that Jordan seized, warning everyone to stand back as he popped the cork. Even prepared, the loud bang startled her.

All of a sudden, music filled the tiny glade. Stella swung her head to see Margie's tarnished teeth flashing as she swept her hands toward a prehistoric contraption.

"A wind-up gramophone!" She clapped in delight. "I've been hiding this gem for quite some time. Jordan and I found it shortly after last year's party. And this—" She cocked her head, humming to the music, "—is the Beatles for those of you too young to know."

The record was severely warped and the fat needle bobbed unevenly atop it. Still, the lyrics were identifiable.

It's been a hard day's night…

Amen to that, she thought.

Jordan crossed over and grabbed his wife's hand, drawing her outside the café's ring to a flat spot where they could dance. The moves were comical and certainly not in sync with the music, but they made Stella laugh. Frederic rushed forward and changed the record when it was done. There appeared to be a pile consisting of four or five pieces of vinyl. The selection would be minimal, but it certainly energized the atmosphere.

At the next upbeat song, Jill grabbed Daniel's hands and urged him to dance. He shook his head back and forth, quite adamant in his denial. She dropped his hands but danced in a circle around him until he, too, was smiling.

Frederic picked up his ukulele and attempted to play along with what must have been Elvis Presley or one of those rock and roll guys. With two strings, it sounded more like a pogo stick, but everyone laughed and clapped.

Loren put on the next record, and there was a ballad of sorts. The warped record made the crooning voice sound out of tune, but it didn't stop Jordan from circling his arms around his wife as they slid into an awkward waltz.

Etienne took Sarah's hand and slowly drifted back and forth to the music. Their arms were stiff, their bodies barely touching, but they were smiling. Stella supposed that was the most romance Sarah would ever get from that man.

To her surprise, Stella felt Colin tap her on the shoulder.

"May I have this dance?" he grinned in that sexy way of his.

Stella blushed and nodded. She felt his arm slip around her back, and his other hand guide hers up to his shoulder. The tune didn't matter. They rolled lazily to it until she relaxed and rested her head against his collarbone, feeling his body sway as she matched the rhythm. Stella opened her eyes to see that Jill had finally convinced Daniel to give it a try. He held her, but his body shifted stiffly until Jill finally coaxed a rhythmic motion out of him.

Loren accepted Frederic's invitation as Don stood on the sidelines, sipping his beer. Stella continued to rest against Colin's shoulder, feeling the pulse at the bottom of his throat against her forehead. She burrowed closer, never wanting to let go. This might be their first and last dance together.

The music ended all too quickly but was replenished with another ballad. Stella looked up into Colin's eyes.

"Give me a moment, but please don't go far. I want to do that again."

Colin looked curious as she backed away, and then he smiled when he saw her intentions. Stella walked up to Colin's father and said, "Mr. Wexler, may I have this dance?"

Don looked startled, and then a slow smile crept over his lips.

"I didn't dress up for the party," he explained, glancing down at his white t-shirt and shorts.

"It's an informal affair," she whispered in conspiracy.

Don took her hand and held it high while maintaining a light touch on her hip. They danced awkwardly to the warped music, but it was worth it to see a smile on Don's face. It was worth it to catch the approving grin on Colin's as they drifted by him.

At the end of the song, Col appeared. "Can I have her back?" he asked.

Don nodded, and looked at Stella. "Thank you," he said earnestly. He moved his gaze to his son. "You take care of her. She's special."

"I know she is," Col agreed. And then his arms were around her even though the music had stopped.

All things considered, it turned out to be an enjoyable evening. If nothing else, it was the perfect distraction for the nerves and adrenaline slowly creeping in.

"Okay, everyone." Margie waved her arms to corral her flock. "Loren has poured us all glasses of champagne. Please grab one and take it over to the bell. Frederic will be ringing in the New Year!"

They filed past the café cabinet, each picking up a glass as they marched down the path to the brass bell hanging from the soaring peak. Forming a semicircle around it, they watched as Frederic made a theatrical motion to check his watch. He had no such adornment on his wrist. With a big grin, he held up five fingers and shouted, "Five!" as one finger dropped. "Four." Another finger dropped.

The group joined in, shouting, *"Three. Two. One."*

With a wiggle of his golden eyebrows, Frederic grabbed the rope and yanked. The clang sounded like the song of an ancient ship. At that evocative peal, a cheer rang out. Margie screeched and hugged Jordan. She then spun around and squeezed Frederic in a bear hug. After that, she formed a queue and embraced everyone.

Jill stepped up to her father and hugged him and then spun around to embrace Daniel. Colin raised his eyebrow at Stella. She shrugged and laughed and then looped her arms around his neck.

"Happy New Year," he whispered into her ear.

He held her tight, and she clung to him, suddenly trembling with nerves. The time was imminent.

Etienne and Sarah moved down the line, congratulating everyone on the occasion. When they reached Colin and Stella, Etienne lingered. He took Colin's hand and shook it emphatically.

"Perhaps this year, you will have more faith in us."

"Perhaps." Colin held his grip and then added, "And perhaps you'll have a little more faith in *us*."

Etienne bowed his head and dropped his hand. "Perhaps," he murmured as he backed away and announced that he and Sarah were retiring for the night.

Don immediately made a similar announcement after saluting everyone.

Margie then leaned in, her cheeks flushed from celebration. "Well, for the rest of us, the party is just getting started. Let's head back to the café. We've got a few bottles to finish."

Jordan latched his hands onto her waist and hollered, "Conga line!"

He started humming a drum beat, and Frederic, also looking a bit toasty, latched onto his hip with one hand, the other swinging in the air to beckon more followers.

Jill stepped up to Colin and kissed him lightly on the cheek, whispering in his ear. She then looked at Stella with intense blue eyes that seemed more vibrant with the pool of tears around them. She touched Stella's arm and mouthed the words, *be safe.*

Wiping the tears away, she called out in great theatrical style, "I'm in!" and timidly grabbed Frederic's waist as she danced off after them.

Loren flashed a look at Stella and Colin and offered a perfunctory nod. Stella wanted to hug this sullen young woman. Without her, they would never have had this opportunity.

Daniel gave them a quick head bob and made as if he was following the procession to the café. It was decided earlier that Colin and Stella would sneak away first and that Don and Daniel would join them later after they confirmed that their departure was unnoticed.

Colin reached for her hand. "Are you ready?"

Stella hesitated. "There's something I want to take with me. Can I go grab it?"

A dark eyebrow rose, but he nodded and added in a soft whisper, "Hurry."

Stella jogged into her bungalow and crouched down to retrieve her journal. Inside it was the folded newspaper Colin had given her. She read the entire thing last night and desperately wanted to keep it, but Margie stated it belonged here. She respected that.

With little time for deliberation, Stella yanked it out and placed it on the desk. She wrapped the notebook in two plastic bags she had found and tucked it under her dress inside the waist of her shorts. It would suffer some water damage, but she hoped it retained enough of the print.

With a hasty glance around the gloomy dwelling she had called home for a month, Stella rushed outside to join Colin.

The Beatles distorted crooning mingled with laughter. Jill glanced over from her spot at the café. At seeing Stella, Jill quickly grabbed Frederic's arm to spin him in a dance move that would prevent him from spotting the stealthy exit.

Stella felt a hard pang of sadness at leaving her friend behind. She recited the mantra, *we will be back to save you*. That was the only thought that kept her going.

Colin was alert, guiding them off the trail whenever possible so that the shadows could mask their getaway. The only way out of the Underworld passed before Etienne and Sarah's shack. It appeared dark and dormant inside, but still, Colin and Stella were vigilant as they progressed, pausing afterward to see if anyone had stirred. The driftwood home remained lifeless.

"Let's hope Dad and Daniel get by them," he whispered.

Once they were out of Etienne's range, they hastened their pace, jogging until they reached the outskirts of the cavern. There, they grabbed two torches and started the long trek through the tunnels to reach the hidden pool. As they advanced, all traces of ambient light were left behind. Only the torches cast quivering shadows on the curved walls—reflecting fanciful caricatures of themselves.

"Col, call me paranoid, but I have this feeling that we're being watched."

"You're paranoid," he quipped with a hasty grin thrown over his shoulder.

She could tell the smirk was forced. He was as edgy as her.

"We're almost there," he assured.

Stella glanced behind her. People had called her tall in the past, but never as tall as the long shadow she cast. Just beyond the tip of that shadow, she sensed motion.

"Daniel?" she called. "Mr. Wexler?"

Colin stopped, and she collided with him.

"I don't see them back there. Let's keep going," she urged, pushing against his back.

A scuff sounded behind Stella. They both whirled, their torches casting dueling circumferences of light over an empty cavern.

"It must be Dad or Daniel," Colin remarked quietly. "The acoustics carry far."

Stella's palms perspired.

"The pool is just ahead," Colin encouraged.

She pressed forward, eager to reach it, but another scrape jerked her into an about-face. At the torchlight's furthest scope, a figure hunched, its profile barely visible. The flames reached the luminous green eyes, and she shrieked.

"Run!" Colin urged.

They sprinted, slipping on loose rocks but

catching their balance just as they reached the pool's ledge.

Colin dropped his torch on the ground and yelled, "Dive!"

Stella didn't hesitate. She tossed the torch to the side and, in full stride, dove into the water, aiming for the wide hole that would usher her into the submersible cave. Black water surrounded her, and the obscurity catapulted her into full panic mode. She kicked her legs and thrust forward into the dark until a soft glow beckoned. As she surfaced with a gasp, she saw several torches—a few diminished to just smoldering sticks. Just ahead, the sphere-shaped submersible bobbed in the water, its top hatch open like the spout of a tea kettle.

Colin's hair broke the surface beside her. He whipped his head, shaking water out of his eyes. They both tread water momentarily, staring back at the black passage they had just passed through. Nothing emerged.

"Come on," he urged hoarsely, "let's prep the sub."

CHAPTER 20

Colin dropped two plastic containers into the cockpit. One contained fresh water, and the other was a jar filled with canned corn from last night's dinner. And a few cans of beans.

"It's going to be dark, Stel," he warned. "Pitch black. Nothing to orient ourselves."

"Yeah, I get it."

He rubbed her arm. "I'm just warning you. It could be more than either of us can handle in such a tight space—that, combined with the limited oxygen—"

"Just say it. Basically, the worst possible environment you can imagine?"

"Not the *worst*," he hedged. "You are going to be sitting on my lap."

Stella smiled and tucked her head. She had gotten a glimpse of the small cockpit. It had a single seat for a single pilot, but where there was a will, there was a way.

"I'm worried about them," she stared at the black water. "What if that thing got them?"

"I'm worried too. But it didn't actually attack us. We had the torches."

"So much for Etienne's theory that they stay beyond the waterfall."

"I don't buy a thing Etienne says," Colin stated. "For all I know, they're his pets and he sent that creature to try and stop us."

Stella hugged her arms at the thought.

The water stirred with a soft splash.

Colin neared the ledge, his stance wavering between aid or attack. Daniel's head popped up, his longish hair covering his eyes. He used his hand to comb it back and looked up at them with a discreet smile.

"He's right behind me," he assured, spitting some water out of his mouth.

As he swam to the ledge, Don Wexler surfaced, coughing slightly.

"Damn," he barked. "This place is a maze."

Hoisting out of the water, he reached over and clapped Daniel on his back.

"You're a pro. You made that nearly seem easy."

Daniel bowed his head.

"I'm so glad you're both alright," Stella gushed, making room on the ledge for them. "Did you guys see it? The Chimaera?"

Don looked perplexed. "One of those things was here? The creatures you told me about?"

"It was in the cave on the other side," Colin stated. "It was in the shadows. It seemed like it didn't like the flames, but we didn't stick around to find out."

"I think I saw it," Daniel acknowledged. "You left your torches on the ground, and we had ours—it wasn't going to mess with us. And now we have four torches waiting for us on the other side when we go back, so we should be okay."

"You've seen them before?" Stella asked, fascinated.

Daniel nodded. "There isn't much I haven't seen in these caves."

The graveyard?

She stopped herself from asking the question in front of Colin's dad.

From Daniel's level gaze, she gathered that he was well aware of it.

"They've never attacked you?"

"They tried," he shrugged. "You just always need to carry a torch when you leave the Underworld."

"Etienne told me they stayed behind the waterfall. Was that a lie?"

Daniel helped Colin test the weight ropes. "Not necessarily," he uttered. That is where they primarily live because that is closest to their food source—the caves by the thermal vents. But every now and then, they venture out—mostly out of curiosity or searching other pools for new sources of cuisine."

"So they fish in the very same caves that Frederic and Etienne do?" Don asked. "Without incident?"

"None that I know of."

Don shook his head in marvel, then turned his attention to his son as Col began to recite the plan.

"How far do we have to push the sub?" Don questioned.

Colin deferred to Daniel, who hiked up a shoulder. "About six feet or so. Once we cut the weights, the ocean will pull it out on its own."

"Are you sure?" Colin frowned. "I mean, that downwell current that dragged us down here—it's strong enough to haul anything in. I'm worried we're going to float out of this cave only to be sucked back into the grotto we first came in at."

Daniel hefted his eyebrows, but only one was visible under the long bangs. "It's a possibility, but we believe that downwell, as you call it, is very narrow. Like a tight siphon."

"So, the odds of us ending up in that siphon from the surface were extremely rare?" Don asked.

"Yep," Daniel hiked up the corner of his lip. "You're looking at one lucky group here."

They laughed—as much as they could under the circumstances.

Don stepped up to his son and reached for his shoulder. "You have no tools, no GPS, no sextant, nothing to chart where you are when you make it up there."

Stella didn't like that they had no tools, but she did like that Don worded it *when* you make it up there rather than *if*.

"Remember that Orion's belt rises due east and sets due west from every latitude. You can kind of guess your latitude by the height of the North Star on the horizon, but—"

Colin gripped his father's arm. "We will find you again. If we make it up there, I swear we will find you again."

Don's eyes were sad. They all knew the odds of ever finding the downwell current again were one in a million.

"I believe you will," Don uttered huskily. "Your Mom will guide you."

Colin dropped his head to avert his eyes. The two Wexlers embraced, Don patting his son across the back.

"I'm not comfortable with the risks, son. Neither of you have to do this. You're safe here—mostly. You're alive." He reached up and cupped Colin's face. "Alive," he repeated.

"I have to go, Dad," he pleaded. "I have to *try*."

The elder Wexler gripped his son tight. "I'm sorry, Col. You and I didn't always see eye to eye. I want you to know that I'm proud of you. I'm proud of you for pursuing what you clearly excel at."

Stella could tell by Colin's profile that the apology hit its mark. Pain and relief took turns gripping his jaw muscles. Emotion took care of the rest.

"Take care of Jill," Colin uttered huskily.

"I will. I've been going through a tough time, but you've given me some clarity back."

"Dad, the weights, are you sure?"

"I'm not that old. And look at this badass." He held up an eight-inch knife with a blade that wasn't as sharp as Colin might have hoped.

Daniel pulled his knife from his belt. It looked in slightly better shape.

"We'll get it done," he assured.

"And you," Colin turned to her, his voice softening. "This is it, babe. You don't have to do this. Like Dad said, you're alive."

What type of life would it be, never knowing if you made it to the surface?

"I'm going. *We're* going. We're going to do this," she finished, beaming.

Her smile was infectious. She stuck her hand out palm-down, and Colin glanced at it, curious. Then he smiled and placed his on top of hers. Don reached in and placed his palm on top of his son's. Daniel looked at the union and finally dropped his hand on top.

"On three say, *sunshine*," Don suggested.

In unison, they all counted, "One. Two. Three. *Sunshine!*"

After the momentary exhilaration was over, Col announced, "Okay, I'll climb in." He looked at Stella, "Give me a minute, and you'll follow."

"Affirmative." She saluted, but the muscles in her stomach twisted in torment.

Don and Daniel stooped to secure the ropes that moored the sub in place. Colin's weight caused the submersible to dip slightly and then bounce back buoyantly. Stella could see him through the acrylic domed window. As he settled into the cockpit seat, he gave her a thumbs-up.

Stella turned towards Don and Daniel. Both men looked sober. Both struggled to seem optimistic. Don gave her a meaningful nod.

"Take care of my son."

"I will." Her voice cracked as she hugged him.

She looked at Daniel and mouthed the words, *thank you.* He gave a brief nod, and then she was maneuvering through the hatch, poking her legs down to straddle Colin's. Finally in position, she sat down on his sturdy thighs.

"Comfy?" he tried to joke, but she could

hear the gravity in his voice.

"Extremely."

Through the murky acrylic, they saw Don gesture towards the hatch and heard his distant voice say, "I'm closing it."

Colin gave another thumbs-up, and they both tipped their head back to watch the heavy flap lower over them. The only light inside the submersible was the minimal glow from the outside torches.

A grating sound came from above, and Stella swallowed as the flat latch wrenched into place.

"He can lock it from on top, and we can twist that latch to open it again."

Once the latch was secured, silencing all noise, Colin's voice sounded tinny.

"Probably not a good sign if my ears are plugged already," Stella remarked.

"It is good. It means the seal worked. When they let go of those ropes and we start to sink, we'll know for sure whether it's locked tight. If it's not, we'll have to reach for that latch real fast."

Stella glanced around but couldn't see much of the interior in the dark. "No seatbelts?"

Colin wrapped his arm across her stomach.

"That'll work," she murmured.

"Okay." He dragged in a slow breath. "This is it. I'll give them the signal to drop the ropes. The sub will submerge. They are going to swim underwater and give us a nudge, and then they are going to cut the weights."

"What if they can't cut the ropes?"

Colin remained silent.

"Col?"

"Then we sink. We'll pull that latch and swim like hell."

Stella clutched the arm clamped around her abdomen.

"Okay. Let's do this," she whispered.

Colin squeezed her.

"Would now be a bad time to tell you I love you?" he asked huskily.

Stella smiled even though he couldn't see it. "No, now is the perfect time," she murmured. "But, I'll tell you when we reach the surface."

Colin tipped his head up and kissed her cheek. "Deal."

And with that, he gave the thumbs-up sign again.

There was a hasty wave of hands through the domed window. She couldn't tell if it was Don or Daniel. Her stomach rolled when they began to sink. Within seconds, water covered the acrylic window, and she lifted her hand, holding her palm up beneath the hatch, testing the rim for leaks.

"So far, so good," she whispered.

There was a weightless sensation, and then they felt the nudge as they were pushed into the darkness.

Stella's spine was rigid as she listened to every little sound that reverberated inside the cockpit. Unidentified pops of adjustment. The touch of someone's hand on the hull. The thuds of the knife strokes. She silently urged Don and Daniel on, aware of each second that they remained underwater. Soon, they would be forced to retreat for oxygen.

The submersible listed as Stella reached out to support herself.

"One down," Colin chronicled quietly.

A knock sounded against the hull—a quick sequence of three strikes, a farewell signal from someone's knuckles, and then a sickening lurch as they began to drift.

CHAPTER 21

A series of harsh clangs echoed ominously as the submersible collided with the tunnel's ceiling.

"Daniel said it wasn't far to the open water," Colin tried to sound encouraging.

"Do you think they're okay?"

"Yeah. It went exactly as planned. It didn't take them too long to cut the weights, and they gave us a good shove."

"But we're still stuck in this tunnel."

Another loud clunk from above testified to that.

"We have no control, Stel. We have nothing left but faith. Daniel said it would be a short distance. I know it feels like forever—"

"Oh!" Stella grabbed his arm and flattened her other palm against the inside of the hull. It was cold to the touch.

"Do you feel it?" Colin asked.

"We're moving," she replied in a hoarse whisper. "Up."

Outside the thick window, there was nothing to see now. It was a black sheath, as was the entire cockpit. Only motion and sound, like the momentum of an ascending elevator, gave them any sense of progress.

Sickening groans sounded from the steel hull as the water pressure tested its resiliency. A loud pop caused Stella to scream. Any second now she expected to hear the rush of water hissing through a hole. What had Col and his father mentioned? *Crush depth.* The maximum pressure a hull could withstand without imploding.

"The hull is just compressing under the pressure," Colin explained gruffly.

"Compressing? Like a waffle iron? I don't want to be a waffle."

"No," he answered quickly. A little too quickly.

More groans ensued, but the submersible didn't turn into a trash compactor, and there was no water on the bare toes poking out of her sandals.

"Look!" she pointed.

A tiny flash of light meandered in front of the domed window and then sped off.

"Bioluminescent fish."

Stella leaned forward on his lap to search for it.

"Hey," he said, arresting her attention. "Stay still. I'm trying to gauge when to drop the next set of weights, and you wiggling around on my lap isn't helping my concentration."

Stella froze.

His hand splayed across her stomach. "It's okay. You don't have to be a statue."

She could hear the smile in his voice, and she relaxed slightly.

"When do you release them?"

"We'll do it together. To your left, I want you to feel for the lever I pointed out earlier. It's like a vertical door handle. When the time comes, you're going to flip that handle up."

Stella's fingertips blindly roamed over the icy steel, encountering a few buttons and switches but nothing that felt like a door handle. Another loud pop made her hand jerk. She froze, waiting to see if this latest racket proved to be their demise. When nothing exploded, she continued her search and located the handle.

"Okay, I found it. How do I know for sure it's the handle you're speaking about? What if this is some auxiliary hatch release?"

"That would really suck," Colin uttered behind her.

She thwacked his thigh.

"I inspected the inside of this cockpit with a torch several times. It's the only handle over there. You're good."

Stella would have thought that information would lift the heaviness from her chest, but the pressure was mounting. She felt like she was trying to breathe with a concrete slab over her rib cage.

"Col," she tested quietly, "do you feel weird?"

"How so?" The concern in his tone was immediate.

"My chest is so tight, and my ears—hurt."

Colin reached around and held her in both arms.

"Easy," he coaxed. "Just take slow breaths. Remember, the pressure in here is atmospheric—static. If we have any pressure adjustment issues, they will most likely happen on the surface. What you're feeling is natural panic."

It sounded like a sales pitch to her.

"Try the nose trick for your ears."

Stella reached up and squeezed her nose and then tried to blow out. It only intensified the pain.

"Oww!"

"Okay, okay." Colin sensed her unraveling. "I don't know how far we've come, but let's release the weights. That will accelerate our speed."

"Yes," she cried. "Just get me to the surface."

She hated the shrill sound of her voice in this urn, but Colin was right, she was freaked. When was the first time someone discovered they were claustrophobic?

"Put your hand on the latch, but don't pull until I say. I want to keep us upright."

Stella nodded, even though she knew he couldn't see it.

"Three. Two. One. Now!"

Yanking the handle, she whimpered when it wouldn't budge. Panicked, she felt the muscles in her fingers cramp with her redoubled efforts. Colin's side came loose as they tipped. In that second, she wrenched the handle up, and the submersible stabilized.

The feeling of ascent was pronounced. She envisioned them slicing through this black sludge and leaned towards the window in anticipation, waiting for the telltale brightening of the ocean water, the sun's filtration, and the glory of the sky.

It never came.

Up. Up. Up.

Weightless, Stella felt perspiration bead up on her forehead. Colin's arm locked around her waist, stabilizing her. She focused on that connection as the nausea kicked in, and her whole body broke out in a sweat.

Colin coughed. His chest quaked behind her, the rugged beat of his heart drumming against her back.

Up. Up. Up.

"How long has it been?" she choked out.

"I can't tell." He leaned around her side, trying to see through the domed window.

"Dammit," he cursed.

The palm that was pressed against the hull curled up as she was ready to claw her way through the steel. Terror wrapped around her throat, choking her. To hell with drowning. She was going to suffocate right here.

There was a sudden lurch that sent her stomach soaring and about to pop through her teeth, followed by a tumultuous bobbing that unsettled her further. Yet, amidst this chaos, the previous sensation of ascending through the depths had halted, replaced by a disorienting stillness that suggested they were no longer climbing.

"Col?" she cried.

Colin leaned forward.

"I think we made it, Stel," he uttered with reserved enthusiasm. "With our crap luck, it just happens to be night."

"Col, I'm gonna throw up."

"All right. Let me get up."

Stella lifted off his lap and crouched to the side; her feet pinched together on the tight floor space.

Colin pressed his face to the window as they could hear the slosh of waves lapping against the exterior.

"I'm going to open the hatch a crack. If water comes in, I'll close it immediately."

"Hurry!" Her stomach rolled with each pitch of the sub.

Colin climbed onto the pilot seat. She couldn't see him, but she could feel the stretch of his body as he reached above for the hatch. Grunting with effort, he twisted the wheel.

The vacuum around them suddenly eased as her ears popped. A splash of water trickled on her face, followed by another. They felt blessed.

"It's okay," he called from above. "That's just spray from the ocean." There was a slight pause, and then he added, "Stel, we made it!"

Stella climbed up onto the chair, using her hands on his chest to guide her up.

"Col," her stomach heaved. "Now."

Colin threw back the hatch. Saltwater sprayed over them as Colin hoisted her up until her fingers could wrap around the ledge and her head could reach over. Unable to hold back anymore, she retched over the exterior hull. As her body racked a few more times, she finally managed a weak "Okay."

Colin's hands were under her armpits as he lowered her back onto the pilot seat.

"I don't think I'll ever eat crabmeat again,"

she joked sickly.

Colin pulled her into his embrace and kissed her forehead.

"Do you feel that?" he asked with a smile in his voice.

She did.

Air. Glorious air.

Salty, but with a crisp freshness that had been denied in the Underworld.

It took a few minutes for her chest to expand enough to suck it all in. She coughed when some salt spray dipped into her lungs.

The Underworld.

It seemed so far beneath them. A surreal place scarcely imaginable now.

Together, they tipped their heads back and stared up at the stars. Pinpricks of light dotted a black sky. It wasn't so black, though. A three-quarter moon scored a brilliant path across the water. In that light, the ocean rolled in tame waves.

"Grab your notebook, Stel. We need to try and draw the stars as best we can."

Stella crouched back down and felt along the floor for the plastic bag that held her notebook. When she pulled the pad out, she could feel that it was damp around the edges. She fished for her pen and scrambled back up.

Opening the notebook, her eyes adjusted to the soft glow of moonlight. After all, hadn't they mastered night vision? Did they really need the sun? Was it just a matter of time before their eyes started to glow green?

Stella tried her best to sketch the night sky, but both knew it was almost futile. No drawing would ever pinpoint their exact location. Still, she drew it all—a three-quarter moon and her best guess at its position above the horizon—the situation of the stars, jotting down the names of the constellations she recognized.

"I think I have it. I mean, it's crude."

"You did good," he rubbed her back. "We're going to have to close this hatch until morning. We don't want to take in too much water."

Stella hated losing the fresh air, but he was right. "Okay," she pouted.

Colin chuckled as he reached above her to haul the latch back into place. He then spun the wheel, and immediately, her ears plugged in protest.

"Come on," Colin urged. "Let's sit down. Judging from the moon's position, I'd say it's a few hours until sunrise."

"I want to see that, Col. I want to see the sun rise."

"I know," he whispered. "So do I."

He dropped back into the pilot seat and guided her down onto his lap. This time, she was seated sideways, her legs dangling over his thigh, her arms wrapped around his neck. She rested her head against him, feeling his assuring pulse on her cheek. After some time, she must have drifted off to sleep because the next thing she knew, Colin was whispering in her ear.

"Stella, look."

Stella opened her eyes and blinked. Actually, she winced at the soft pink glow that illuminated the cockpit. Sliding one leg off his lap, she leaned into the domed window and could see a brilliant path of gold slice through the ocean. Milky green water undulated outside the acrylic hole.

"Let's go up," she urged.

Colin scooted out from under her and climbed up to twist the hatch, shoving it open.

Cool air brushed over their faces.

What month was it? September, October?

Her eyes finally adjusted as they silently watched the sun climb out of the water. Darkness surrendered to the light. Cumulus clouds with their heavy pink bellies slowly blossomed into downy white pillows.

Colin twisted, searching the watery vista.

"No seagulls. No land," he reported. "But hey, now I know why they paint these things yellow. Surely someone will see this big, bobbing tennis ball."

The upbeat tone was forced. As she looked around, hopelessness began to set in. They had done it. They had escaped the Underworld and risen to the surface. Now, they were in the middle of the ocean with no flares, no communication, no means to draw attention, and no ships or planes on the horizon.

Colin reached for her face, cupping her cheek. In the sun, his eyes flashed with a million beguiling colors—jade, brown, caramel. She could see his face so much clearer now. There were no heavy shadows to conceal how attractive he was. She reached up and dusted her fingers across the bridge of his nose.

"Your nose," she began.

Colin frowned. "Yeah, what about it?"

"What happened?"

Shaking his head, he grinned. "A fistfight in a back alley with two six-foot-five thugs."

Stella's mouth twisted in disbelief.

"Seriously?"

"Nah. I got too close to the swing set when we were kids. Jill was swinging, and her foot clipped my nose. It hurt like hell."

Lifting onto her toes, Stella kissed the slight bump. "I like it. It makes you look human. If your nose was perfect, you'd be too intimidating."

"Intimidating?" He lowered his eyebrows in staged menace.

"Not like that," she laughed. "I mean, if you were that perfect, there's no way you'd like someone like me."

"So, because I broke my nose, I can like you?"

"Something like that." Her voice trailed off as she listened to the constant ebb and flow of the waves. Her head lolled on top of her neck in the same rhythm.

"Col," she began futilely.

"Shh. Someone will come. Have faith, Gullaksen."

She closed her eyes, pressing her face into his palm.

"I love you," she whispered.

He reached forward and leaned his forehead against hers. "That's a relief."

That made her smile as she kissed his hand.

They stood in that embrace for a few minutes until Colin stirred. "Hey, let's close it up. Now that we have light in the cockpit, we can do a better search. Maybe there's something in here that we can use."

Yes. A plan. A task.

Stella dove back into the cockpit with renewed enthusiasm, hearing the deadening clunk of the hatch drop shut behind them.

Inside the sphere, Colin narrated every device he could identify.

"Look at all this handy stuff," he said, pointing to one black screen. "Depth gauge." He moved to the next panel. "Handheld radio." He continued to identify components that were literally dead in the water.

Stella followed his hand and caught a reflection of herself in one of the empty steel panels. A grain in the alloy made her slightly fuzzy, but she could see long dark hair now in chaotic waves. All the tan from the summer was gone. Foggy brown eyes stared back from a pale face.

The murky reflection seemed appropriate. It was as if she had lost herself, and all that remained was this altered image.

She still had the white dress on over her clothes because it was cold at night. Reaching to tuck the tangled hair behind her ears, Stella frowned.

"Col." She ran her fingers along the plate that was screwed into the bulkhead. "Couldn't we use this?"

Puzzled by her attention, he followed her gaze. Comprehension widened his eyes.

"Yes." He stepped in closer to examine the screwed-in handles. "It's reflective enough to catch the sun's glare. Maybe even moon glare at night."

Stella felt some much-needed adrenaline kick in.

He spun around. "There are three empty panels. Daniel threw in a coil of rope for us. We could use it to fasten these just outside the hatch."

"It's got to help, right?" she asked, hopeful.

Colin was already crouched down, digging his hand under the pilot's seat.

"You bet! Look for drawers—anything that might hold a tool we can use to unscrew these."

Stella started cautiously yanking on handles, afraid she might accidentally trip a latch that would drop open the bottom of the sub.

"Here!" Colin pulled an orange plastic kit from an unmarked compartment.

He opened the box and looked dismayed.

"I was hoping for a flare, but hey, this is very helpful." He pulled out a sheathed diving knife. He inserted the tip inside the slotted screw and tried to turn it. The blade slipped out. With a muttered curse, he tried again, pushing as he turned.

"I felt a bite."

Redoubling his efforts, they both murmured *yes* as the screw began to loosen. It took time and patience, but by midday, he had removed all three panels and cut sections of rope with the knife.

"All right, I'll climb up, and you hand me one of the panels," he instructed.

They affixed the three panels and flinched when the sun hit one. The glare was piercing—until the clouds poured in.

Stella sat with her butt wedged into the domed window, facing Colin. Her forehead dropped onto his shoulder.

"We have no more water," she whispered hoarsely.

"We just need it to rain." Gone was the robust strength in his tone. "We can capture the water in the container we brought."

Hunger poked at her gut with rigid fingers. They had nearly exhausted their limited food supply. A few commercial jets had flown overhead but far too high to ever see them. The ocean's vast emptiness stretched in every direction, overwhelming them with solitude.

What had it been, two days? Three? Four?

"You promised me a dinner out," Stella murmured. "What restaurant do you want to go to?"

Colin was quiet. For a moment, she thought he might have fallen asleep. They were both so tired—so utterly drained. They were struggling to keep what little food they had digested down.

"For our first date," he said hoarsely, "I'd just want it to be you and me. Like this."

"Like this?" she laughed weakly.

She felt his lips curl up against her forehead. "I mean, just the two of us. No one is ever going to understand us, Stel. No one will ever comprehend or believe what we've been through."

What he said was true. The only people to understand remained beneath the ocean.

"Would you cook me dinner?" Her voice was fading.

"I would. If you'd eat macaroni and cheese."

She smiled, envisioning the creamy sauce smothered over pasta. A loud grumble sounded from her belly.

"I'll take that as a yes," he chuckled.

"Col," she sighed. "Can we take a nap?"

There was more silence, but she was already diving into slumber, diving into the dark water. Down, down, down into the caves, where luminous green eyes lurked, watching for her. Inside that dank cavern, a loud horn blared. Stella frowned. It should be a bell, not a horn.

"Stel," Colin shook her shoulder. "Wake up."

Stella mumbled, still caught in the Underworld.

"Stel, there's something out there."

Yes. A Chimaera. It was moving in—crawling closer—hugging the shadows of the bungalows—peering in the glassless window at the sleeping prey.

The horn must have been an alert.

Run, she thought. *Run*.

"Stella, wake up."

Colin's voice broke through. She grabbed her head in both hands. It ached so much. The sun hurt her face—her eyes.

The sun.

So bright.

The reflective panels above lobbed the rays back at the orb with molten swords.

A horn sounded. Closer this time.

"Col?"

"Come on," he urged. "I've got you."

Colin clutched her arms, guiding her up the tight barrel. As she climbed up into vivid daylight, the wind lashed her hair into her eyes.

"Look," Colin cried.

There was enough urgency in his voice that she obeyed. She swept her hair back, squinting against the sun's glare. Was that harsh light playing tricks with her eyes? Was any grip she had on reality gone? That seemed more plausible than the notion that she saw the distinct outline of the ship slicing a wedge through the ocean. The tip of that V formation was aimed directly at their submersible.

The horn blared again, breaking through her lethargy. Stella gripped the rim of the hatch with one hand and cupped the other over her eyes as a shield.

It looked like a fishing boat—a large one. Perhaps the light had tainted perspective. Colin climbed higher, pinning his thighs to each side of the hatch so that he could wave both arms overhead.

Stella hefted up, her arm slicing over her head with a weak wave. She began to shout. Where the sound came from, she'll never know, but she yelled for twenty minutes until that boat reached them, and she could see the men on the bow waving back.

"We did it, Stel," Colin hugged her. "We did it."

There was nothing to say, and she wouldn't be capable of speaking if she tried. She had poured it all out. Her throat scratched and closed, and all she could do was clutch him and cry.

EPILOGUE

Stella stood on the stern of the SUMMER FIN, the fishing trawler from Sandy Hook that had come to their aid. Colin's arm was looped around her shoulder. They watched a flock of seagulls swoop and soar, trying to gauge their prospects for food. To the left, a thin blue score of land came into view. She didn't gasp at the sight. Excitement eluded her.

They had been missing for almost two months, and now she feared the inevitable questions—the certain doubts. Perhaps Loren and Daniel's reluctance to rise to the surface was founded.

Colin squeezed her arm, nodding at a yacht cutting through the surf. Music glided across the salty mist.

Life.

No, they were wrong to want to stay below. They deserved the light. The light represented life. What they were experiencing down there. That wasn't life.

"You asked the captain for the coordinates where we were located?"

She knew she'd asked Colin this question several times, but he patiently assured her he had.

There was no telling how far they drifted in those days before the SUMMER FIN arrived. Would they ever be able to find the spot again? Would they ever locate that peculiar siphon— that water tunnel to the underwater cavern known as the Underworld?

She looked up at Colin's stubbled chin. He caught her staring and met her eyes. She saw it there. His gaze mirrored the ocean, or maybe it was emblazoned there. Also reflected there was her own conviction.

They would never stop trying to get back to the Underworld. They would never stop trying to save their loved ones. They would never stop until they were once again beneath.

BENEATH

HORIZON DIVIDED

In this exciting sequel to BENEATH...

Stella and Colin search futilely for the rogue Atlantic current that dragged them to the shadowy Underworld just a few months ago. With an ill-defined area to explore, their futile attempts cost too much money, and their resources are running out.

When it appears that all hope is lost, a miracle occurs in the form of a retired Hollywood producer-turned-explorer who is willing to use his ship and equipment to support their quest. Although no one believes their tale, he is the most accepting person they have met. Whether his intentions are honorable or not remains to be seen.

With a crew full of skeptics, Stella and Colin locate the downwelling current and once again find themselves dragged into the subterranean network of caves deep in the Atlantic Ocean canyon.

Time is running out for the Underworld, though. Will anyone be left to rise from beneath?

HORIZON DIVIDED

ABOUT THE AUTHOR

USA TODAY bestselling author, Maureen A. Miller worked in the software industry for fifteen years. She crawled around plant floors in a hard hat and safety glasses, hooking up computers to behemoth manufacturing machines. The job required extensive travel. The best form of escapism during those lengthy airport layovers became writing.

Maureen's first novel, WIDOW'S TALE, earned her an RWA Golden Heart nomination in Romantic Suspense. Initially, she wrote for Harlequin's digital imprint, but when the little voices in her head called for her to craft the young adult science fiction BEYOND series, it didn't quite fit into the Harlequin world. So, she put on her big boy pants and ventured out on her own.

The grownup in her still writes romantic suspense, but the inner girl enjoys young adult adventures.

Find more about Maureen at
http://www.maureenamiller.com/

Printed in Great Britain
by Amazon

57039444R00182